DEAD AND
BURIED

DEAD AND BURIED

A WILKIE JOHN WESTERN

TIM BRYANT

PINNACLE BOOKS
Kensington Publishing Corp.
www.kensingtonbooks.com

PINNACLE BOOKS are published by

Kensington Publishing Corp.
119 West 40th Street
New York, NY 10018

All Kensington titles, imprints, and distributed lines are
available at special quantity discounts for bulk purchases for sales
promotions, premiums, fund-raising, educational, or institutional
use. Special book excerpts or customized printings can also
be created to fit specific needs. For details, write or phone the
office of the Kensington sales manager: Kensington Publishing Corp., 119 West 40th Street, New York, NY 10018, attn:
Sales Department; phone 1-800-221-2647.

PINNACLE BOOKS and the Pinnacle logo are Reg. U.S. Pat.
& TM Off.

ISBN-13: 978-0-7860-4231-9
ISBN-10: 0-7860-4231-1

First printing: June 2018

10 9 8 7 6 5 4 3 2 1

Printed in the United States of America

First electronic edition: June 2018

ISBN-13: 978-0-7860-4232-6
ISBN-10: 0-7860-4232-X

CHAPTER ONE

People who live out in the sea of sand that is West Texas tend to have strong beliefs in God and the devil. It's not really any mystery. When you walk out into the landscape and take a look at the mountains and plateaus, the cliffs rising up dramatically out of the earth in streaks of reds and browns and even a few greens here and there, it's real easy for these people to see God. Even a nonbeliever like myself can be swayed. Walk out farther into that same landscape, try to ride very far across the flatland, into or around one of those mountains or maybe through a pass between them, hang out for a while with just you and your horse and the sun, it gets pretty hard not to see the devil, too. You can hear him rattling, cooing, and cawing at you. He might show up in the form of a black bear or a javelina. He might even show up as a man.

I found the bones of a guy out there in the middle of nowhere, and I just as well might have been looking at my own self. I was out of water, my horse Little Cuss was down and dying, and I had good reason to think I was following shortly behind.

When I say the man I found wasn't nothing but bones, I'm speaking in the most literal of terms. There were some leather chaps less than ten feet away, and the ripped remains of a shirt pulled over some scrub brush. The only other thing was bones bleached pure white in the sun, gleaming like the teeth of some dust devil.

Of course, everything was starting to look white. The sun was bleeding into everything and washing out enough of my eyesight that I was blind to just about anything farther away than ten feet. I was hoping I didn't step on a rattler or run up on any of the black bears that called the area home.

"Hell's Half Acre got nothing on you," I said.

I had been talking to myself ever since I left Little Cuss back a few miles. I had reason to believe there was an army encampment just over the hills to the south, and that's what I was aiming for. If I made it by nightfall, there was a chance they could send back for the horse. At least that's mostly what I was telling myself.

I had spent a considerable amount of time in Hell's Half Acre, the area of Fort Worth where gambling dens rubbed up against the most spectacular whorehouses you ever saw and made the sweetest music ever heard by a sinner's ear.

What I was standing in right here was more hell than Fort Worth ever thought of raising. A week out of camp in Fort Concho, I'd followed the Pecos River down to the Pacific Railway and then turned west. It had been days since I'd seen smoke behind me. I was on the part of the map that was a big blank. And I could see why.

The bones strewn out in front of me weren't me. I was pretty sure who they were. If I was lucky, they belonged to a man known among the Apache Mescaleros as Phantom Bill. His true name was Manley Pardon Clark, from Chicago, and he had been on his way to Chihuahua with a sackful of money taken from a train from Santa Fe.

I'd stumbled across the carcass of a horse the day before, so I expected to catch up with the Phantom. I just thought there would be more to him.

"The Tonkawa ate your horse like it was a fine steak, Manley," I said, "and, from the looks of things, they got their teeth into you, too."

That didn't bother me much. I'd heard tales of the Tonkawa eating captured families and then dining on the family dog for desert. They were a hearty bunch of people. Great trackers, too.

"What I want to know is what you did with the money, my friend," I said.

I knew him well enough to know he would have hidden it before letting Indians get their hands on it. You could tell by a few drag patterns that Manley had been dragged due south, either by the Tonkawa or by bears that came along and took what was left. I walked back north and scanned the horizon. It was all white. If I was going to do this, I was going to have to do it on my hands and knees, a few feet at a time. If I did get down there, I had serious doubts if I'd be able to get back up.

I don't rightly know how long I searched for that damn money. Time kind of bled all together like the light did. I stopped to rest frequently and slept a bit, too. Somewhere along the line, my knees and elbows folded up and left me stretched out across a bunch of rocks, another easy meat stick refreshment for a passing band of renegades.

"Wilkie John."

In my dream, it was a woman's voice. Not just any woman's voice. It was Sunny, a colored girl left behind in Fort Worth. Only now I was back there with her in a big house called the Black Elephant, and she was coaxing me into a nice, warm bathtub.

"What are you doing down there? Wake up, you fool."

I opened my eyes to the sensation of lying naked in a place you shouldn't be naked. I reached down and fumbled around for my different parts. My clothing was soppy as a dishrag, but it was there. I looked up into the light, like a heathen looking into the face of God.

"I can't see a damn thing, Jack," I said.

Gentleman Jack Delaney. Probably the last person you would expect to see me with. The same Gentleman Jack Delaney whose father I had killed in Clara, Texas, the previous year. The same one that had me hung in downtown Fort Worth. Jack was something to see, if, in fact, you could see. He was wearing a new blue suit that looked like it was made from fancy brothel curtains. I might have questioned the suit's practicality, but I would have been given the speech on wind and sun damage and the importance of shielding yourself. He had proven right about that much, but I had heard it all before.

It wasn't exactly true that I couldn't see anything. I could see the shod front feet of the fastest quarter horse in all of Texas. I was pretty certain of it because she had caught me and Little Cuss even with a morning's head start the previous day, and I took no enjoyment at all in that fact. In my mind, that whole episode had been responsible for Little Cuss cutting his leg. If he hadn't been trying to prove something to himself, he'd still have been right there beneath me instead of the rocks and sand.

"Manley Pardon Clark is laying right over there against them rocks," he said.

Gentleman Jack Delaney waved his rifle, which cut through my white light like an angel of death slicing through fire.

"Think I don't know that?" I said. "I was the one who found him."

I listened to the man swing down from his horse and crunch his way toward me.

"No money?" he said.

I shook my head, and the world seemed to tilt and spin backward in reaction. I turned away from Jack and vomited a stream of clean water that polished the rocks beneath me. I suddenly recalled that I had done the same thing before. Just minutes, maybe hours or even a day ago, but at some earlier time.

"Should I trust you or search you?" Jack said.

I couldn't figure out how he was standing there, cool and composed, while I lay on the ground, closer to Manley Clark than Jack Delaney.

"Little Cuss hurt his leg," I said. "We need to go back and see if we can save him."

Jack laughed. Not so much like he was laughing at me. Just laughing at the ridiculous situation.

"Little Cuss didn't cut his leg, Wilkie John. Snake got hold of him."

It depended on how you looked at it. He may or may not have run up on a snake, but the bite threw him off-balance enough that I came off the tail end and Little Cuss went down. That was when he'd cut his leg. I was sure of it. Somehow, in my fall, I had totally missed the snake.

"Don't worry," Jack said. "I made a tourniquet and cut the bite out. Gave him some water. He'll probably make it."

He bent over and grinned down on me.

"You, I'm not so sure about."

I was just about as happy to see the man as I could have been, generally speaking. He'd spent considerable energy trying to kill me the year previous, and I'd sworn revenge on him for it. Now, back down in the lonesomest part of the state, I ran into him when he was running down Manley Pardon Clark, or Phantom Bill, and I was sitting around, trying to decide what to do next. To be specific, Jack had sent word to Fort Concho: he was looking for a soldier or two to help in the capture of the outlaw. Then he sent word again and made mention that the reward would be split in an equitable manner.

When still no soldier was provided, he showed up at the fort, looking exactly like himself. At six and a half foot tall, his legs were long for his horse, and he still insisted on wearing a top hat that made him look odd and even taller. He wore a suit that fit perfectly, even if it didn't befit the situation. Sure, it was important to dress well, to guard against all the things the desert might spring on you, but he was still dressing for a night out on the town, and that didn't appear to be in the cards.

"Manley Pardon Clark was here at Fort Concho three days before he held up the train," I said.

Neither Gentleman Jack nor I had any thought that Clark would be coming back that way again, but the stop at Concho had proven helpful. Two different soldiers, neither of whom had a clue who Clark was at the time, said he'd mentioned going to Chihuahua when he left. That information narrowed the trail enough that I was now out in the middle of hell and just a few yards from what remained of Phantom Bill himself. Seemed he hadn't been so much a phantom after all.

Neither soldier reported any mention of train robberies or other plans for misbehavior along the way. In fact, being told who they had been talking to, neither believed he was the man. Not him, they said. He didn't have it in him to do such a thing.

Now I was lying in the desert, half-blind and wondering where the money was.

"How hard would ten thousand dollars be to hide?" I said.

I was looking at Jack's suit and counting pockets. I didn't trust him as far as I could see him, and he was moving in and out of eyesight.

"A hundred hundred-dollar bills. Two hundred fifties," Jack said. "Not enough to slow you down a whole lot, Wilkie John."

I scanned the sand between me and Manley, like I was expecting a bill to come fluttering by on the wind.

"Hell, bears could've eat up the money, too," I said.

I had no idea how much time had passed, but I knew I was quickly running out of it. I had four more days to find the stolen loot and return it to the railway people in Alpine, Texas. After that, they were leaving for California and half of the reward money was going with them.

Gentleman Jack Delaney had asked me to come along for one reason. He was considerably more likely to find both Manley and the loot with me helping. He knew it, and he knew I knew it, too. I also knew something else, and I wasn't completely sure if he was aware I knew that part of the deal. He wasn't planning to split any reward money with me. Not a chance. In fact, he had no intention of taking the loot to Alpine at all. Why would he take ten thousand dollars into Alpine and get five thousand back when he could take ten thousand to Chihuahua? How did I know what he was doing? For all his faults, and they were numberless, he was too damn much like me. I wasn't interested in some reward money doled out by the railroad or the government. I also had no interest in vacationing in Chihuahua with Gentleman Jack. I would leave his bones with Phantom Bill for the devil to find.

Then again, he had saved my life and maybe even the life of my horse on that day we found the bones in the sand. And there was that thing about being a Texas Ranger. Damn. Things, as usual, were bound to get complicated.

CHAPTER TWO

Several days earlier

Becoming a Texas Ranger had an interesting effect on my life. Womenfolk took more notice of me. Maybe I walked a little taller. At least I didn't think of myself as so small anymore. I wasn't perfect, but it reminded me of something a Fort Worth preacher had once told me.

"Being saved doesn't make me perfect, but it makes my imperfection into something God can work with."

I didn't know about all that, but if you counted that the Rangers had saved me from a life of crime, it certainly did go on to make my weaknesses something easier to overlook. So even if Reverend Caliber had got the letter of the law wrong, he'd at least got the spirit of the thing. There was no question I was a better Ranger than I had ever been a non-Ranger.

I'd had it in mind to visit Indian Territory. In fact, I was in Meridian, Texas, and headed north, stopping only to pay respects at the gravesite of my older brother, Ira Lee, when word came that the Colorado and Concho rivers were flooding and there were German immigrant families stranded and possibly in danger of drowning. I went down there and, with the help of another Ranger from Leon Springs and a soldier from San Antonio, we brought out eight Germans of varying shapes and sizes and two Cherokee women with their children.

The soldier had already set up a camp on high ground by the time I arrived, and we carried our survivors there behind two mules. I call them *survivors* because we saw more than a few who weren't. A dead boy in a tree that spooked me good, the look on his face so real, I tried to talk him down before I realized he wasn't alive. There were several people washed up in bushes and against fence posts. Most looked like farmers, farmers' wives. We didn't move any of them. Where would we bring them? We didn't have the tools to dig graves, and, if we had, we'd have just dug into more water. The soldier said a solemn prayer over each of the bodies, and I was completely respectful.

"Which way you going from here?" the soldier said.

The rain was gone, but the Colorado had flooded its banks, and the water was still rising. You couldn't make out where the river began and ended. Standing on high ground and surveying the scene, it looked like the whole world had become the raging Colorado.

Half of the Germans wanted to stick it out. I couldn't get over that. With everything underwater or washed downstream, they wanted to stay put. Start over. The other half had had enough. There was nothing left to pack, nothing to save. They were ready to go back East right then.

"All I know, I'm moving upstream," I said.

I was like that half of the Germans. I'd seen enough water. I'd seen enough of what it could do. I was going elsewhere.

"You mind carrying these people over to Fort Concho?" the soldier said. "They'll be okay there until they can get a coach or maybe a train back to where they come from."

"No coach take us back to Bremerhaven," one of the ladies said.

She didn't appear to be talking to us, so I didn't answer.

By then, the Indians had slipped off, never to be seen again. There was no need to look for them, no need to worry. They could look after themselves.

It turned out Fort Concho was less than forty miles away, and, if it wasn't in my preferred northerly direction, at least it was out of the flood's path. And it was a direction I'd never taken before. I said yes, and we decided to go ahead and move out that afternoon, so we stood a good chance of arriving in camp the next day.

"Wait until tomorrow," said the Ranger, who turned out to be Roy Lee Deevers from San Antonio. "You don't want to travel by night."

But I did.

"There will be a full moon tonight. Plenty of

light, and much cooler for the horses," I said.
"Plus, maybe he will sleep."

I nodded to one of the German men, who had
a badly broken leg. He wouldn't be easy to deal
with. He was a mean son of a gun who didn't seem
the least bit happy to have been saved from a more
horrible fate than traveling back East.

The San Antonio Ranger cleaned up the break
as best he could and made a real decent splint with
one of the many sticks scattered around us. When
the German argued against it and tried to get up
and walk to prove his case, Roy Lee knocked him
over the head with the butt end of his rifle.

"I've done just as much good with that end of
the gun as the other," he said.

I drug the German and his family off in peace,
making good time through the night. Watching
the moon come up right in front of me, climbing
up into the night even as we climbed into the
hills. At one point I stopped and made them all
look at the beautiful sight before us, split equally
between the valley below us, the sand seeming to
glow under the moonlight, and then the sky, so full
of stars they seemed to be crowding each other
out, trying to get in position to look down upon us.
I saw a hundred rabbits and even some hyenas,
one of which I drove away with a single shot from
my gun. Overall, it was a perfect example of why I
like to move at night and sleep during the day. To
make it even better, we arrived at Fort Concho in
time for a late breakfast of ham hocks and eggs.

Fort Concho was built on a grand scale. So grand,

I thought I found it and left it, only to find it a second time. Turns out I had never left and wouldn't exit the grounds for two more days. It was bigger than Mobeetie. Enough men to whip Attila and all of his Huns. I never did figure out who the supreme commander was, but there was one lieutenant with the name Zephaniah Swoop, who seemed to have a pretty firm grasp on the situation. Most of them seemed to bow to him, in spite of his name.

Swoop had a heap to say. Mostly about this outlaw the Indians called Phantom Bill. The Phantom had robbed the Pacific Railway train three times, each time getting more brazen and getting away with more cash. It was embarrassing the railway people, who had put three Pinkertons on the last train. His ability to get away seemed supernatural. That's how he got the name Phantom Bill.

Orders had come down to help some bounty hunter track him down and kill him. Swoop was hesitant.

"I don't mind taking my orders from President Arthur," he said. "These orders are coming from Pacific Railway. I don't work for the railroad."

I could sympathize. I wasn't much of a railroad guy, either. And I damn sure didn't take orders from California. I had delivered my Germans safe into the care of the U.S. Army and was planning to pull out for Indian Territory the following day.

Swoop awoke me while it was still dark. I thought I was dreaming.

"Say again?"

I blinked hard and shook my head, trying to force myself to attention.

"This bounty hunter is named Jack Delaney. He says he knows you. Wants you along to track this Phantom Bill fellow. He seems to think highly of you for some reason."

It was quite possibly the last name I would have ever expected to hear from the man's lips. In fact, I'm not at all sure of what else Swoop did say. When I heard Jack's name, everything else kind of played second fiddle.

"And what exactly does he want me for?"

With a few hard blinks, my vision had come back to me and was focused on this man, tugging on his beard like maybe he would pull the answer out of it. I recall wondering, ever so briefly, if pulling at your beard would make it grow longer like Swoop's. Mine grew to a certain length and then seemed to just stop. I had never pulled on it much.

"Phantom Bill's robbed the Pacific Railroad three times now in two months. This guy's looking for someone to ride with him. I'm not sending any of my guys out there with him. If they get that money, they won't come back. If they don't, they'll be dead. This fella seems rather fond of you."

One of the privates was standing right at Swoop's elbow. He looked like maybe one of the men who wanted to go and didn't get the call.

"Said he's going back to California with a hat made of Phantom Bill's skull," the private said.

Swoop elbowed him in the side.

"It's Gentleman Jack's skull I'd be more comfortable wearing," I said.

The idea of a hat made from a human skull was worthy of contemplation. Hunting down an outlaw with the man who'd tried to kill me only a year before wasn't.

"Why don't you send one of the Germans?" I said.

It was an admittedly weak argument. The only one who might have been up to the job at all had bone sticking through his leg and was delirious from either fever or the medication he'd been given. The only other, a boy obviously the man's son, was watching over his father and feeding him water from a canteen. Maybe it was beer.

"You are a Ranger, aren't you?" Swoop said.

Even if the ladies did look at me differently, and even if I did walk more like five foot and six inches than five foot and one, there were times I'd just as soon not wear the badge.

"I'm not afraid of no Indians," I said, "and I'm sure as heck not afraid of this Phantom Bill. But you can count me out of this one. I'm not signing up."

Swoop and his boys watched me for a good while.

"He didn't say he wasn't afraid of this Jack Delaney," one of them said.

I was saddling up Little Cuss just as the army medic arrived to patch up the new arrivals and prepare to ship them to Savannah, Georgia. My instructions, if I wanted to meet up with Gentleman Jack, were to ride due south. Pass Lonetree Mountain and then proceed thirty miles. There I would meet up with my old foe and proceed to track down and smoke out the outlaw Phantom Bill. Manley Clark. Whoever he was.

I wasn't going to do it. That much I knew.

"You have an alias, Wilkie John?" Zephaniah Swoop said while I checked my supplies.

I thought about it. I'd been falsely identified as John Liquorman, but it hardly qualified as an alias. I'd toyed with calling myself Long Gone Liquorman, but I'd never put enough effort into it for it to catch on.

"People named Wilkie John Liquorish and Zephaniah Swoop don't have much need for an alias," I said.

Swoop laughed and nodded.

"I never trusted anybody with an alias," he said. "Don't much matter if they're good guys or bad guys."

Swoop had a handle on things, all right. He'd taken one look at Gentleman Jack Delaney and had taken the measure. All in all, I'd have rather chased the Phantom down with Swoop and told him as much.

"I don't reckon I believe much in phantoms," he said.

I mounted Little Cuss and tipped my hat.

"Real phantoms probably don't have to call

themselves phantoms," I said. "Same goes for gentlemen."

I left riding south, and I cussed myself for it. It was the one direction I wasn't interested in. I was potentially riding into a trap. Even if I wasn't, I was surely riding into trouble. I wasn't teaming up with Gentleman Jack. He could count on that much. I looked down at the peso badge on my coat. In ways, it had surely changed me, its pin poking through layers to jab at me, prod me. Sure, part of me was a little intrigued. Had Jack really asked for me? If so, why? We hadn't separated on good terms. In fact, I had promised his daddy I was going to shoot him dead. That was right before I shot his daddy dead. I was more interested in following through on the promise I'd made to his daddy than wasting bullets on some damn ghost.

CHAPTER THREE

You could see Lonetree Mountain a day before you got there, such were its surroundings. It was like a bad guy with no cover, and I was thinking of it in those terms from the get-go. As I approached, I spied what looked to be the best route over it. Because it lay dead center in a ridge of smaller mountains, going around would add a day or more to the trip. To the left of the mountain's peak you could see a trail that rose precariously in a spot or two but seemed to have been used by plenty before me. The trail went from right to left across the northern face of the mountain, and I was moving up toward it, maybe a hundred yards from where it took a turn, when I heard the quick crack of three or four gunshots. I watched the sand kick up, far enough in front of me to be of no big concern, but I stopped and waited. If the shooter was aiming at me, he was a terrible shot. If he was aiming to get my attention, he had done so. I knew who he was, thanks to a few of Swoop's men.

I looked up into the rocks and tried to spot his position.

"Tom Pascal."

I didn't put much wind behind it, but it echoed up into the hills with more vigor than I would have thought. He moved when he heard his name, and I saw where he was taking cover. It was a far piece, but I could've at least scuffed the rock he was hiding behind.

"Who wants to know?" he called back.

Pascal was well known enough that several of the troops at Fort Concho had pitched in when it came to relating the details. Pascal fairly owned Lonetree Mountain, at least the portion of it that contained the pass-through, and he had set himself up in the business of taking toll for passage.

A government man had come down from Austin, aiming to put an end to his livelihood, and had promptly been turned back with legal papers and threat of a lawsuit against the United States government. That was pretty much where things stood when I met up with Tom.

"I'm Wilkie John Liquorish," I said. "I'm a Texas Ranger."

I had been advised to announce myself that way. In fact, they had suggested that I mention the Texas Ranger part in advance of my name. I got down from Little Cuss and held my hands in the air, my badge in the left one. As if he could read it from where he was.

"Got a badge?" Pascal said.

I raised it up higher and waited for what seemed like an unusually long time. He finally came out from his hiding place, a rifle trained right on me. I doubted his ability to hit me from there, at least with his first shot, but I didn't see any need to prove it.

"Come on up, but you don't have a legitimate badge, you won't make it back down," Pascal said.

I had been told he would say something along those lines. I had also been told he was a real bad guy, but he was predictable, and that was something I liked in bad guys. I led Little Cuss up the trail, a step or two ahead to make sure he stayed on steady ground, and approached the rocks that Tom Pascal had shot from about half an hour later. He was no longer there.

I had traveled over terrain similar to this during my move north out of San Antonio a few years earlier. Hills don't bother me much, and they don't bother a good horse, either. Little Cuss wasn't in any hurry to get anywhere, and we slowly made our way up Lonetree, not really noticing the progress unless we turned around and looked behind us. Halfway up, you could almost see back to the wooded area around Fort Concho, and looking back east, you could see smoke drifting away from the horizon. That was Comanche land, and it made me realize the true value of owning a piece of land like Lonetree Mountain. Maybe only an angry god could remove you from the top of such a place, and it surely must have been one of the only places in Texas that a man could sit and sleep with little concern for Indian attack. The government was right to be kicking themselves for letting it fall into the hands of someone like Tom Pascal. The man was sitting on a gold mine.

I eventually found Pascal again, all the way up the north side of Lonetree. There wasn't really a single tree on the mountain. There may have been as many as twenty or thirty, but most of them were scrawny little things, half-dead from lack of water and no taller than Little Cuss's haunches. There was a single tall tree which stood at the crest. It could be seen from some distance but then disappeared as you moved up into the shadow of the mountain and remained hidden from that point until you finally approached the summit. It was there, lounging beneath the tree, his rifle still at the ready, that Little Cuss and me came upon Tom Pascal.

"I was just about to give you out," he said, standing up and walking toward me.

I had pinned my badge back onto the lapel of my coat, thinking if I turned it over to him I might not get it back without shooting him first. I was back on Little Cuss at this point, preferring to look down on this man than having to look up to him. I stand five foot and a single inch, and I don't take kindly to remarks about it. All said, I was doing Pascal a favor. Not giving him cause to comment meant not giving me reason to shoot.

"I had to stop and take a piss on your mountain," I said. "I hope that don't cost extra."

I hadn't really, but I wished I had.

"One dollar to pass," he said, "unless you've got that badge."

I showed it to him and let him take as long a gander as he wanted. I looked down on his old bald head and thought how easy it would be to crack it open like a watermelon.

"How did you come to buy a mountain?" I said.

He looked up and shielded his eyes with his right hand. I knew right then he was a rank amateur. You shoot right-handed, you don't use that hand to do anything else. Not while you're standing directly in front of someone who might have reason to shoot you down. Another day, that would have been cause enough to do it.

"Didn't buy it, mister," he said. "Won it fair and square in a card game."

I had never won more than a dollar or two in poker. I obviously traveled in different circles.

"Who in their right mind would put Lonetree Mountain on the table?" I said.

I was genuinely curious. He paused for a minute like he was trying to figure out if I was tricking him into revealing something. Maybe I looked like the kind to hang around with government lawyers. I had never met a lawyer I could stand.

"He's in the Texas State Legislature," Pascal said.

I feel about those guys about the same as I do lawyers. It suddenly seemed like I was overdue making my way down the south side of Lonetree. I pulled a silver coin out of my vest pocket and flipped it to the old man. He didn't even look at it. I hawed Little Cuss back toward the trail.

"I don't want your dollar," he said to my back. "If you're a true Ranger, I'll take something else in exchange."

I turned back to him. He handed the coin back.

"I'm not fighting the government for you," I said.

He shook his head *no*.

"That ain't it," he said. "It's my boy."

Tom Pascal wound up inviting me to dinner that night, in a little one-room cabin on the east face of Lonetree Mountain. He warmed up calf's head soup and johnnycake, and we swapped stories. He wanted to hear about my adventures as a Ranger, but they were yet sparse, so I told other ones and let him think they were Ranger stories. I told him about Gentleman Jack killing my wife on the streets of Fort Worth, I told him about my cook who had once cooked for the king of Mexico. He told me what he claimed to be the real story of Phantom Bill.

"Phantom Bill ain't no more that fella from up north than you or I," he said. "That Clark fella's sitting over in Mexico, sipping on tequilas with a senorita sitting on his lap."

He had asked to see my peso badge. Now I asked for proof.

"Here's the proof I got," Pascal said. "Phantom Bill is my son, William Pascal."

I was skeptical, but the soup was smelling good,

it was making my mouth water, and so I sat and listened. The story got better.

"I saw William a year and a half ago in Austin," he said. "He'd already held the damn train up once at that point. Had a Pacific Railway bag in the lining of his coat, stuffed full of fifty notes. Tried to give it to me, but I wouldn't take no part in it. What did I need money for? What was I going to do with it?"

I watched Pascal as he poured a bowl of soup and handed it across the table to me. I thanked him, held it up to my face, and drank.

"So what is it that you do want?" I said.

He broke a piece of the johnnycake off and handed it to me.

"I want a promise that you're not here to kill my son, and that you will not kill him."

I held the food in my hand, thinking that, if I dared to take a bite, it would be the same as making a promise. Did he understand this? Was he buying my sympathies?

"If your son is indeed Phantom Bill, I'm afraid I can make no such promises."

He was obviously disappointed.

"Even for free passage across Lonetree?" he said.

I wondered if the poker game had really happened. Had Tom Pascal purchased Lonetree Mountain as leverage against the Texas Rangers as they pursued his son? If he was in the habit of playing cards with Texas congressmen, anything was possible. It made me think that maybe Pascal was

right. Maybe Manley Pardon Clark wasn't Phantom
Bill after all.

"Catch him if you must," Pascal said. "Bring him
in safely . There's no reason to kill him. He ain't
never hurt nobody."

I told Pascal that, if I was attempting to bring his
son in, his son might very well decide it was time to
hurt someone. I didn't plan on being the one.

"I can only make you this promise," I said. "If he
comes without much fight, I'll bring him in alive,
If not, he's as good as dead. It will not be my body
they drag away."

The soup was delicious. The johnnycake got a
little dry in my mouth, but it might have been the
conversation that was to blame. I left the little
house knowing more than I did when I entered it,
and for that, I was grateful enough to leave him
with the dollar coin. Pascal seemed almost humili-
ated to take it, but that served me well, too. He
wasn't sure whether he had achieved his ends, and
I liked that just fine. I wasn't inclined to trade
promises for safe passage over Lonetree Mountain.
In fact, I didn't have any specific plans to be coming
back that way.

I had told Tom Pascal that I wasn't planning on
killing his son William. That much was true. I had
killed quite a few people by that point in my life,
but I don't reckon any of the killings had truly been
planned out. Mostly they just kind of happened.
Somebody forced my hand. Some I felt bad about.
I didn't like having my hand forced.

Anyway, I didn't plan much of anything, truthfully. It wasn't in my nature. If things happened, things happened. If they didn't, they didn't. I thought I might run into Gentleman Jack Delaney. I couldn't even make my mind up what to think about that, which was half the reason I wanted to do it. Pure curiosity. Whether I would join him in hunting down Phantom Bill was beyond me. I was beginning to get curious about Phantom Bill, too, though. I thanked Tom for the hospitality and told him the dollar was meant to cover for the food. I might come that way again, I said, and, if I did, I didn't want him shooting down the mountain at me.

When I say most of those killings just kind of happened, I don't necessarily mean it as an excuse. It seems like life in general seems to go that way, far as I can tell. Like I told Little Cuss as we rode away, I was just along for the ride.

CHAPTER FOUR

I hadn't got out of sight of the tree on top of the mountain before I had a thought and turned Little Cuss back. Tom Pascal was still standing right where I left him and didn't seem the least bit surprised when I rode back up.

"Want a little more of that johnnycake, do ya?"

He didn't come across as such a bad guy when he wasn't shooting into the ground around your feet. I thought maybe the boys at Concho had been a little peevish in their assessment of him.

"No, but I do have a question for you," I said. "There's a man supposed to be somewhere around these parts. A big, tall fella. Name's Jack Delaney."

I didn't even get to my question.

"He wear one of them Lincoln hats to make himself look even taller?" Tom said.

Anybody in the area would have almost certainly come through the same pass. Why I had almost neglected to ask about Jack, I don't know. I had been on the wrong side of the law many a time.

When you were on that side, you had to remain sharp at all times. I wondered if I was losing a little of my edge.

"That would be him," I said. "How long ago did he come through?"

Tom was clutching his rifle again, but he didn't appear to be in any mood to use it. I was watching for a move that wasn't going to come.

"First time or the last time?" Tom said.

I scanned the horizon for any sign of travelers approaching. The Comanche smoke was still rising to the northeast. Everything else seemed as still as God's stopwatch.

"How many times has he been this way?" I said.

I was already thinking. If Tom Pascal gave me an even number, I couldn't be sure he was still in the area. If it was an odd number, he was south, where he was said to be.

"Five, six times," Tom said.

I wasn't in any mood for guessing.

"Well, which one was it?" I said. "Which way was he going, last time you seen him?"

He had one hand on his gun and the other on his hip, and he looked like a woman trying to figure out how to answer or whether he should say anything at all. You could tell he had seen his share of lawyers, and I guess I must have looked a little like one to him.

"Has he done anything illegal, Mr. Liquorish?" he said. "Is that what this is all about?"

I knew it was useless to push. I was wondering

if I could still get some of that johnnycake for the trail.

"Not at all," I said. "I was supposed to meet him. He's planning to hunt down your son, I guess."

He pulled his rifle up into a defensive position, like if he wasn't so far away, he might aim to clobber me with it.

"You gave me your word, damn it," he said.

I didn't recall doing any such thing, but I was tired of talking.

"Just tell me which way he was going, I'll be on my way," I said.

It made me mad, but I was giving up on the johnnycake.

He pointed his rifle up and to the south, to indicate that Jack had been traveling west on his last time through the pass. I knew good and well, in my mind, that's what Tom Pascal was doing. My reflexes thought different, though. They saw that rifle come up and got jumpy. I grabbed my Colt .45 Peacemaker and shot. Got him right in the head. Pascal was dead before he hit the ground, never knew what hit him.

I didn't have any plan to kill that man. If you ask me, he provoked it, first by raising his voice with me. Then he had to go and raise his rifle. You don't do a fool thing like that. Not with me, not with anybody. Especially if you're being quarrelsome.

I buried him behind the little house, where a failed attempt at a garden at least made the earth a little more forgiving. Going six feet deep was near impossible, so I compromised at two, hoping there wouldn't be many wild critters hanging around at that altitude. I moved myself into the house and, over the next two days, ate all of the soup and the johnnycake, too. When I wasn't eating or sleeping, and I did that with one eye open, I was planning. Looked to me like I had stumbled upon an unusually favorable find, and I would make good use of it.

To begin with, if Gentleman Jack Delaney had passed through on six occasions, it would surely be just a matter of time before the seventh. Instead of trying to hunt him down out there in the miles of dust and desert, I could sit and wait for him to come to me. I would have the advantage as he approached, just as old Tom had. And I was fairly certain, if it came down to it, I could shoot from up above and put a bullet or two in him. At the same time, if Jack was used to paying Tom Pascal to pass through, he might not be all that joyous to see the new toll collector.

The little house was simple. It reminded me of the room me and Mama and Ira Lee lived in back in San Antonio's Sporting District. There was a stove in the middle of the room that Tom obviously used to cook on, as well as to heat the place. It assuredly got more work doing the latter. The location was high enough that, even on the east side of the mountain, the night wind could go to the bone, right up until the hottest heat of summer. There was a cot that looked suspiciously like the

one I'd slept on during my stay with the U.S. Army
at Fort Griffin. I pulled the dusty sheets from its
frame and burned them, along with a few photographs and personal items that didn't suit me, and
remade the cot with a quilt that had been nailed
up in a window. Soon enough, it looked more like
a room I could wake up in, in the middle of the
night, and feel like I wasn't someone else.

The following day, I got my first traveler passing
through and decided, from that point on, travel
through the Lonetree Mountain pass would be
free and painless. Delivered with a wave and a word
of warning against the ravages of desert heat and
sandstorms if they were going in a southerly direction and a warning against the Comanche if they
were going north.

Two days after I buried Tom Pascal coyotes and
wolves dug him back up and made off with various
parts of him. I found bits and pieces of him as I
scouted what I now thought of as my mountain.
One of his legs was halfway down the south face of
the mountain, the other one was north. I didn't
find his head, which seemed to have been ripped
right off his shoulders. I gathered up as many
pieces as I could find and cooked them up for a
son-of-a-gun stew. I never ate any of it, but I fed it
to three or four travelers over the next few days,
including a German woman who spit it out and
told me it tasted like human flesh. I wondered if
she was some kind of witch and kept a wary eye on
her from that point until she and her family left. If
she hadn't been traveling with them, I would have

killed her, too, just for making such a mockery of my hospitality. I didn't want to kill her two dirty-faced kids or her sickly-looking husband. The western desert would do that soon enough.

The day after the German family came through, a solitary man showed up from the south. It was a rainy day, and there was a misty cloud cover hanging low enough, when he came riding up, his silhouette cut through ahead of his features. I guess maybe mine did, too. He appeared startled to see me and acted suspicious of me right off the bat.

"Where's old Tom?" he said.

He was riding a beautiful palomino. Its saddle and blanket looked like the kind the Kiowa Apaches used. I had one in my bag from my old Kiowa Apache friend Long Gun, who had joined the U.S. Army with me in hopes of being a scout. He was dead now, and this guy was no Apache.

"Tom went up to Austin," I said. "Asked me to look after things here until he got back."

I stepped up and stuck out my hand.

"I'm Wilkie John Liquorish, Texas Ranger."

Most Kiowa Apaches I knew wouldn't readily jump to shake a white stranger's hand, and, if they did, it would be like shaking a dead rabbit. This man squeezed like a snake, which made me the rabbit.

"I don't give out my name to strangers, stranger," he said.

I could have just as easily shot him then and there, but part of me was intrigued. I thought he might be William Pascal, if there really was such a thing. Maybe Tom's story had been a bunch of hogwash, but, even then, this could've been Phantom Bill. If there was such a thing as him. I didn't have much to go on, and this guy wasn't helping me any.

"Any good reason for all the secrecy?" I said.

I gave his bags a look-over. They didn't look to be holding much. If there was money in them, it wasn't much. He could have hidden some in his coat, but I wasn't inclined to ask him to get down from the horse so I could pat him down.

"I'm no outlaw, if that's what you're thinking," he said.

I motioned for him to continue on and was irritated when he didn't do it.

"Mean to tell me there ain't no toll?" he said.

I told him I didn't have any interest in his money unless he had pulled it off the Pacific Railroad. I made sure he saw my badge, just in case he thought I wasn't playing straight with him. He reached down for his sideshooter. As long as his hand rested on it, I was fine. Once he made a move, I was shooting to kill.

He knew I had the jump on him. He nodded and hawed the palomino, and they silently moved along. I watched until they disappeared halfway down the north face and then saw them a little while later, moving slow to the northwest. My instincts were that he was a bounty hunter out of Austin looking for a little easy reward money. It occurred to me the desert might be scattered with folks like him. Maybe it was why Jack needed my help.

As if on cue, Gentleman Jack came along the following morning. I could identify him from half a mile away, the hat letting me know that it was either him or the ghost of Abraham Lincoln coming to call. I stood there in the same crag where Tom Pascal had hidden himself, settling my long gun right on his face and then on that stupid hat. I never shot.

A quarter of a mile from me, I heard him let out a long whistle. I knew it was a signal, but if I was supposed to whistle back, it would have done me no good. I couldn't whistle to save my life. I waited until the whistle came again. Something about Jack put me off, to where I knew I was standing on top of the mountain and still felt hemmed in. I propped myself just behind the lone tree, readied my rifle, and waited for the whistles to grow closer. They never did. I stood there beneath the tree until darkness fell and then slipped back to the house. I didn't sleep at all that night, alternating between lying there on the cot with my gun trained on the door, listening for every movement out in the darkness, and walking out and looking for any sign of Jack sneaking around under the moonlight. He was already getting to me.

He didn't show up the next day, either, much to my irritation. A waste of a day, that was, as I could even never let down my guard enough to make a meal or read from a book, much less take a nap. That evening I ate some jerky I'd brought along from Concho and finally fell into a light sleep just as rain returned to pepper the tin roof. Hours later, still in pitch black, I awakened to a nightmare.

Something rustled against the rickety old table, which caused the soup pot to clank out a warning. I thought maybe a wildcat or even a small bear had climbed in through the back window, all agape since I'd taken the quilt down. I sat up and rubbed my eyes.

"You move another inch, I will shoot you," a voice said. "Maybe I can't see you, but I will shoot at the noise and take my chances."

I knew the voice like I knew my own. It was a voice that could wake you from a nightmare and make you wish it had let you sleep.

"Jack," I said, "what the hell are you doing?"

I wanted to reach down and light the lamp sitting next to my left foot, but I didn't want to get my head shot off, even if I couldn't see it happen.

"Well, it's great to hear your voice, too, Wilkie," Gentleman Jack said. "I was hoping you might be agreeable to helping me root out this fellow—maybe you've heard of him—calls himself Phantom Bill."

He lit a cigar, and, for a short moment, his face cut through the black. He had a handgun in his lighting hand. Then he was gone again. Almost.

"But now," he said, "I fear I'm gonna have to bring you in for the murder of Thomas Pascal instead."

I leaned forward.

"I have my Peacemaker trained on the glowing end of your cigar, Jack," I said.

He laughed, and it glowed even brighter.

"No," he said, "no, you don't, Wilkie."

I didn't want to shoot him. Not there and then, anyway. The only thing I could think of that was any worse was getting shot sitting there on that bed. Just then, a slow rumble came rolling across the mountain, followed seconds later by a deafening crack and a flash of lightning. We both took a good, long look. My Colt, pointed right between his eyes, wiped the smile off his face in a hurry.

CHAPTER FIVE

"Why should I help you catch this Phantom?" I said.

Tom Pascal had obviously been a man who enjoyed a good sunrise, because his house was situated where the first splash of morning light spilled right through the window. It would be there soon, but, as we sat and talked, there was still no indication that this night was coming to an end.

"It'll take two working together," Gentleman Jack said. "One chasing and the other waiting."

I was giving Jack as much of a look-over as the newly lit lamp would allow. He was wearing a brown suit that might have been chosen to help hide a film of sand. I was pretty sure the hat, a dark velvet red, was the same one I'd seen him wear plenty of times.

"So you chase him into me, and I shoot him dead," I said.

He grinned and I noticed he was down one tooth

since I'd seen him last, on the top left corner. I wondered who knocked it out and under what conditions. No doubt Gentleman Jack had it coming.

"I was thinking you do the chasing," he said.

I knew that. I just wanted him to see that I knew what he was doing. Jack wanted to be the one to ride away as the killer of Phantom Bill. He would take the lion's share of the credit, and he would try to take the lion's share of the loot, too. And yet, to hear him tell it, Bill would go scot-free without my assistance. I had a good hand.

"I got a lot better things to do than ride around in the desert looking for a damn phantom," I said.

"You were on your way to see me, Wilkie," Gentleman Jack said.

I had no interest in pursuing that kind of talk. He sounded like an old lady trying to tell me how to make biscuit gravy with nothing but a pan of water and two sticks.

"Have you laid eyes on this Phantom Bill?" I said.

I wasn't sure how much he knew about the Phantom. Maybe I had information that he could use.

"I saw him in Pine Bluff, Arkansas, in last year, winter of '81," he said. "He didn't seem that bright to me then. He tried to rob the First National Bank there in Pine Bluff and got away with less than a hundred dollars."

If it had been my hundred dollars, I would have been pretty sore. Still, it seemed that if this was the same man robbing the Pacific blind, he'd polished his act a little.

"How you know it's him?" I said.

He looked at me the way he had back in Fort Worth, when he thought he was leading me to my slaughter.

"Phantom Bill is a guy called Manley Pardon Clark," he said. "He's a Yankee. Came down south because he had a price on his head up north. Comes from Chicago, I think."

Sometimes it's good to not tell everything you know. I know that to be true. I'm not very good at it, though.

"Phantom Bill is a man named William Pascal."

Gentleman Jack responded like he'd just been told a joke.

"Tom tell you that before you killed him?"

I was beginning to wish I'd blown Jack's head off when I'd had my chance.

"I didn't kill nobody," I said.

He reached down into a bag he had slung across his nonshooting shoulder.

"He says you did."

He pulled old Tom's head out of the bag by a handful of hair. It had been chewed over good, but there was no mistaking it for anybody else. Jack was like a kid with a new ball, pushing it closer and closer into my face, daring me to grab it or maybe kick it. Tom seemed to grin at me as he dangled from Jack's hand.

"He even says you shot him right through the smeller," he said. "See where it comes out the back of his head? Must have took his whole upper story right out with it."

He lifted Tom up against his own head, almost

cheek to cheek with the dirty remains. I looked out
the window, my brain seeming as empty as the one
Gentleman Jack was holding.

"I could take you into Austin, but I'm not gonna
do that. I need you with me this time. You help drive
this Phantom Bill out of the desert and across my
path, you'll go free. On that, you have my word."

I didn't trust his word. But it made no sense to
argue. If he thought I trusted him, that would be
his first mistake. Who was I to stop him?

I poured some stew and put out some hard
bread while Jack made the coffee. Grabbing the
cup, I poured some down my throat and found it
to be the worst I'd ever had. We had a mostly silent
but satisfactory breakfast, the first meal together
since sitting in the Black Elephant Saloon in Fort
Worth. I had to admit it, he cut as imposing a
figure in the little house on Lonetree Mountain as
he did in the fancy house in the city. Maybe, for a
while, we could make a team.

"The old man also told me his son William was
Phantom Bill," he finally said, drinking down the
last of the coffee like it was something to be proud
of. "I thought maybe he was right, too, until I went
down to the border. Little town down there called
Piedras Negras, close to Fort Duncan but over in
Mexico. They know of William Pascal down there.
They called him El Fantasma because he escaped
from the calaboose. William Pascal's hiding out in
Chihuahua."

He glanced over at Tom, who was sitting on the

floor next to him but, thankfully, out of my line of sight.

"Sorry, Thomas," Jack said. "Phantom Bill he ain't."

I watched Gentleman Jack swallow the last spoonful of the stew, his taste seemingly less finicky than the Germans'.

"Tom said he admitted to holding up the Pacific," I said.

Jack grabbed a handful of Tom's hair and placed him on the table between us. Everything Jack did was for effect. He looked at me and waited for some kind of response. He was testing me.

"Tom made you promise not to kill William," I said. "You probably worked out a deal. Twenty percent of the haul from the robberies, you would throw the scent off. Tell everyone he went to Chihuahua, wherever. Make everyone believe Phantom Bill is someone else."

I looked at Tom, sitting there on the table between us.

"Tom, you in on this deal? Did Gentleman Jack Delaney kill you for your share?"

I wasn't easily fooled, and, if Jack needed reminding, I was happy to do so. I had no idea whether Jack had cut himself in on Phantom Bill's business. I didn't know if William Pascal was Phantom Bill. But, if I had been a worthy opponent the last time Jack had seen me, my experience had only sharpened me, made me both tougher and more cynical. I would fall for nothing.

"Or maybe you're bringing me down here to set

me up. Maybe instead of driving the Phantom into your clutches, you'd have me driving myself there. You shoot me out there in the middle of nowhere, plant a bag of money on me, and drag me into Austin. Tell everyone *This is Phantom Bill.*"

Jack studied my face silently, like he would a poker player's, and then burst out laughing.

"You would make for a good Phantom Bill," he said.

He was right about that. I could have been Phantom Bill if I'd wanted. I liked trains, though, so I probably wasn't as inclined to rob one. I would have been better suited as a bank robber.

"Lots of people would," I said. "I suspect there's more than one of them."

After a while, the game grew tiring, and we gave it up. Jack went outside to tend to his horse, and I sat down with a worn copy of George Eliot's *Middlemarch,* which I had taken from a hotel in Lampasas, trying to make sense of it. I was hoping Gentleman Jack would see that I had no interest in his schemes and would ride off. When I heard horses approaching, I vainly thought it was Jack preparing to leave. It turned out to be the last thing I wanted. More company.

"You the owner of this place?"

The voice had a twang to it that said it didn't come from these parts. Alabama maybe, or Georgia. I knew it wasn't talking at me. I wouldn't have troubled myself to walk out on the porch if I wasn't afraid of how Jack might answer.

"The owner recently passed away," Gentleman Jack said. "I'm in charge, for the time being."

"That time being passed now, too," I said. "The owner's name was Tom Pascal. He left me in charge of things. What can I help you boys with?"

There were three of them. The two behind were squirts. I was just an inch over five foot, and they looked small to me. Schoolkids.

"Detective Bennet Salter, Pinkerton Detective Agency. I'm down here doing some work for the railroad. There's been a robbery resulting in a couple of deaths about fourteen miles south of here. Anybody at all come this way over the past several hours?"

I looked at Jack and counted back in my head. It was possible he could have come that far, that fast. Not many could. He had definitely come from the same direction.

"No," I said.

Jack was looking back at me with an expression I couldn't read. It didn't look grateful or relieved as it could have been. Maybe more like intrigued or bemused.

"We've got a dead conductor and a couple of passengers down there," Salter said. "Puts it in a whole different category. I expect you'll be seeing a whole lot more people that look like me."

I had seen enough Pinkertons to spot them a mile away. I didn't like them, even if we were now working the same side. Maybe I even liked them a little less because of it.

"I heard they already hired a bunch of you guys to ride the trains," I said.

I kind of hoped he wouldn't take any personal offense at the implication, but I mostly hoped he would.

"On some of the trains. Not all of 'em," he said. "Whoever robbed the train knew we weren't on board or else he got lucky."

"We'll sure keep an eye out," Gentleman Jack said. "Any idea how many of 'em?"

I could tell what he was thinking. If they shot the conductor and got away with loot, there was bound to be at least two. One to do the shooting and another to do the looting.

"It's Manley Clark that done it," Salter said. "Pretty sure it was a solo job."

I didn't know what to think. A lot of people seemed to be convinced this Manley Clark was pulling off the longest string of train robberies in America, and now he was upping his game. I wasn't about to say it wasn't him, but, in a funny way, I felt like maybe I owed it to Tom Pascal to at least check out his son William. It was this nagging doubt which produced a curiosity in my mind, and that was the real reason I decided, right then and there, that I would take Gentleman Jack Delaney up on his offer. I would ride south with him, into the hardest land in a state full of it. I might drive Phantom Bill into the arms of Jack, but I would most certainly drive him into his own demise. I was a Texas Ranger, and I sure as shooting wasn't going to let a lousy Pinkerton get this one.

Salter left, going back to the scene of the crime. It seemed like the thing to do.

"You can hang around here with ol' Tom," I said, "but I think I'm gonna follow that Pink on down to the railway line."

I got my hat, and me and Little Cuss were ready to ride.

CHAPTER SIX

Gentleman Jack proved to be a decent enough riding companion. When he got to talking, it reminded me of those few days back in Fort Worth, where he would sit around in the bar at the Black Elephant and tell tales of life in New Orleans and then chasing scoundrels all over the South. Most of the stories I had heard at the Elephant, but I let him go on with them. Partly because I wanted to see if he changed any details and partly just because they were good enough to hear one more time. It didn't matter that I knew half of them to be complete fiction. Jack had either forgotten that I knew better, or maybe he'd just plumb forgotten himself.

It was almost enough to make me forget I had shot and killed Jack's daddy in Clara the previous year. I had made a promise to the old man, a preacher I killed inside his own church, that I would finish the job by sending Jack on to meet up with him. I wasn't too foolish to overlook the fact that this gave Jack motivation to send me there, too. It was a Mexican standoff of sorts for now. Who knew what would happen when we were done with this Phantom Bill. Or Manley Clark. Or whoever he was called.

Some of the things Gentleman Jack talked about sounded too amazing and far-fetched to be real, but he had been born onto a cotton plantation during the years before the War of Northern Aggression, so who was I to say anything. I grew up poor, with a dirt floor and a roof leaky as a fishing net, but I belonged to myself and the backstreets of San Antonio. My mother made money entertaining soldiers from the base right around the corner from the Sporting District, but the money she made was for the most part hers to spend as she wished.

Gentleman Jack claimed to have been born into slavery, owned by a man named Guilbeaux and his daughter Sabina. Owned like a man might own a mule or a plow. I asked him if he could remember any of that time.

"I purchased my freedom and became a man on February 13, 1860," he said. "I wasn't a man before that day. There's nothing to remember."

He didn't seem inclined to dig further into that so I let it go. I had plenty of reason to suspect that Jack's life, before he had become a man, didn't take place in New Orleans at all. But if that was the case, it appeared that he had spent some time there afterward. He threw names around like someone who wasn't having to think about it. More than that, the man dressed like New Orleans.

Whatever his connection to that sinful city, it was something he seemed to share with at least two other people I could name. And they were both quite possibly named Henry John Liquorish.

Starting with the here and now and working my way backward, I could construct a certain amount of storyline, even if it was a mix of speculation and educated guesswork. First, there was my father, Henry John Liquorish. He had come to Texas with the New Orleans Greys, only to be killed by Comanches. Since I was little more than a suckling when that happened, I never knew the man, but I knew the name as well as I knew the name George Washington. And then there was the inebriate who showed up in Wheeler, Texas, carrying an envelope with the name Henry John Liquorish and a New Orleans address scrawled on it. That seemed to attach him to New Orleans at some point previous. Found crawling along on his hands and knees by the sheriff of Amarillo, he had been a far piece from that New Orleans address and going in the opposite direction.

He had been looking for me and my brother Ira. I was as sure of that on the night he showed up too drunk to convey any message. Then he disappeared. That disappearing act was troublesome. I still hadn't sorted it out. If he was a true Henry John Liquorish, he was a Henry John Liquorish who had heretofore not been known of by us San Antonio Liquorishes. That meant he was a cousin or a half brother at best. It also meant he may have been coming to Mobeetie to introduce himself. Ira and I had discussed that possibility. I had also talked it over with Greer.

"But why would he run off like he did?" I had said.

We had given him our warmest blanket, over the objection of Greer. We allowed him to sleep off his condition, a charity which had been returned with indifference.

"Likely as not he was embarrassed by his drunkenness. And wouldn't you be?" Ira had said.

I didn't make for much of an alcoholic. I preferred tonic water and fizzy drinks. Still, I could see Ira's point, and, even if I wasn't convinced, I didn't argue.

This strange new Henry John Liquorish opened up some dark trails in my mind, even to this day. I came to see him not as Henry John Liquorish at all. I began to see him as a man with an agenda. He had come with expectations to kill us and claim some reward or maybe an inheritance that we knew nothing of. Maybe he had been drinking to build up the nerve to do it, and then, waking up to find himself a guest in our very household, had gone cold on the idea and fled. If that was the case, and I could almost convince myself it was, I could also make myself think he was hiding behind every tree or around every bend in the road, his courage reassembled and his rifle loaded.

This is where things got a little complicated. It

was kind of like following a trail and suddenly coming up on a river that you had to cross. You could do it. You had to, if you wanted to keep going. You just had to be careful that your horse didn't lose his footing and get swept downstream and clear off track. There was one reason I had cause to know Gentleman Jack and one reason only. He had made it his job to see that I was hanged for a cattle drive that went drastically wrong. It was a terrible situation. Ira died on that trail and so did a lot of cattle. I wasn't any more to blame than General George Custer, but Jack had come damn close to hanging me for it anyway. I had survived only due to a rope that got stretched a little too long.

Here's the thing, though. Gentleman Jack had also been in New Orleans previous to showing up in Texas. That made two people from the same town who both came to Texas hunting me down.

Was there a reason Gentleman Jack came into Fort Worth wanting me dead that didn't have anything to do with red water disease on the drive or Leon Thaw the coach driver showing up in town with a bullet through his noggin or however many people getting sick from eating tainted meat in Wichita Falls?

The more I poked on it, the more suspect the whole thing became.

And what about that man with the envelope, that other Henry John Liquorish? Was he trying to tell me and my brother, Ira, something? I was sitting there on Little Cuss, staring at the back of Jack's head, when it hit me so hard, I almost yelled it out.

What if Gentleman Jack had poisoned that boy? I had no evidence that Jack was anywhere near on that night, but I had none that he wasn't, either.

"You spent some time down in New Orleans," I said.

We had been riding along in silence for the longest stretch of the ride, and I was beginning to feel like it was my turn to make a try at conversation.

"That a question or just an observation?" Jack said.

I brought Little Cuss up against his horse, a Thoroughbred named Alice that stood two hands over Little Cuss. The trail was wider than the Mississippi River at that point, so there was no call to ride in file.

"My father lived in New Orleans," I said.

I watched him as close as I could without being obvious. I had picked up on a habit of Jack's. I'd never noticed it when he was dandied up and thrilling the crowds in Fort Worth or playing for high stakes at the poker tables at the Black Elephant. He had seemed invincible then, and any flaw was covered over by brashness and bluster. But in Clara, where he had been stripped down into nothing but a preacher's son, a sinner amongst sinners, it had sat there as plain as the eyes on his face. When he felt vulnerable, when he felt trapped, when he felt the heat begin to rise under his collar, he rolled his eyes. Like he couldn't believe anybody would lower themselves to the point of questioning something he said. It stuck out to me because it didn't go with everything else I knew about him.

"A lot of people live in New Orleans, little friend," he said. "You should travel there yourself someday."

I hated when he called me *little friend*. Unfortunately, he knew it.

"His name was Henry John Liquorish," I said.

He turned and looked into my face.

"Think he would be disappointed in what you've done with yourself?"

I may have rolled my own eyes at him. I couldn't believe he would say such a thing. Of course it didn't have its intended effect, mostly because it was a question I had an answer for.

"I'm a Texas Ranger," I said. "My father loved Rangers."

It was the one card I held over Gentleman Jack, who liked to appear as if he had the winning hand, even when he didn't. I wanted him to roll his eyes at my answer, just to prove me right, but he turned and squinted blankly into the distance instead.

"They'll let anybody be a Ranger these days," he said.

I let him sit and stew for a while. I knew I'd got the best of him. Even so, he'd slipped out of my question, so maybe he was thinking he'd got the best of me. I decided to take a different approach.

"A man come all the way to Wheeler looking for me and Ira last year," I said. "He was from New Orleans, too."

Maybe I couldn't see Jack's mind at work, but he looked like a man studying a board of checkers for his next move.

"Like I told ya, a lot of people . . ." he trailed off.

I was beginning to wonder if I needed to look for a third way to kick the door in when he stopped Alice in her tracks and turned back toward me.

"What did he say he wanted?"

Ira was dead and buried, and I hadn't seen our drunken visitor since the night in question. I felt pretty free to answer as I saw fit.

"He warned me about people from New Orleans," I said.

I smiled and winked, feeling like I had crowned my checkers piece right in front of him.

"I'm not from New Orleans," he said. "I just lived there."

It was a distinction like saying he wasn't a man until he was set free from his slavery.

"Yeah, he warned me about people from New Orleans, Louisiana, and Clara, Texas," I said.

He laughed and rolled his eyes. It was quick, but I saw him do it. Just like he had rolled his eyes the year before when he found himself under scrutiny in Clara. I immediately doubted myself, like a man who asks for a sign in the heavens and then, upon receiving it, decides he is seeing things. I tried to recall if I had ever seen him do such a thing in Fort Worth. When I stood on the gallows, when I had fallen through the trapdoor, surely when I had been rescued from a slow choking death, Gentleman Jack had looked to the gathered crowd, if not the heavens, and rolled his eyes.

But yes. Maybe he had given himself away, in just the manner I had hoped he would. Maybe there were still secrets to be uncovered about Jack's past in Clara and in New Orleans. It was enough to go on. It was enough to think, just maybe, if I went along with this plan to chase Phantom Bill into the arms of the law, I would also be able to deliver Jack into the same long arms. It was enough to keep me moving south into the hardest part of a hard country, with a man who had tried to kill me once. I knew that turning and riding away would mean riding away from whatever truth lay out there to be discovered. As a Texas Ranger, as a man, as Wilkie John Liquorish, I was not about to do that.

CHAPTER SEVEN

The train lay across the desert like a dead snake, a likeness made more noticeable by the stench coming off it. It looked to be carrying mostly cotton, but I'd never known cotton to smell that way, even when you set it on fire or manured it. There was a cluster of detectives gathered around the engine, and then another gathered about half-way back. We were aiming for the front until I spied a figure waving us in from the other direction. I couldn't tell if it was Salter, but it was a bet that paid off, if not handsomely.

"There are three bodies," Detective Salter said. "Conductor up front. Lady and her kid back there."

He pointed three cars back. Suddenly the story had shifted. A dead lady was enough to get the attention of the Pinkertons. A kid was gravy. Put them both together, I was beginning to see the picture more clearly.

"Not a passenger train, though?"

The detective shrugged.

"One passenger car. The occupants may be members of the Pacific Railway family."

I wasn't sure I understood. I guess neither did Jack.

"Family of the conductor?" he said.

The Pinks didn't seem to be very far ahead of us.

"Somebody important enough to get their own railcar," Salter said.

Gentleman Jack had a look of concern that I wasn't used to seeing. I wanted to think it was annoyance at Salter, but it looked more like genuine concern that a child had been victimized. Maybe it was all those years of being victimized himself that were coming out.

"They found the woman and child this morning when a little girl walked up to a station one mile down," the detective said. "Told them she'd left the mother and little boy asleep back on the train and they wouldn't wake up."

First station down the line was San Saba. It wasn't a real station. It was a watering stop. A lot of times, robbers would hit a train when it was at a water stop. It didn't normally happen a mile away from one.

"Don't seem to be the work of one person," I said.

I was riding that pony all the way, fire or floodwater.

"Kid said it was one," Salter said.

Looked like floodwater in the forecast.

"The kid," I said.

How believable was a kid who thought her mother was just catching a nap, I wanted to know.

"How old is she?" Gentleman Jack said.

Detectives are supposed to know things like that, but Salter shrugged the question off.

"I don't know her," he said. "A kid. You know."

Jack and I both took a look at the engineer. He was slumped up against the firebox, burned to a well-done state on one side. He was obviously dead, but Jack pushed the body away from the box, and we watched it slump to the floor and fall sideways, bumping hard against the floor. There were two bullet holes, one in the right cheek, the other through the left eye.

Jack stood in for the poor guy, going through the motions of how he might have been looking straight ahead when the first shot hit him and then turned to catch a fleeting glimpse of his killer, as well as the bullet in the eye. It was a convincing play, and I had nothing to add except for the fact that, if things had occurred as Jack acted them out, the shots would not have left him slumped up against the boiler like he was.

Jack looked backward, trying to place where the shooter might have been to pull off such a feat.

"You're right, Jack," I said. "He was shot from where I'm standing. But the killer came into the cabin and moved him up against the firebox."

I jumped up onto the engine with Jack, and he momentarily flinched, like I was about to demonstrate just how it all went down. I wasn't interested. What I was looking for were the pop-off valves on the boiler. Because of my size, I could shimmy up onto a train with ease. I had done it in Fort Worth once or twice when one parked itself between me and something I took a liking to. I knew if the train had been coming into the San Saba water station, the engineer would have had the valves open for sure. I had a hunch that our train-robbing killer had climbed aboard for nefarious reasons. What I found didn't change my mind.

"Valves are closed," I said.

Gentleman Jack jumped down from the cabin like he was jumping off a wild bull. I couldn't help laughing at his coattails slapping in the breeze. He reminded me of a turkey trying to take flight.

"Get off that damn thing," he said.

He knew what was going on, but, from the steam dome, I could tell the train wasn't hot enough to blow.

"Somebody came up and closed the valves," I said. "And they shoved the engineer up against the firebox while they were at it."

It was my turn to walk through the scene, playing it out in my mind. Gentleman Jack wasn't dumb. I knew he was thinking the same thing.

"So whoever did it intended to blow the thing sky-high," Jack said.

And he wanted to make sure the driver went with it.

"Only it didn't blow," I said.

That was a puzzle, but not one worth pursuing. There were a dozen different reasons a train might not have blown up, including just because it didn't.

"Our Phantom Bill is a vindictive little son of a gun," Jack said.

The Pinkertons soon descended on us. Salter was telling a couple of new guys to go over the engine with a fine-tooth comb and look for anything that might have been missed. I heard him mention the safety valves as well, so I knew we were still playing catch-up. As Jack and I walked toward the cars, I did notice one of the Pinkertons quietly sketching the body as it lay there on its side in the cabin. I didn't tell them that I had moved it. I guessed they could see that for their own selves.

The third car back was an atrocious sight, the likes of which I never wished to see again. Unfortunately, I would see it in my dreams for years. The mother lay to one side, flopped over onto her son, who was almost hidden beneath her. She was wearing a gray dress, calico with a flower print. It was similar to one my wife, Greer, and a hundred others like her had worn. Now drenched a dark, wet bloodred, it did its best to cover her wounds, all being in the torso. Her face looked down, soft and white, eyes blue and wide open. Trails of blood from one ear and her mouth were the only noticeable blemishes there.

The boy had been shot once, right in the face. Because of the placement, you could tell that he had been shot first.

"If the engine had blown, it would have taken this car with it?" I said.

I wasn't sure, and, because Salter insisted on

following along with us, I decided to make use of him as I could.

"By gum," he said, "it could have taken out everything for a quarter mile."

Jack was poking around on the boy, trying to fish him out from under his mother's protection. I was wishing he'd just let the kid be.

"I imagine you would have seen her blow from Lonetree Mountain," Gentleman Jack said.

He turned around and looked at me.

"What are you thinking?"

He wasn't asking me because he wanted to know. He was testing me. Or maybe he was testing the Pinkerton.

"I think that lady right there was the reason for all of this," I said.

Salter shook his head.

"They took a lot of money."

That ended the conversation. Whatever I had to say on the matter would not be said in front of that jackass. Gentleman Jack followed suit, and we did whatever looking we had left and departed in the direction of San Saba. There was a kid there that I was wanting to talk to.

On the way, we did plenty of talking. We made for a decent enough team when we had something proper to talk about. It kept the past from coming up, and I could almost forget who I was talking to.

"They didn't hit that train for the money," Gentleman Jack said.

I was willing to entertain the notion, but I wanted

to know more. Like how much money they did get. He said it didn't matter.

"They grabbed the money because it was there," he said. "Why not take it? But they didn't shoot a lady and her kid, sitting three cars back, just because they were there."

Okay, I could grant him that much. And I could raise the stakes.

"He wanted to hurt her before he killed her," I said. "First of all, he shot the boy right in the face."

Gentleman Jack pulled Alice right alongside Little Cuss, and we were going at a pretty good clip, but it was so quiet on the midafternoon desert that it sounded like he was whispering in my ear.

"And he shot her in the gut."

She might have lain there a long time, using her son's dead body as a pillow, listening to his heart not beating in her ear. It had surely taken the girl a while to walk the mile to the water station. Why had the little girl not been shot? Or had she? She had been in another car. Probably riding with the freight. Where had she been going?

"I'm still wonderin' about the valves, and I'm surprised the whole thing didn't blow, what with the release valves shut up and all," I said. "But that sure looks like somebody wanted to destroy the evidence."

Any engineer would notice if the valves weren't working. He would have already had his hands full before Phantom Bill or Manley Pardon Clark or whoever arrived on the scene.

"He was cooling his engines, getting ready to

stop in San Saba," I said. "Maybe the boiler was cool enough that it just never got hot enough."

Jack admitted it was possible. Still, it was pretty cold comfort. The conductor and passengers were dead anyway. Only the train had been saved.

"I'm still not sure why he stopped the train a mile before San Saba," Jack said. "Something just doesn't feel right."

We rode along in silent agreement for a while. Then Gentleman Jack spied a bunch of turkey vultures to the south and adjusted, partly out of curiosity and partly because Jack wanted to whoop and holler and run through them, waving his arms and sending them in all directions. I came along behind and found the carcass of a sheep at the center of their attention.

"I always heard a vulture wouldn't eat anything that had been dead for more than a few hours," I said.

We rode along at a faster clip now, Jack still using his momentum from scattering the turkey vultures and me just trying to keep up with him.

"It's true," he said. "They like a fresh kill."

I wondered what a freshly killed sheep was doing out in the middle of nowhere. I hadn't seen any flocks roaming around anywhere. I remembered Sister Mary Constance, the nun who schooled me back in San Antonio, telling the story of the little lost sheep. I couldn't remember the details, but it was something about Jesus leaving his flock of sheep and going out to rescue the little lost lamb. Maybe there was a big bad wolf involved, but that might have been another story entirely.

As I looked over my shoulder, a few of those damn birds were already starting to reassemble. Didn't look like the Lord had mustered up enough interest to do anything, so it sure wasn't any of my business.

The sun slid down just to where it stared us right in the eye as we entered San Saba. We came in with our arms up over our faces, seeing nothing where there was nothing to see. Just a water tower full of water and a hand pump with no hand. Nothing else but a track and a bunch of sand and rocks.

"The little kid came here?" I said.

Gentleman Jack nodded into the distance, and, north of the tracks about a mile, you could see a couple of buildings rising out of the flatland. If the little girl had walked all the way to that house, after watching her family get shot, I wanted to meet her. Not just to ask what she had seen. I wanted to see what kind of kid could survive such an ordeal and have the gumption to save herself and then go for help.

CHAPTER EIGHT

What we had seen in the distance there at the San Saba water station was the Spiney McSwain Ranch. I had no idea who Spiney McSwain was and said so right away. That tickled Gentleman Jack to no end. No sooner would he stop his guffawing than he would commence right back again.

"It ain't Spiney McSwain," he said finally. "It's a hundred thousand acres belonging to the Isaac Spiney family from Austin and the Charles McSwain family from right here. Each family has fifty thousand acres, but it runs, for the most part, as one big ranch."

I didn't have to ask what kind of ranch it was. The cow dung blowing in from the northwest was so thick you could lick it off your lips. There's nothing like it in the world.

"I wonder how much cattle they got," I said.

I had helped run one cattle drive. It was paltry by any definition. I had never seen a ranch the size of the Spiney McSwain Ranch, even out in the farmland around Mobeetie.

"Probably three, maybe four," Jack said.

I was thinking of the eight hundred head of cattle I'd driven into oblivion a year earlier. It was a thought I didn't like to light on any more than necessary.

"Four hundred?" I said.

He looked at me like I was crazy, something he was prone to doing on a regular basis. It only troubled me when I knew I had messed up. I always knew.

"Four thousand, Wilkie John. Four thousand."

His words burned in my ears like when Lieutenant Granville Hanley of the U.S. Army had dressed me down for not doing this thing or another thing as quickly, as perfectly as he wanted it done. I reminded myself that I had shot Hanley right through his ear hole.

Somehow, the McSwain family were expecting us. Maybe they had just seen us coming from a distance and decided to welcome us hospitably. The old mama of the house, whom I presumed to be Mrs. McSwain, brought out whiskey and cigars and even took a splash from the bottle, maybe just so we'd know that it wasn't poisoned. When she understood that we were looking into the train killing and, more important, that we weren't Pinkertons, she asked one of the young ladies in the kitchen to go and fetch the young girl who had walked up to the house the previous day.

"She's staying in the little room out back," Mrs. McSwain said. "You understand."

I said sure, I did, even though I didn't really know yet what I was sure about. We sat there and sipped at our glasses, the whiskey burning off a layer of dust as it went down my gullet and found a warm place inside of me. I watched Gentleman Jack stir his glass with his finger and tried to remember when I had seen him do such a thing before. Undoubtedly, it was in the Black Elephant in Fort Worth.

"You've got a nice place here, ma'am," I said. "How long have you been here?"

The lady seemed happy for a little attention.

"I came here in '36," she said. "We were living in Gonzales. The whole town evacuated because the Mexicans were coming. We'd heard what they did at the Alamo, and we didn't want to stand around and be part of a massacre like that."

Thirty-six. I tried to count back and figure her age. She seemed as old as the hills. Maybe she had even known Crockett and Travis.

"You must have been a baby," Gentleman Jack said. Every once in a while, he really was a gentleman. Mostly, it was out of sheer luck.

"You flatter me, sir," she said. "I was sixteen years old and as naive as a newborn calf. My father moved me and Mama and my two brothers here, onto this land he purchased from a friend of Stephen Austin. It was twice what we have today, too."

"Was it always a cattle ranch?" I said.

I was adding up the numbers. I wasn't as good in my head as I was with a piece of paper, but, to the best of my ability, I was putting her somewhere in her sixties. If that was true, she still seemed full of vim and vigor. Or piss and vinegar, as I'd sometimes heard it.

I looked up and saw the kitchen door swing open, and into our presence came a girl. She was a kid, all right. Maybe five, six years old, best I could tell. But she didn't appear to be the correct kid.

"She's colored," I said.

Mrs. McSwain looked over her spectacles at me and then at the girl, like she hadn't noticed until I said something.

"We thought this was the daughter of the woman on the train," Gentleman Jack said.

We had both assumed this. We hadn't been told any different. It didn't trouble me that she was a colored girl. I found an affinity with colored females, even. It just hadn't been what I was expecting.

"What is your name?" I said.

When she stepped forward, I could see that her left leg and arm were both wrapped in medical bandages. She had a black eye and a small cut on her left cheek to complete the package. Still, when she spoke, her voice was strong and clear.

"Bess Harper."

"Bess?" I said.

She nodded, never lifting her eyes from the floor in front of her.

"You're a brave little girl," I said.

She was fidgeting with a little cloth doll that

looked like it had spent as much time in San Saba as Mrs. McSwain. I wondered if Mrs. McSwain brought it with her from Gonzales. I looked down and caught myself fidgeting with my shirtsleeve. I didn't know how to talk to kids. Never mind that she was colored. Or that she was a she.

"Where were you going on the train?" Gentleman Jack said. "Could you tell us?"

Bess shook her head *no.*

"How old are you, Bess?" I said.

She held her hand up with all five fingers present and accounted for. I couldn't see a five-year-old colored girl riding a train by herself, not knowing where she was going. I was beginning to wonder if she was even on the train.

"How did you get here, Miss Bess?" Jack said.

I didn't like the way he said "Miss Bess," and I don't think she appreciated it, either.

"I walked."

I got down on my haunches, thinking maybe if I was on her level, she might at least accidentally look me in the eye.

"But you were riding the train when the bad people stopped it," I said.

She looked me dead in the eye.

"It was a man with teeth."

I wasn't sure what to make of that. I decided to concentrate on the first part.

"It was one man?"

Bess nodded her head.

"Did you see the man hurt the lady and her little boy?" Jack said.

I could see Mrs. McSwain was getting antsy. It wasn't conversation for a proper lady, much less a young girl. And yet, here we were, face-to-face with the only witness to the crime.

"He was gonna shoot Pete, but I wouldn't let him," she said.

"Pete?" Mrs. McSwain said. She looked at me with an expression that made it clear this was new information to her, too. "You didn't tell us this before."

Gentleman Jack, sensing I was starting to get more from the young girl, dropped to one knee in such a dramatic fashion, I thought he was about to launch into a verse of "Moonlight on the Lake."

"Pete was the little boy with the lady?" he said.

She immediately went back to her head-shaking.

"That little boy was shot in the face, if you'll recall," I said.

Mrs. McSwain shushed me after the fact.

"Was there another little boy on the train?" she said.

Bess looked up at the old lady, and I could tell she wanted to be anywhere in the world but in that room.

"Eli said Pete could ride with me."

I could barely make out the words.

"Eli?" I said.

The girl turned tail and ran out of the room, and Mrs. McSwain followed her. I turned to Gentleman Jack and shrugged.

"A colored girl," he said.

We hadn't gone through the rest of the railcars

out there on the track. Now I was kicking myself for assuming the Pinkertons had done the job right when it was theirs to do.

"You reckon there's more bodies out there?" I said.

It wasn't a far piece back to the scene, but after what I had already seen, I was in no hurry to go back for more.

"Could be," Jack said.

We stood there in the drawing room and waited for Mrs. McSwain or Bess or somebody to return. I was beginning to think they'd both run off. Soon, I heard the back door shut to, and, in a minute, a young man with a thick head of red hair and a face that bore a strong resemblance to Mrs. McSwain's came stepping into the room. He look as surprised to see us as we were to see him.

"I'm Robert McSwain," he said. "And who might you be?"

I told him my name and added that I was a Texas Ranger. I made no move to explain my partner. Robert McSwain looked at him and waited.

"I'm Jack Delaney," he said. As if anybody knew who that was.

"He's a bounty hunter," I said. "Goes by Gentleman Jack."

The young man looked him up and down, I suppose to check his gentlemanliness. He seemed satisfied enough.

"Y'all hunting down Phantom Bill?" Robert said.

His mother returned to the room, but without her small guest in tow.

"You won't be questioning Bess Harper any further."

The matter didn't appear to be up for debate.

"I don't believe much in ghosts," Gentleman Jack said. "I am in pursuit of Manley Pardon Clark for holding up the Pacific Railroad and killing three people on it."

Robert stepped across the room and shook hands, first with Jack and then with me. He was young and scrubbed down until he gleamed. He looked like he'd never shaved before.

"We were trying to talk to the little colored girl who witnessed it," I said.

I looked at Mrs. McSwain for support. She looked back like she was watching me talk for the first time in her life.

"That colored girl didn't see Manley whatever-you-said," Robert McSwain said. "You ask me, she probably come along after it all happened. Why would a colored girl be on a train like that?"

I thought his logic was something less than logical.

"What would she be doing walking along in the middle of nowhere?" I said.

I wanted an answer, but I didn't get one. What I got was another question, this time from Gentleman Jack.

"Well, she said she was with Pete. Maybe if we can find Pete, that'll at least be a start."

That kind of shut us all up for a little bit, as we all stood there in the room and reviewed where the discussion had taken us. It was into the lull that little Bess burst again. She made a beeline for Mrs. McSwain, who used her whole body to block her from the rest of us.

"What you two fellas need to do is go talk to a man named Cookie Zamora," Robert said. "He lives just south of the river. Used to be a darn good blacksmith."

I wasn't sure why I should care what he used to be. I wasn't sure I needed to see him, either.

"I don't need a blacksmith," I said.

It wasn't really true. Little Cuss could have used a reshoeing.

"He don't shoe horses anymore," Robert said. "Mostly he just drinks and talks about Phantom Bill."

It didn't seem like a combination I could put much stock in.

"Boys?"

I turned on my heels toward Mrs. McSwain, who was face-to-face with the little colored girl and leaning against her.

"What's the problem, Mama?" Robert said.

The little girl was in midcry, but it was one of those silent, nonbreathing kind of cries that only kids are brave enough to do.

"She wants you to go find Pete," Mrs. McSwain said.

There was something in her face that reminded me of my dear friend Sunny, the most beautiful call girl at the Black Elephant, who cried the same way on the night before Gentleman Jack was supposed to throw a necktie party for me. Her face was something I wasn't ready for.

"Where is he?" I said.

The little girl pointed toward the back of the house, but Mrs. McSwain motioned the other way.

"Last time she saw him, I think he was somewhere out there between here and the train," she said.

If I had ever wanted to believe in God, it was right then, even if it was for all the wrong reasons. I wanted to curse him for leaving that little lamb out there in the desert to die alone. I looked at Bess, though, and was glad she had made it through. I didn't know where she came from or where she was going, but that didn't make much difference. I could say the exact thing about myself. We might eventually end up food for the turkey vultures, but we were keeping a step or two ahead of them for now. In the heat of the Texas desert, that was good enough.

I waited until Bess left the room.

"Ma'am, I sure hate to tell you this," I said, "but I'm afraid ol' Pete is vulture food."

Mrs. McSwain's lip trembled. Whether it was at the thought of Pete's demise or of having to tell the girl, I don't know. I was glad I wouldn't have to do it.

CHAPTER NINE

Cookie Zamora wasn't anywhere he was said to be. First, he wasn't in his house on the southwest side of the San Saba, where it ran crooked through the small patch of pecan trees and then snaked its way in the general direction of Mexico. If I had been a grown man named Cookie, that's where you would have found me, because there was more shade there than I had seen since I left Fort Worth, and the rush of the water made for at least a false sense that everything wasn't drying out and dying before our eyes.

Cookie wasn't there, and he wasn't anywhere in the surrounding area, either. Not fishing in the river or swimming in it, like Robert had said he might be. Not up on the hilltop passed out drunk after drinking in the stars all night as Mrs. McSwain warned. There weren't a lot of other places to look. You could cast your gaze in any of four directions and, for the most part, see for miles. No Cookie.

We watered the horses and were getting ready to

go back in the direction of the Spiney McSwain Ranch when he came walking over a distant horizon, his horse a good three lengths behind him. I wasn't sure what to make of it.

"*Bueno*," he said, two, maybe three times as he got nearer.

I had learned in San Antonio not to answer in Spanish, even though I was somewhat capable of it. If I did, they would assume I spoke the language and would launch into a conversation that quickly left me in the dust. My Spanish started and ended with what few words I learned as a kid in Sister Mary Constance's classroom. That was more than Gentleman Jack knew.

"I thought *bueno* meant 'good,'" he said. "Not 'hello.'"

He was muttering beneath his breath, although Cookie was still an eighth of a mile away.

"It does," I said. "*Hola* is 'hello.'"

I wasn't sure he was paying me any attention, or that he even believed me, but about a minute later, Cookie was close enough that you could see the bottles of beer balanced across the back of his horse. It looked like enough to get all the troops at Fort Concho drunk.

"*Bueno*," Cookie said for maybe the fourth time.

I tipped my hat to him.

"*Hola*," Gentleman Jack said.

I didn't have any time to warn him. Cookie let loose with a barrage of words that included something about cerveza and maybe *bienvenido* or something. I just looked at Jack and smiled. Jack, of course, had a way of cutting right through to the heart of the matter.

"I hear you know a little about this man they call Phantom Bill."

Cookie stopped suddenly and held his hand up.

"Phantom Bill is no man," he said. "He's what my people call a *fantasma.*"

I liked Cookie Zamora immediately, in spite of his belief in ghosts. When it came to ghosts, I was a skeptic. I treated ghosts the same way I treated God and Jesus and most other things I had never seen. There was no good reason to believe in them. I had never seen one. I'd never even seen the wind move behind one. If they were out there, they had always kept a wide berth. Of course, I preferred it remain that way. As for his Spanish, I was pretty quick to find that Cookie's Spanish didn't go a lot further than we had already seen demonstrated. In his house, which looked more like a small fortress against the world once we got inside, he was quick to tell us his entire story, completely in English. Thank God.

"I was born in Chihuahua," he said, "but I don't remember it. Chihuahua, I mean. Although I don't remember being born, either. The first I remember, I was living in San Antonio next to the mission. We used to play around the mission. We didn't have no conception of what it meant. I wondered why everyone else liked the mission so much. Why no one would let us play. My mama, she spoke Spanish only. Can you believe it? When I was small, that's what we spoke. Later, my mama passed away, and so did the Spanish."

He looked sad, so I wanted to stop him, but he wasn't paying me any attention. I drank his beer, which was hot but wet and went down smooth.

"We packed up our things and went to live with a gringo family. It was the same city but very different and far from the mission. Only much later, I found out that this white-skinned man in this family was my true father. His name was Sidney Brashear.

"Now everybody called me Cookie. Called me that way back when we lived over there by the mission, and when we went to live with the white folks, they kept right on calling me that. My Christian name is Juan Pablo. You tell me, do I look like Juan Pablo Brashear?"

I didn't see anything wrong with it, but I didn't want to argue with the man about his own name. I had enough trouble with my own. People calling me Willie John or John Willie or maybe on a good day John Wilkie. Even Gentleman Jack Delaney had mangled it, most times on purpose.

"So I had my mama's name. I am Cookie Zamora, in honor of her."

Jack had had enough of not hearing himself speak.

"Well, Juan Pablo Zamora is a fine name."

That statement hung out there for a while like a high limb no one wanted to jump for.

"Robert McSwain says you might know a thing or two about this fella that goes by the name of

Phantom Bill," I said after some time had passed to mourn the death of Jack's comment.

Cookie stood up from the chair where he sat, almost knocking his beverage sideways.

"Phantom Bill. El Fantasma," he said. "I have seen him with my two eyes. He comes up from the south and follows the train line, but he always turns back before he gets this far west of San Saba."

I could tell Jack wasn't buying in. He was sold on the Manley Clark thing the same way I was sold on it being more than one person—or ghost, if you insisted—that was doing the killing and looting. The more I heard about Clark, the less I thought it was him. I just didn't much think we were dealing with a Yankee. Problem was, the more I heard about El Fantasma, the less stock I was putting in him, too.

"You aware the latest holdup resulted in three dead passengers?" I said.

Cookie seemed surprised to hear the news.

"The whole thing has gotten out of hand," Jack said. "You think this Phantom was responsible for killing those people?"

We gave him a moment of silence to absorb the information. I was beginning to think he had said all he was going to for that day.

"Who did he kill?" he said. "He killed the conductor?"

I tried not to imagine the scene I had witnessed on the train, but just trying not to do it required doing it.

"A lady and her little boy, too," I said.

I wondered if Cookie had ever had a wife and kids. His expression said maybe he had.

"Oh, Phantom Bill would not do such a thing," he said.

Jack was growing frustrated with the whole discussion.

"Maybe he wouldn't because he's a figment of the imagination," he said. "But maybe Manley Pardon Clark would do it."

Cookie emptied the last few drops of drink onto his tongue and reached for another bottle.

"You must understand. El Fantasma's vexation is with the banks and the railroad men who put their tracks down across people's property," he said. "They didn't pay a penny for it, and, if they did, it was just a penny. El Fantasma has no issue with the people who live down here or with anyone who's just passing through. You must look for someone with the heart to kill. You are on the wrong track."

His thinking made sense to me.

"You got any ideas who might have that kind of hate?" I said.

He looked at me with a faraway look that might have been caused by the alcohol but maybe not.

"Look close at people on the train," he said. "They will tell you who did it."

I was beginning to wonder how often he rode off and came back home with a saddle stacked with cerveza. The way he was going through it, even discounting the ones Jack and I were sipping along on, he was going to need another trip by the time the rooster crowed again.

"They're dead, Cookie," Jack said.

Cookie was wearing thin with Gentleman Jack. He didn't give people nearly as much leeway as I did. I liked to study people, study their differences, what made them tick. Jack didn't give a darn. The only person who was worth his time was Jack himself. That was both his best selling point and his worst defect.

"They're no deader than El Fantasma," Cookie said. "Their spirits will speak to you, if you have ears to listen with."

That reminded me of preacher talk. Something about every ear hearing and every knee bowing down. I didn't care for that kind of talk coming out of a preacher's yap, and I didn't like it coming from Cookie, either.

We were slowly working our way toward the door when Jack brought up Bess Harper. I was mad at him for it. I was ready to get gone.

"There was a little colored girl who walked to Spiney McSwain Ranch and said she was on the train. So the killer either had a soft place in his heart for coloreds or for children or maybe just for colored children."

That seemed to interest Cookie Zamora a great deal.

"I'd think the little girl was in another car," he said. "Pacific is the railroad that lets colored folks and Mexicans ride, but they put us in a separate car. Always."

I guess I knew that, even if I had never really stopped to think on it. I had never ridden a train before, so any information I did know had come secondhand.

"You think maybe there was more there we didn't see?" Gentleman Jack said.

I couldn't imagine that the Pinkertons wouldn't have checked out all of the cars, but, then again, I didn't have a high opinion of the Pinkertons, so it was completely possible.

"Think she would've been riding alone?" I said.

We both looked at Cookie, as if he had become the ranking expert.

"Maybe she belonged to the white family," he said.

Did he not know the slaves had all been freed almost twenty years earlier?

"Slaves, field hands, what's the difference?" he said. "My people work fields alongside those people. They aren't slaves, but you wouldn't know for sure. That colored girl was maybe the little white kid's playmate or something. Somebody to entertain while Mama's off sipping tea with friends."

That scenario seemed as plausible as anything else I had heard.

"Might have been another kid," I said. "She said something about someone named Pete."

Cookie looked at me like I had lost my mind, and, for a minute, I wondered if I had said something different from what I heard in my own head. What swam to the top of my thoughts was a confused and garbled thought altogether.

"Do you have a boy named Pete?" I said.

It never made any more sense than it did there in the moment I said it, but in my defense, he looked like he had peered over the edge of all darkness and found its cold, dead heart.

"There's a kid out there, wandering around in the desert, and you're sitting here talking to me?" he said.

Gentleman Jack must have sensed my momentary confusion and stepped in.

"We're pretty sure Pete's already dead."

We had that discussion on the way to Cookie's riverside hideaway and came to a mutual agreement. If Bess had asked to bring Pete along but had left him behind somewhere out on the hottest, most barren part of the trail, not knowing that there was a ranch house not too much farther on. If she had not mentioned him at all to Mrs. Mc-Swain until much later, when she cried out and begged us to rescue him. If all of those things were true. Then Pete was almost certainly the little lost sheep we had found on our way to the ranch house. It seemed obvious. Why would a single sheep be out there in the middle of nowhere? There wasn't a sheepherder that I knew of anywhere in the territory.

It hit me right there in midthought.

"You know where any sheepherders are located around these parts?" I said.

Cookie looked at Jack. I knew Jack didn't know. We had already discussed it. That's why I was asking Cookie.

"Me?" he said.

"You."

I sat up and knocked over a bottle that knocked over another bottle before crashing to the dirt floor. All were empty. No loss.

"Sure," he said. "There are two ranches that raise sheep. One is very small."

He stopped for a minute. I thought he was going to pick the bottles up off the floor, but he kicked them aside instead.

"If you're looking for trouble, you might want to check the Alameda Ranch. They're the big sheep ranch. Got thirty herders, each with a thousand, maybe two thousand."

I had heard of the Alameda. It was back east of the train robbery. Over a hundred thousand acres, it took up part of three different counties. Cattle and sheep.

"Why do you say it's trouble?" I said.

I hadn't heard of any trouble on the ranch. Granted, I hadn't spent any time in the area until the past week.

"The guy at Alameda, a man from Scotland named Charles Stirling, has been skirmishing with some of the cattlemen on a few of the other ranches. They don't like the sheep taking over the grasslands."

Didn't seem like that big of a problem to me. Surely they cold hammer out some sort of agreement by which the sheep and the cattle could share a few hundred thousand acres of land.

"Maybe not," Cookie said. "There have been threats of killings for a year or more now. They flair up, then they settle back down. That's part of the reason I moved here. I used to work for Robert McSwain, but I didn't care for the fighting. It looks now like maybe that first death has finally occurred."

At first, I thought he was referring to Pete the lamb, but soon enough, I realized. Cookie thought the whole train robbery was connected to the Alameda Ranch.

"I don't think I understand why the ranches would be involved in something like this," I said.

"I'm not saying they are," Cookie said. "I'm saying look for connections. Anytime someone dies around here, if it isn't the desert heat, it's got something to do with the sheep-grazing fields that used to belong to cattle."

If he was right, Spiney McSwain looked to be prime suspects.

CHAPTER TEN

It's a good thing we found the little lamb on our first pass through the area between the Spiney Mc-Swain Ranch and the train because, on our second pass through, there weren't enough bones left to identify what it had once been.

"I'd give Pete a proper burial if there was enough to bury," Gentleman Jack said.

I was surprised at his gentleness. Was it provoked by the little girl Bess? By the little lost lamb? Or by something he carried inside of himself? He would certainly not tell, so I didn't bother asking. We left that spot and traveled south of the trail we had followed on our approach to the Spiney Mc-Swain Ranch, following a ragged range of hills and bluffs. It was from that area I suspected our robber and now killer approached. The hills would have given him cover both before and after the robbery, and I knew he hadn't come from north of the tracks. I was hoping we might find something that would reveal his previous whereabouts, if not his current ones.

Right up against the rocks, there was a small trail of mud that had been a stream feeding into the San Saba earlier in the year. Now there was no water to be had. I was walking ahead of Little Cuss, going west along the dried-up stream. It was wide enough that you could jump it, but you would be lucky not to leave a boot print, and so we were hunting for boot prints. Half an hour later, I heard Gentleman Jack let out a whoop that echoed against the side of the rocks, so loud I figured Cookie himself could have heard it.

I came running, but I was cussing him with every step. My initial thought was Jack had captured Phantom Bill by himself. If that had been the case, I probably would have shot Jack dead and maybe the Phantom, too. We had walked ourselves far enough apart that he was just a small speck against the horizon, but I could see he was alone.

"Who in tarnation are you hollering at?"

My voice seemed to fade out in the air. Jack threw his hands in the air as if to show me where he was. He slowly got larger until I could see that he was holding his hat in his hands. He yelled out something about his feet, and I could see he was looking down.

"What happened?" I said.

My meaning was, "What happened to your feet?" He was still pointing down, but now he was laughing. I could hear his laugh from a quarter mile away.

It was a laugh that stuck out in a crowd, and it stuck out in a desert, too.

"Not my feet," he said.

I couldn't see anything where he was pointing, but he seemed to think it was funny and highly interesting.

"What you laughing at?" I said.

We were now close enough to talk at a mild shout. I could still see nothing that looked like that big of a deal. A pile of rocks in the middle of the desert. I thought maybe something was written on them. Directions on how to find Phantom Bill, maybe.

"I think I found Pete," he said.

I stopped running. It was like my brain couldn't think it through at full gallop.

"I thought Pete was a lamb," I said.

Gentleman Jack looked down at the pile of rocks, which had reassembled itself enough that I could see it might not be a pile of rocks after all.

"Maybe so," Jack said. "But maybe not."

There, halfway in the muddy creek bed, lying with his right arm actually buried in the mud, was a dead colored man. It looked like he had been trying to dig his own grave and just gave up on the idea and died. He was still fresh enough that the birds hadn't found him.

"He ain't been dead for long," I said.

Jack was standing right over him, his left boot rubbing right up against the wool trousers.

"I was scaring the vultures away, Wilkie John," he said. "Shooing them away."

I didn't mention that I thought he was whooping for me, but it felt like he knew. I thought seriously about shooting him right then and there. I could have done it. I could have said that the colored man lying facedown in the mud had done it. But I didn't.

"You think this man is Pete?" I said.

Gentleman Jack kicked at him as if to prove he wasn't just napping.

"Think about it," he said. "A five-year-old girl on a train to California. She's going to take a lamb with her? Old Pete here was escorting her."

It seemed at least plausible. It didn't explain the dead sheep, though.

"Little girl is being sent out West. Maybe she has family there. I don't know," Jack said. "She asks if Pete can go with her. Didn't she say something like that? Maybe he's her uncle. Hell, maybe he's her brother. I can't tell how old he is. His face is in the mud."

I bent over and got as good a look as I could. Looked to me like Pete was grinning, maybe out of embarrassment for his situation. His right eye was filling with blood.

"Don't see no evidence of him being shot," I said.

It was fairly obvious, but I had learned that you start with the obvious. And truthfully, it shouldn't have been obvious at all, considering he seemed to be crawling away from the scene of a triple murder.

"Guess we need to flip him over," Gentleman Jack said.

He stood there and watched, hoping the "we" he was talking about might be the "we" he was looking at. I didn't fall for it. While I waited, the vultures started trying to swoop back in, which caused Jack to doff his hat again and swing it around like he was fighting off bees. I was close enough this time to see that he had grown completely bald-headed on the top of himself. I wondered if that was his reason for always wearing the hat or if always wearing it had caused his hair to just give in and fall out.

"I'm not sure we can get his arm unstuck," I said.

He was in up to his elbow, and it was a dark, sticky sucking kind of mud that was almost like quicksand. I didn't want to get caught up in it.

"I'll pull on him. You yank on the arm," Jack said. "And hopefully, his arm comes unstuck from the mud and not from his body."

I hadn't thought of that, and I didn't know if it was a thing that could be done or just Jack talking. He counted to three, and we both pulled. His arm came flying out of the mud with a loud popping sound, like the earth was spitting him out, and his dead hand slapped me across my cheek and sat me down on my ass before I knew what happened. Gentleman Jack laughed for a short moment then pulled in the reins.

"Oh hell," he said.

I pulled myself up and took a gander.

The right side of Pete's face looked, I'm guessing, pretty much as Pete had looked in life, with the possible exception of that grimace and the bloody eye. The left side, the side planted in the mud, was another story altogether. Eaten up with grubs and crawly things that I couldn't even name, they were passing each other by, in and out of the hole that had once been his left eye, and they were starting to work his nose over pretty good as well. I suddenly knew why he was making such a face.

"Got something to wrap him in?" I said.

We could have left him there for the critters easy enough. Could have ridden away and never said a word to anyone. Gentleman Jack was surely thinking the same thing. On the other hand, we would have to secure Pete enough to haul him back up to the Alameda Ranch and see if they recognized him, and, if they did, whether they wanted him back. We didn't have a wagon, so the ride would be rough, but, if we wrapped him good and tied him right, he would at least arrive in one piece.

"No."

I looked at my supplies. I had a blanket, but it was a good blanket from home in San Antonio. I wasn't aiming to part with it, but I knew there wouldn't be anything left of it after a ride to the Alameda Ranch. Even if there was, who would want to sleep in it after Pete had taken his last ride in it?

"We're gonna burn it," Jack said. "Keep the damn buzzards and wolves from getting to him."

And so we went to collecting pieces of wood,

most of them no bigger than my hand, and stacking them up there by the dry creek bed, right next to where we found him. It took a while before Jack said we had enough—quite a while after I thought we did—but he said it took a little to burn halfway through a human body but a lot to burn it all the way through.

"You want to walk away and leave old Pete halfway burned up and halfway sitting here like he's waiting for the creek to rise?" Jack said.

I kept foraging, going in larger and larger circles to where we were almost as far apart as we had been earlier in the day. We timed our circles, with a little practice, so that one or the other of us would be close enough to the body to flap our arms and yell anytime the vultures would start circling again. If anybody had been riding by on a train in the distance, and if they could have looked out the window and managed to see us, they might have thought we had gone crazy from the heat. Maybe we had. It was a bit crazy not to just pack up and ride away. We had no allegiance to Pete. He might have been a real bastard and deserved his fate, for all we knew. But if Bess had asked for him, then he deserved some small piece of dignity. I wouldn't have wanted to look that little girl in the eye and tell her we rode away and left him with bugs crawling in and out of his left eye and nostril.

We burned Pete up good that evening as the sun was starting to set down on us. I had been getting hungry, but the smell of Pete cooking turned me right off that notion, and I spent my time instead vomiting up my innards into the creek bottom.

"We do need to pay the Alameda a visit," Gentleman Jack said.

It would be easier to do without Pete coming along for the ride. I was ready to look for a quiet place to lay my head down and get some rest, but I knew a visit there was in order.

"Need to go back and tell Mrs. McSwain, too," I said.

Gentleman Jack thought for a moment.

"We'll just tell Bess that Pete decided to go on down the road."

That seemed like a kind enough thing to do. His response intrigued me once again.

"You ever have any children, Jack?"

He spit into the fire and then apologized when he realized what he had done. I don't know if he was apologizing to me or to Pete.

"I had a boy and a little girl, I think, once upon a time," he said. "But that was before I bought my freedom. They sold my boy to a woman in Opelousas. That's all I know. I know even less about the girl."

I couldn't think of anything smart that was worth saying to that, so I let it be. Jack had said that he was born on the day he purchased his freedom, but it was plain that there was a whole other life back there on the other side. I had a good suspicion it was that life that made the one I knew today. I resisted the urge to feel too sorry for him, though. He was living his current life on his own terms, and they had once included a serious desire to end mine. I wasn't sure that had changed, and, if it had, why. I needed to know more about this man, Gentleman Jack Delaney, but I wasn't going to ask him any more questions. Not then anyway. I would wait and watch and ask when his guard was down.

CHAPTER ELEVEN

The trip to the Alameda started out promising. Never mind I was getting sleepy and the moon was not so full in the sky and partially hidden by a low band of clouds. Gentleman Jack seemed to be in good spirits. Not high spirits, which often vexed me to no end, but good spirits. Talkative enough to keep my mind alert but not enough to be a nuisance.

"Reckon why they called it the Alameda Ranch?" he said.

It was a question I might have gone forever without entertaining had he not brought it up. Once brought up, it was intriguing enough to help pass most of an hour.

"There might have been a place called Alameda in Scotland or wherever they came from," I said. "Didn't they come from Scotland?"

I couldn't remember the family name, but I thought I remembered Jack saying they were Scottish, and I thought their name had sounded suitably so. Alameda sounded like some castle far away on a Scottish hillside, if Scotland had hillsides. For all I knew, it was as flat as a griddle cake, just like most of central Texas.

"Alameda," Jack said. "Sounds Spanish to me."

He repeated it again, I guess to show me how it did. The fact that he pronounced it with a Mexican flair didn't make much difference to me.

"I still think it's Scottish, not Spanish."

The matter went on like that for miles, neither of us moving the other. We finally let it die away, riding on through the night and listening only to the sound of earth beneath our horses' hooves and the regular howl of wolves, sometimes near but mostly distant. Once we thought we saw a light in the east and went to investigate, only to find nothing. For the most part, we were silent. In fact I had drifted into slumber once or twice in my saddle, only to be awakened by the sensation of pitching sideways.

"I think it's Spanish, Wilkie John," Jack said.

I looked ahead at the man in front of me. He never looked back, and I thought for a moment I'd dreamed it up.

"What's that?" I said.

"Alameda."

If it was a dream, I was going all in.

"Why's that?" I said.

"It sounds like Alamo," he said. "It must have something to do with Alamo."

Jack had me there. It did sound like some variation of the word *Alamo*. Maybe he was right after all.

I didn't concede defeat, but neither did I argue the point. I wasn't even planning on arguing the point, but, if I had, I wouldn't have been able to.

"Jack, look," I said.

He stopped and followed my pointing across the eastern plain, where a dim light danced above the horizon like a lightning bug.

"What the hell is that?" he said.

I didn't have any idea. It was high enough off the ground, if it was a man walking with a lantern in his hand, he would have to be twelve, maybe fifteen feet tall.

"It's not a campfire," I said.

We debated altering our course and scouting it out.

"I don't know," I said. "Could be Apaches. Could be riding right into a trap."

I had known a few, and most weren't nearly as bad as people made them out to be. Leastwise, unless you crossed them. Still, it was a dark night, and I was tired. Too tired to leave it to chance.

"That ain't no damn Apache," Gentleman Jack said. "If it is, it's the tallest damn Indian I've ever come across."

It was decided that we would travel a way in the light's direction and try to determine what it was.

"Maybe it's a star on the horizon," I said.

It seemed like a smart idea, but it wasn't. Riding at it, you could see it was too close, too big to be a star.

"Maybe it's Phantom Bill smoking a cigarette," Jack said.

He said it because it seemed like a funny thing to say. He didn't no more believe it than the man in the moon. I didn't like him saying it, but for some reason I kept it going.

"Maybe it's not his cigarette but it's Phantom Bill himself."

It was like a chill going through me when I spoke it, and I immediately wished I hadn't. With God, I had never felt my soul stirred if I had a soul to be stirred, and I never felt that He had any special concern for stirring it. Some people might see Him coming in the clouds with a band of angels at his heels, but they never seemed to get here. With ghosts, it seemed they were already here and waiting, and they took pleasure in letting you know they were here. They liked to mess with you. Maybe especially if you didn't believe in them.

Mama made money dating soldiers from the base near to the District where we lived. Sometimes that meant letting them have their way with her for a while, but sometimes they only wanted someone to hold them and listen to them talk about home and the mamas and girlfriends they left behind. And most times, Mama would come home with a coin or two for her troubles, but there would also be times when she would come home with gifts, things to make her more beautiful or things to place around the room we rented to make it more homey.

It was one of those times that she came home with an oval-shaped mirror that was almost as long as I was. It looked to me like the kind of thing that had once hung in the drawing room of some queen or princess. More likely it came from a whorehouse in Galveston. We had no business with anything like it, and we sure didn't have a drawing room, but Mama put it up in the little room that housed her and me and Ira, and we all took turns looking at our own reflections in it. I never did look like myself in it, as far as I was concerned, even if Ira said I did. He probably got tired of me always standing in front of it, plastering my hair down with spit and elbow grease and trying to make the image look more like what I had in mind.

"They took it out of a house where a man got murdered, you know," Ira said.

I hadn't learned to question Ira except to ask why. Which is precisely what I did.

"What you mean *why*, Wilkie John?" he said. "Ain't it obvious? This mirror caught the reflection of a man getting stabbed to death by his own wife. It's haunted by it. You can take your chances, but I wouldn't gaze into the glass too long if I were you."

I spent the next day or so dodging around the walls of the room, trying to make sure I didn't get caught in the mirror's reflection. Ira would egg me on, threatening to wrestle me to the ground in front of the thing until, on the third day, I finally just didn't come home until after dark, when the mirror's powers were diminished. Mama had enough of it by then and sat it out in the alley for somebody else to worry with, but by then, I was good and spooked, whether it was by my own imagination or a rotten older brother or the ghost of a murdered man.

"So if you believe in ghosts," Gentleman Jack said, "do you ever feel haunted by the people you've killed? What do you think they have to say?"

It was the first time he had made any mention of my past.

"Who said I believed in ghosts?" I said.

I wanted to ask if he ever wondered what his God was saying when he let me slip through that hangman's rope and out of Jack's hands in Fort Worth. I should have.

I rode away from him in the opposite direction of the light, which was still hovering a substantial distance above the ground to the east. If he wanted to ride out there and check it out, that was fine by me. With the freedom to go where I chose, I decided to go north, back to the McSwains' place and not northeast to Alameda. Not yet. I had more questions I needed answers for, and they wouldn't let me be. I didn't need to waste time with Apaches or ghosts or whatever was hanging around out there with Gentleman Jack Delaney.

I could have ridden away for good that night. Could have washed my hands of the whole thing, gone to bed, and woke up the next morning in a whole new town. Maybe back at the Black Elephant with Sunny lying in my arms again. I tossed the idea around for a while and, seeing as I was already moving in the general direction of Fort Worth, might have actually thought I was doing it for part of the night. The girl who weighed most heavily on my mind that night, though, was little Bess. Bess, who clutched at the hem of Mrs. McSwain's dress and cried. Bess, who asked no more of us than to go out and find Pete. And if one of us was content to spend the night chasing ghost lights on the prairie, I would at least ride to see the McSwains before I made my decision about riding farther. It was the proper thing to do. The Texas Ranger thing to do.

CHAPTER TWELVE

I didn't see Gentleman Jack again that day or for the next few. I arrived at the Spiney McSwain Ranch late for breakfast, but Mrs. McSwain greeted me like I was one of her sons and sent the help out to the henhouse to ask for one more plate of eggs. This she paired with a side of breakfast steak. I hadn't eaten so well since the last time I woke up in Fort Worth.

"Steak for breakfast," I said.

It was a rare occasion that I had steak at all. I had never had such a thing for breakfast.

"We're a cattle ranch, Mr. Liquorish," Mrs. Mc-Swain said. "Most days, we eat beef for all three meals."

"When we don't, we have it for four, don't we, Mother?" Robert McSwain said.

Robert had eaten his fill previous to my arrival but insisted on sitting right across the table from me and peppering me with questions. I returned the favor by talking with my mouth full of food.

Mama taught me better, but she also taught me to recognize trouble when it stared me in the face.

"What happened to that fancy man you were with before?" he said.

"Did you kill him? Is he dead? Did you find Pete? You do know that the little girl Bess isn't here anymore, don't you? Why are you so worried about a little colored girl?"

He was like a small child inside the body of a man. I could scarcely scramble up one answer before he was off to the next question. No. I decided he was more of a cross between an unruly child and an overzealous lawyer. I took the Fifth.

"Will you leave the poor man alone," Mrs. McSwain said.

She was in and out of the room, making sure my cup of coffee was filled and that everything was just so. I liked her being there, because her son would relax his spurs a little bit. He didn't have a clue why I wasn't answering him, and I think my silence made him angrier, but I was sitting there thinking about how much my life had changed in the last year or so. There had been a fairly long stretch of personal history where I would have pulled my .38 and stopped him asking questions for good. I had killed folks for less. In fact, I was going over the list of people I had shot for one reason or another and comparing them all to Robert McSwain. He wasn't sizing up well.

"Ma'am, I do have a bit of news I can deliver," I said, "even if the main recipient isn't present."

Robert leaned forward.

"My, my, Mother, will you listen to all those words. He sure is trying hard to impress you, Mother. The 'main recipient.'"

He repeated it again, for no good reason.

"The main recipient."

Mrs. McSwain had her hands full. I didn't expect her to send him to his room or stick him in a corner with his nose in a circle. At the same time, her mere presence was pretty near saving his gizzard, and I'm sure neither one knew it.

"The little girl Bess," I said.

It was at that point, sitting at the table looking at the last forkful of eggs and one more bite of steak, that I looked at Robert and put things together. It was something I had become better at as a Ranger, if mainly because I didn't always shoot first and then think it over.

"Where did you send the kid?" I said.

If what Cookie had said was true, I wasn't sure I trusted him with a child, even a colored child of one of the Alameda Ranch helpers.

"Someone came by and picked her up in an old buggy," he said. "I can't say how far they might have gone in it. That buggy was pretty beat up, wasn't it, Mother?"

His mother wasn't answering questions any faster than I was. In fact, she washed her hands of the whole discussion and vacated the room at this point.

I didn't like it one bit, but I couldn't help wondering if Robert would have acted different if I had brought Jack with me. Robert had inches on me, but he was no match for Jack in either altitude or attitude. Jack would not have remained silent.

"I apologize for interrupting your morning," I said. "I'll take a moment or two to speak with Mrs. McSwain and be on my way."

I meant it, too. I was in no mood to hang around the ranch with this man. He seemed like someone who would go to deadly lengths over something like the grazing of sheep near his cattle.

"Between you and me, Mr. Texas Ranger, I don't give a hoot about whatever news you brought for that little colored girl. We took her in and gave her a place to sleep. Her people came and got her. I don't expect I'll have cause to see her again."

He stood up, grabbed his hat, pushed it down onto his head, and turned to leave.

"Mother, come back inside and clean up this table," he said. "Mr. Liquorman is through."

I was through. I was through eating, and I was through putting up with his smart mouth. He got just far enough that he was framed by the side door. The door led from the breakfast nook out into the part of the yard where a clothesline stretched. Chicken wire surrounded a henhouse full of hens whose sole purposes were to keep the McSwains fat on eggs. The other side led out to a field of corn and peas and beans and maybe some watermelons, best I could tell.

In the moment that he was outlined by that screen door, I did something I hadn't done in a long time. I pulled my gun. He turned around with a look that I had seen before, right before I would pull the trigger and shoot somebody. It was a funny look. Not just of surprise or anger, although it had a little of those in it. It was more a look of recognition. A coming to terms that whatever he had done up until that point, it was all about to end. It usually came with a small sigh.

I didn't pull the trigger, although I had to fight myself to keep from doing it. I pulled the gun up and smiled. It was enough. He understood then and there that he was a dead man if I wanted him to be. He left the house, moving in the direction of the cornfield. I didn't see him again.

Mrs. McSwain was outside, throwing hands of feed out to the hens and singing a song that sounded both familiar and otherworldly.

"What is that you're singing?" I said.

She shook her head like I had overheard a moment between her and the chickens, and it wasn't mine to hear.

"Where is that Robbie off to?" she said.

I looked down toward the field.

"He didn't say," I said. "Took off in kind of a hurry."

She wiped her hands on her apron and sat down on a rusty old chair that didn't seem to go with anything else on the ranch. There was another one like it, but it had a bushel basket of purple hull peas on it. She grabbed the basket and went to shelling, but I went right on standing.

"I could shell those for you," I said.

I hated shelling peas, but I hated being impolite

to old ladies even more. And I would have shelled them if she had said yes.

"Lands, no, Wilkie John," she said. "Won't take me the shake of a lamb's tail to get these done."

I've learned to spot an open door when I see one. And if there's something I think I might want on the other side of it, I'll let myself in.

"Speaking of lambs, I hear there's a sheep ranch somewhere over, other side of Senterfitt."

She looked up from her bushel basket but her fingers never slowed down, feeling their way as she talked.

"You didn't find hide nor hair of Pete, I take it."

The statement was so to the point, so quick, if it had been a bullet, I would have been dead before I hit the ground. I wasn't sure of the answer.

"Was Pete a lamb, by any chance?"

She didn't know about the little lost lamb in the desert. The one Jesus didn't save and I couldn't save.

"A lamb?" she said. "Lands, no. Pete, a lamb."

She slapped her leg and almost dumped the bushel basket at her feet.

"He was a colored man, right?" I said.

I felt like my chances were pretty good at that point.

"I wouldn't call him just a colored man," Mrs. McSwain said. "Pete Rondell is one of the most loved colored men in all of South Texas, with all the coloreds and a pretty big portion of the whites and Mexicans."

Is. I made note of the present-tense use of the

verb. I wasn't in an all-fired hurry to correct her, though.

"My son Robbie—Robert," she said. "He can't stand the man."

Something about that news made me feel even worse.

"What did he do?" I said. "He a cowboy or what?"

I realized my use of the past tense but only after it popped out. By then, it was too late. She didn't seem to pay it any mind.

"He's not a cowboy," Mrs. McSwain said. "He's a sheepherder. He came to Texas to show the coloreds and even some white families how to make a go of farming sheep. He probably would have done his thing and gone on if it hadn't been for the wars."

The wars? I knew of the War between the States. There were lots of battles in various parts of Texas. I hadn't been alive for most of them.

"The wars between the cattle people like us and the sheepherders," she said. "He spends a lot of his time trying to get both sides to live with each other. Foolhardy man is what he is."

I was beginning to think we shouldn't have been so hasty in our decision to burn the body.

"So was this Pete Rondell signed on with Alameda?" I said.

She stood up and shielded her eyes, looking off down the side of the ranch. Like she was watching for the man himself to come walking up the road. I assumed it was her son she was really watching for.

"Pete Rondell isn't signed with anybody," she said. "He's not a sheepherder."

The more questions she answered, the more I had. I didn't want her to feel like I was interrogating her, but in a way, I was.

"So why would he be riding with that little colored girl?"

Mrs. McSwain was fidgety, like she was fishing for an answer that was giving her fits.

"He was probably trying to escort her out of danger," she said. "Things have been getting more troublesome. It's not really safe anymore."

Mrs. McSwain was a likable person. I had a hard time seeing her as any kind of warrior. I didn't bother her with any more questions. I had the sense that she'd said all she had to say on the matter. I excused myself and prepared to get back on the road with Little Cuss. It would be a two-day ride to Alameda, and I didn't want Gentleman Jack to have too much of a jump on me. We were on the same side, to hear him tell it, but I didn't trust him as far as I could throw Little Cuss. It still felt very much like Jack and I were on separate sides here. Maybe he was a sheepherder and I was a cattleman. But thinking back to my experience with the one cattle drive I had ever been a part of, it seemed the other way around. I was a sheepherder and he was the cattleman. It was a war.

I did ask Mrs. McSwain a final question, after I had watered Little Cuss and gotten everything ready for the journey onward.

"You say you know this Pete Rondell character,"

I said. "You say he may have been trying to get the kid out of danger. Obviously, it didn't end up as he planned it. Do you think it was this Phantom Bill who stopped the train?"

The face she made said she wished I had just gotten along without the final question.

"I'm pretty sure it's Phantom Bill," she said. "I've been here a long time, Mr. Liquorish. When I came here, I didn't have any belief in such supernatural nonsense. But I hadn't seen much back then. Now I've seen too much not to believe it."

I thanked her for her time and hospitality. I didn't care for her son Robert, but Mrs. McSwain was all right. I passed Robert about two miles down the road. He avoided my eye. I tipped my hat to him, but he didn't acknowledge that, either. I thought about shooting him, but I didn't want to waste the bullet. He had one coming sooner or later anyway. That seemed like a solid bet.

CHAPTER THIRTEEN

I enjoyed the peace and quiet on the trip from Spiney McSwain Ranch toward Alameda. It gave me time to think through everything I knew, to look at everything next to each other and see what pieces might fit together.

We had a character named Phantom Bill, and most of the people in the area seemed to believe he was real. In their minds, it was Bill who held up the Pacific Railroad, robbing it several times and finally leaving three people dead in their tracks. What might have caused him to step up his actions, crossing the line into out-and-out murder, was still a mystery. Having killed my own share of people in the past, I tried to put myself in his shoes. Rarely had I killed a man for his money. Almost never had that been the cause of me taking a life. More typically, there was either a sense that he had slighted me in some way that called for an answer or he had done so to someone else. In other words, he had it coming.

I couldn't see any obvious reason that the lady and her son had it coming. Maybe the killer just really had a thing against the railroad. Given that assumption, the engineer might have been nothing but guilty by association. I had killed a few men in that situation myself. However, the killer seemed to have killed the two passengers for no reason other than to do it. The one thing I kept coming back to was the horrible killing of that little boy. I never killed a kid, and I damn sure hadn't shot one in the face. That took a special kind of anger that I just didn't possess. It wasn't the kind you would direct at a kid. For what? Not doing his chores?

For a good while, I mistakenly thought it had been directed at the mother, sitting there in the seat and trying her best to shield him. Her last minutes of life had been as a witness to that kid's cold-blooded murder, and it seemed like a pretty hellacious punishment. But somewhere along the trail, mostly because I wasn't having to deal with the ramblings of Gentleman Jack, it hit me.

The dead woman wasn't who Phantom Bill was punishing. As bad as her medicine must have been, it was thankfully a short-lived and fatal dose. The person Bill was punishing was still out there. Phantom Bill—or whoever he was—wanted some man somewhere to know that he shot that kid in the face right in front of the lady. And once I knew who the lady and kid were, finding the person being punished would be much easier.

It appeared to me that we had two different outlaws to deal with. One might have been stopping the train at water stops and robbing it at gunpoint. But there had been no reports of shots ever being fired. I had already formed the opinion we were dealing with a second, different man with this last stop. Somebody taking advantage of the previous train robberies and using them as cover for something much more sinister. Without Gentleman Jack around to talk me out of it, my opinion was pretty well formed. Without him around to argue with me, my opinion wasn't just well formed, it was more of a strong hunch.

On the way to Alameda, I did run into a couple of guys. I knew right away what they were about. They stuck out like two whores in church.

"Where are you gentlemen from?" I said.

They were sitting next to a pile of sticks that wanted to be a fire. All their best intentions couldn't work up enough heat for a flame.

"He's from Savannah," the older one said, pointing at a kid that looked no older than me, and far less experienced in the ways of this part of the world. "I was born in Vicksburg, Mississippi, but I've done most of my living in Memphis, Tennessee."

They weren't Yankees, but they might as well have been.

"You two down here chasing Phantom Bill?" I said.

The Pacific Railroad money was attracting shiftless no-goods looking for a quick reward and maybe a little fame. They weren't much different from Gentleman Jack, come to think of it.

"Is it any business of yours, stranger?" the older one said.

I didn't care for the attitude.

"I'm Wilkie John Liquorish, Texas Ranger," I said. "How do I know you two aren't responsible for the train robbery and killing that just occurred not far from here?"

I showed them my badge, in case they wanted proof of who I was.

"There was a killing?" the older one said.

The kid was looking more and more uncomfortable with each passing second. Part of me wanted to just put him out of his misery. I wondered if shooting the old guy would accomplish it.

"Three dead in the last robbery," I said. "Don't that strike you as funny?"

I didn't mean funny like a joke. I meant funny like peculiar. Maybe that didn't translate due to them not being from around these same parts.

"Not much funny about anybody being dead," the man said.

I was beginning to wonder if the young guy was a deaf mute. I'd known a couple of them way back in San Antonio, and he reminded me of them.

"It don't seem right to me," I said. "He took ten

thousand dollars. Why would you shoot everybody on your way out?"

I thought it was a valid question. Robbers tended not to shoot people while they were robbing. It was only when something wrong happened that they resorted to killing.

"Maybe they didn't want the people to be able to identify them," the old guy said.

Yes, maybe. But this was the fifth or sixth robbery on the same line, and he hadn't ever shot anybody before. I still was of the opinion that we were looking for two different people. And I didn't think either one of them was a ghost, even if Mrs. McSwain did.

"You guys ever hear of a man named Pete Rondell?" I said.

The old one acted like he didn't even hear me, but the kid finally seemed to notice I was there.

"The Rondells are colored folks. They come from Memphis."

I figured he must have Pete Rondell mixed up with some other Rondells back in Tennessee.

"This is another Rondell," I said. "He worked on some of the sheep farms around these parts."

The kid nodded.

"Pete and his brother Joe David. Ain't nothing but trouble."

The old man was busy packing up his saddlebags. He looked like he wanted out of my company real bad.

"We ain't got no fight with your Phantom Bill,

sir," he said. "We'd be obliged, though, if you told us where we might find these Rondell boys."

That's when I knew I had been wrong. These fellas weren't there for Pacific Railway reward money. They were there to take up arms in this war of the cattle versus the sheep. More than likely, they were there for some Robert McSwain money. Good old Robbie wouldn't be likely to stand on the front line of any war, but he would sure buy a few soldiers.

"You boys looking for the Spiney McSwain Ranch, by any chance?" I said.

The young one had gone stone silent again.

"We heard tell they were looking for help," the old one said. "We come when and where we're needed."

I had, up until this point, done all of my talking from astride Little Cuss, but I sensed a larger conversation in store, so I swung myself down and walked over toward the older one. I didn't draw my gun or look like I wanted to, but he jumped back and declined my handshake. Maybe he was intimidated by the Ranger pin.

"I would rather you turn these horses around and head back where you come from," I said. "We've got our hands full down here already. I really don't need two more folks to keep an eye on."

That much was true. I only had so many eyes, and things were getting more complicated by the minute.

"Are we in Mexico, pardner?" the man said.

He pronounced it like the Mexicans did, but he wasn't Mexican. It didn't endear me to him.

"This is Texas," I said, "and I'm a Texas Ranger."

I thumped the pin again, in case he'd forgotten. I was now close enough that he could inspect it.

"Well, Texas is part of the United States of America," he said, "and last time we checked, we were still a free country. I expect that means I'm free to roam wherever I feel a hankering to."

I told them it was a free country, but they weren't free to go any farther unless they identified themselves. Far as I knew, they were still suspects in the killings on the train. Turned out, they were an uncle and his nephew, a Cates Dorrough and his brother's son Owen. Both had been living in Memphis. They said I could send word back there and it would bear out. I let them go on their way, but not without a little friendly advice.

"First of all, there are a lot of Pinkertons in the area," I said. "I catch you doing anything questionable, I may haul your butts to Austin. They catch you, you're liable to end up somewhere so far away, Memphis will seem a skip and a hop in comparison. Let that be a warning."

The old guy swore to me that they had nothing dishonest in mind. They were going to help someone who needed help. They would keep it all on the up-and-up.

"Now, about that," I said. "We've had some trouble here between the cattle barons and sheepherders. We've got our boot heels on that situation, so I wouldn't come in here picking sides and making trouble. That's a real fast way to spend your time in Texas looking at it through jail bars."

The kid seemed impressed by my speech. The uncle less so. I left it at that and continued on my way. I had half a mind to circle back and follow them a ways, but it seemed mostly like a waste of time to me. I was more interested in what I might find at the Alameda Ranch.

A few miles east, I came to a fork that went north into Lampasas County, bypassing Lampasas Springs. I had no interest in Lampasas Springs. It was a town of hucksters. Could the train robber live there? Sure, he could. But as long as he was in Lampasas Springs, he was as contained as he would be in the San Saba jail. And Lampasas was probably harder punishment. Moving in that direction also brought me back into view of Lonetree Mountain. It was a welcome sight to see when it appeared on my left. Not home, but a place I had hung my hat a night or two.

At first I thought the smoke was coming from north of Lonetree Mountain. That was largely considered Comanche country, and it was almost comforting to sit up on Lonetree and watch it. Heavy at first, then maybe not so heavy, until the fires would go out for a while, only to reappear somewhere else. But I wasn't sitting on Lonetree, and this wasn't behind the mountain. As I looked closer, I could see that the smoke was rising from atop Lonetree. Someone had put a torch to old

Tom Pascal's home. I didn't weep over it. It wasn't enough of a loss for that. It could be rebuilt, and much better. I did wonder who would do such a thing, though. If it was Phantom Bill, he was the busiest ghost I had ever not seen. If it was William Pascal, it was a hunted if not haunted man. Me and Little Cuss put the mountain and the smoke behind us and kept moving. We were more drawn by what lay ahead.

CHAPTER FOURTEEN

The Alameda Ranch was unlike any ranch I had seen. Built into the side of two sprawling hills with the ranch house plopped between them at the bottom, it stretched as far as my eyes could see and then some. And being used to the smell of cattle, which most folks weren't fond of but I'd learned to accept, I found the smell of sheep to be downright pleasant. Like fields of wool.

"You'll get used to the smell," Charles Stirling said.

He was a big man, tall and barrel-chested, hair on his knuckles, red beard, and a hat that was no longer the color it had once been. He looked every bit like Texas. He talked like he came from somewhere in Scotland.

"We used to have chickens," I said. "Believe me, chickens smell much worse."

Charles Stirling had been standing at the gate to

Alameda when I rode up. He welcomed me before I got within hearing distance.

"Pardon me?" I said.

Well, it was partly due to distance. The accent also threw me off a little.

"I said welcome, good sir, to the Alameda Ranch. Charles Stirling at your service."

You had to really listen.

I told him I wasn't used to that kind of service. Maybe it was a Scottish thing. He confessed he had been working on the fence across the front of the property when he saw me coming from several miles away.

"I knew you weren't trying to sneak up on me," he said. "You were throwing a trail of dust up behind you."

I liked the man at first glance. There was a kindness in his eyes that hadn't been worn away by the hardness of the Texas landscape and the people who lived in it. Before I could even introduce myself, he saw my badge.

"A real Texas Ranger you are?"

I looked down at the badge as if my answer depended on it still being there.

"Yes, sir," I said. "My name is Wilkie John Liquorish."

He turned his head around and pointed at his left ear, which was nothing but a normal left ear.

"This is my badge right here, Wilkie John," he said.

I couldn't find a proper answer for him. I must

have looked like the bread man who found too much sour and not enough dough in the sourdough.

"I've got me ear, Wilkie John," he said. "That's the thing. In America, they let me keep it. My grandfather and his father before came to this country with the left ears whacked off by the bloody British. You know why? Care to hazard a guess?"

He had my full attention. That accent made you listen. You were afraid you would miss something. And then it would start to play tricks on your ears in such a manner as to almost leave you under a spell.

"Was it one of those indentured servant arrangements?" I said.

By this time, we were walking along the road that led to the space between the two hills, to a house that looked grand from half a mile away.

"No, but you're on the right track," he said. "Had all their left ears cut off, the British did. Marked them so they would know them if ever they met again. It was all so they couldn't go back home, see? My grandfather lived to be an old fella. Ninety-seven years he lived to be here in America, but as he used to say, he could live to be two hundred and he'd never grow that ear back."

I don't know why Charles Stirling was telling such a story to a man who just rode up and got off his horse. Maybe he went around telling it to everybody, like some Scottish Ancient Mariner, and he finally just ran into me. But I liked him for telling it, and I was happy for him that he had both of his ears.

"We've got a space for you at the table if you'd like to stay a day or two," he said. "I have a guy who will take care of your horse, of course."

I saw no reason to beat around the bush.

"You seen a tall fella in a hat, calls himself Gentleman Jack Delaney?"

He was walking a step ahead, so whatever expression he might have made was not for me, but I could see the surprise roll over him like a shiver on a fever-hot day.

"You kidding me?"

He stopped and eyed me a little closer than before, like there might have been something he missed at first glance.

"Jack's more the kidding type," I said. "I tend to shoot pretty straight."

It was, I thought, an honest assessment.

"I've known Jack Delaney for seven, eight years," he said. "I figured he was long dead, seeing as I haven't heard from him lately. Is he still around?"

It wasn't an answer I was expecting. I wanted to know only if he had arrived ahead of me. Sometimes you ask for a little and you get a lot.

"I'm supposed to meet him here," I said.

There was no need to lie about it.

"How do the two of you know each other?"

I was afraid once we got to the ranch house, Mr. Stirling would excuse himself and go about his business. Surely running a sheep ranch with thirty herders and sixty thousand sheep was an around-the-clock job. I might not have any one-on-one time again with him, especially once Jack did show up.

"Me brother Henry is the reason I came to America," Charles Stirling said. "Jack Delaney is why I'm in Texas."

He told the story as we walked. How brother Henry had been pushed off the Isle of Skye for grazing sheep on private land. How Henry came over to America and wound up with four hundred acres just south of Saint Louis. How Henry then talked Charles into coming over and helping with the business, even though Charles said he didn't know a sheep from shinola. They ended up being just about to be the biggest sheep ranch in all of Missouri when Henry got sick and passed away. Left Charles flummoxed or some such thing. Charles thought of selling it off and returning home. Would have returned with enough to live decently on. He had his ears, he said. There was nothing keeping him here.

"That's when I met Jack Delaney," he said. "At a card game in a brothel in Storyville, down in New Orleans. I was planning to sail out of the port of New Orleans the next morning, going back to Scotland."

I had heard stories of fates meted out and fortunes made and lost in places like that. The fact that my own father had lived in that same city meant nothing. I had only stories.

"Jack Delaney lost this place to you in a card game?" I said.

I would have found some small satisfaction in that. The fates weren't interested in my satisfaction.

"No, he lost the card game," Charles said, "but he bought the ranch from a man at the table. And by the time the sun came up over the Mississippi River, he'd damn well convinced me to stick around and run it for him."

My spirits sank faster than a bottomless boat. Gentleman Jack, owner of the Alameda Ranch? My allegiances were swinging back to the cattle barons.

"Wasn't anything but rocks and dirt when he first took ownership, mind you," Charles said. "Didn't look much different from what you've been riding through. A month into it, we were already getting bother from the old man back over the way."

He thumbed over his shoulder.

"You're saying you and the same Jack Delaney I know were in cahoots on a sheep farm," I said.

It didn't smell like a coincidence. It smelled like something fishier.

"If there's two of the one I know, God save us all," Charles Stirling said.

We walked a good ways in silence, me slowly realizing how big the ranch house was as we kept walking and still didn't get there. The house revealed more and more of itself as we continued, though, until I finally remembered a loose thread and pulled at it.

"You say there was an old man."

At first, he looked at me like I made it all up.

"Old man that caused you trouble," I said.

You could see the light flicker and come alive in his eyes.

"Oh yes, the old man," he said. "Well, he was a mean old man. McSwain was his name. Come from Scotland, same as me, so they say. Must have been the Lowlands. Didn't sound Scottish to me at all. And he darn sure didn't act it."

I knew Mrs. McSwain was a widow, but so were half the women above the age of thirty. If the war hadn't done the job twenty years earlier, measles or yellow fever or cholera or just old wounds from the war had.

"So he didn't like that you were bringing sheep in?" I said.

He nodded, but he was walking ahead and he was dragging the conversation ahead with him, dangling it like a carrot in front of a mule.

"I think the people over there still think I killed the old man," he said. "I found him out on the trail one day, a lot closer to his own land than mine. I was looking for a couple of sheep that had scattered and found him instead, facedown in the sand. Took him back to his wife and kids, laid over the back of his own horse. Never opened his eyes again. A week later, the doctor from Austin pronounced him dead and departed. I would have done better to leave him lying in the dirt for all the good it did me."

As we approached the house, I knew my free time with Charles was most likely coming to a close. I had to wrap things up right quick.

"So that's what this feud is all about? You bringing the old fella home to die?"

He shook his head.

"No. That's behind it all maybe. The argument has always been over grazing the sheep. They say we're using up the land, overgrazing. Leaving nothing for their cattle. The sheep stay mostly on our land, but both ranches use some common land. They've bought up land all around us, hemmed us in."

He had a negro boy maybe two or three years older than me who came out and took both horses. I grabbed my bags and followed Mr. Stirling up the steps of the house. I made note that the main ranch house was made mostly of stone and sprawled north and south while several smaller wooden houses sat east and west. It was in one of the eastern houses that I would be set up, after a meal of lamb, venison, corn, and beans. I felt like a prince visiting a neighboring kingdom. Once in my room, a woman came and drew a bath for me, and I was able to wash off three layers of dust and dirt.

I had just climbed into a feather bed taller than Little Cuss when I heard approaching hooves out in front of the house. I wondered if it was Gentleman Jack, and I thought I should get up and take a look. I looked at the roof and listened for voices instead and soon fell into a deep slumber. I don't know if the folks at Alameda went to sleep counting sheep or cattle or trains or what, but such was the magic of the place that I never found time to even count my fingers before I was out. It was the most comfortable bed I'd lain in since I'd shared a whore's bed in a city that felt farther away than it was.

CHAPTER FIFTEEN

To my surprise, the horse arriving as darkness fell over the ranch the night before was not carrying Gentleman Jack. I would have been happier to see him. Instead, we got two more Pinkertons, both arriving in the area from points north and east. Both of them met me at a long breakfast table, which also held a handful of herders and other ranch hands. The breakfast table was set with eggs and ham, biscuits piled high, and jars of mayhaw jelly. I couldn't imagine that such a spread was offered every morning, but I was assured that it was the case.

"Wait around till tomorrow and see," one of the cooks said.

A colored woman, she appeared to have seniority over the other kitchen help, most of which appeared to be white and possibly, although I couldn't say for sure, of Scottish heritage. I couldn't say because none of them spoke a word, but just nodded and went to work doing whatever the colored woman said.

One of the Pinkertons was too busy watching the girls float in and out of the kitchen to pay me any attention, but the other watched me like he was starving and I had the last biscuit, although that was far from the case.

"What's the latest on the train robber?" I said. "Y'all broke the case yet?"

I knew the two tenderfoots wouldn't know a thing. I thought it might be a good idea to remind them of that fact.

"He killed three people, including a two-year-old boy," said the one giving me the eye. "And there's a colored man missing."

I knifed some of the jelly onto one of the biscuits and bit into it. The taste of mayhaw took me back to the army camp at Fort Griffin and a cook named Jacobo. I had grown to love the man, and I had especially liked his biscuits from the first taste. The biscuits at Alameda Ranch weren't as good but almost.

"They identified the lady and boy yet?" I said.

The detective watching the cooks took a sudden interest in me.

"You could get more eating done if you'd do less yakking."

He seemed like good enough Pinkerton material. Scrubbed free of any trace of life and stiff enough to make me wonder if he slept propped up in a corner.

"Oh, they knew who that lady was before the sun

went down that first day. They still don't have a clue what happened to Mr. Pete."

I turned around to find the cook backing out of the room with a tray scattered with coffee mugs. The Pink seemed to be chirping with laughter as she said her piece, and if there was any question who she was talking to, he answered it.

"Pete Rondell knows when it's time to move on," he said. "That man stirs up more trouble than a snake in an outhouse."

Not even the coffee mugs thought that was funny.

"You just best hope he turns up but soon," she said, and disappeared, leaving a quieter breakfast table behind her.

As a Texas Ranger, I was afforded just as much respect as I demanded and not much more. If I sat there and stared at my jelly biscuit, the Pinkerton would wipe his feet on me on his way out the door. If I stood up to him, he would be shown as the waste of a uniform that he was. I stood up.

"It's a foolish man that pesters the woman in charge of his meals," I said.

I excused myself, letting myself out through the same kitchen door that all of the help disappeared through. I wanted to talk to the cook. Unfortunately, I found only a couple of her more timid helpers. The moment they saw me coming, they scurried away like mice. I washed my hands and went in search of the young man who had taken Little Cuss from me the previous evening. I found him easy enough in the stable. Little Cuss was nowhere to be seen.

"I hope you haven't lost my mustang," I told the boy.

He looked smaller than I remembered, younger.

"No, sir," he said. "Mr. Stirling took him and the mule for a ride to the blacksmith. He told me to send you down there. He's having your horse reshoed."

Little Cuss was in need of new shoes, something I'm sure Mr. Stirling noticed while we were walking to the ranch house. The rocky Texas earth was hard on horses. It might have been hard on sheep, too. I didn't know. I did appreciate Mr. Stirling's generosity and would tell him so as soon as I found him.

"That's a fine little horse you've got there," he said. "I used to have one like him. Traded an Indian three sheep for her. She was a beauty."

Stirling liked me because I was a Texas Ranger. He said he had heard of the Rangers even before he came over from Scotland. I hoped I was living up to whatever image he had of us. I was trying my darndest.

"Sir, what exactly are these Pinkertons doing here at your ranch?" I said. "I know about the train robbery, but they're not going to solve it up here."

I hadn't seen him interact with either of the detectives at breakfast, but I knew he hadn't personally escorted them onto the ranch.

"They're looking for Pete Rondell," Stirling said. "The little girl said the man who robbed the train told both of them to scram, Pete and her. Pete showed her exactly where to go, pointed the way, and she walked straight to Spiney McSwain. But Pete didn't follow."

That was only slightly more information than I already had.

"You think they did something with him?" I said.

He shook his head.

"Who? The killer? Maybe. I'm starting to wonder if it's not just as likely Pete did something with them."

It clicked in my head, like a bullet clicking into the chamber.

"Inside job," I said.

I wondered if the Pinkertons were thinking the same thing. I thought about Cookie Zamora's warning. Watch for connections.

"My property goes north, all the way up to Still Creek," Stirling said. "Just got word that a body was found up there. These two fellas came in from Shreveport and rode right past it."

I admit I thought of Gentleman Jack. He hadn't shown up at the Alameda.

"They get a description?"

"No description yet," Stirling said, "except a man. I think they said it was a man."

Everyone knew the colored man who was missing. Pete Rondell. Most even seemed to know him or at least know who he was. Sitting around that morning, waiting for word, I went through several different scenarios in my head. If it had been a colored man, we surely would have received word that it was. They would have done everything except confirm it being Pete. That made me think it might be Jack, although I couldn't imagine how he would have gotten far enough off track to wind up at Still Creek.

I also couldn't really decide how I felt about it, if it did turn out to be Gentleman Jack. I wouldn't shed any tears, but would I continue on with plans to find Manley Clark or Phantom Bill? If I knew myself at all, I would continue with the plan. I wasn't sure how well I knew myself anymore. The badge pinned to my overcoat was still poking at me a little too much to make me comfortable.

I decided it would do me good to move on. I aimed to visit the smaller sheep ranch, Still Creek, which turned out to be the one Bess and Pete had been traveling from. I still wanted to talk to Bess and find out any additional information she could provide. And, with any luck, I might even be able to get a look-see at the body at the creek and satisfy my own mind.

"It's not Pete Rondell," Charles Stirling said. "Latest word is, it's a white man."

I had almost killed Gentleman Jack myself on a few occasions, but I didn't like the feeling that someone else had done it for me. I didn't know it was him. But he wasn't where he was supposed to be. It could have been Jack. I started to tell Stirling my suspicions, but I held my tongue.

I learned where the name *Alameda* came from that day before I left.

"It's a Spanish word," Stirling said. "Funny thing,

your friend Jack Delaney told me it meant 'steps,' like on a staircase. I thought the way the two hills were built ridge upon ridge, it gave the appearance of a set of stairs. Turned out later, one of my herders told me it didn't really mean 'steps' at all."

I asked him what it really meant. He said he couldn't even remember, and that was the whole point. It wasn't anything worth remembering. He said it still just made him angry all over. I was amused by the thought of Gentleman Jack naming it and getting it wrong.

"Ever think about renaming it your own self?" I said.

He was carrying Little Cuss's saddle and I had my bags. We were walking to meet Little Cuss at the smith shop. I wanted to think Mr. Stirling was walking along because he had genuinely enjoyed my company and not because he was trying to speed my exit. He stopped in his tracks, pulled his left hand free, and waved it across the expanse.

"What in the world would you call this?" he said.

I had no quick answer, for once, and my hesitation was interrupted by a loud yell from the area that stretched south from the entrance to the ranch. The same area I had walked with Stirling the day before. It was an unmistakably human noise, but it sounded like trouble. Reminded me of Apaches.

Stirling laid Little Cuss's saddle down and ran back in the direction of the main house. I stood there listening to the yelling get louder but no less understandable. Part of me wanted to turn around and keep going. Then I saw the hat.

Gentleman Jack Delaney came in almost twenty hours after me, and, as usual, his entrance was more dramatic. He came off Alice at near full gallop and used the momentum to fling himself directly into the path of our Scottish friend. Part of me was cussing him for being alive before he even shook Stirling's hand. I was unburdened of my bags and already halfway across the yard.

"My friend, I apologize for greeting you under such circumstances, but there's been another terrible attack."

I heard Stirling put voice to the words in my own head.

"Another train."

But no. Jack was shaking his head. No, it wasn't a train. Not this time, he was saying.

"They killed the old lady," he said. "She hung on through the night but died at sunup."

I got there in time to hear that Manley Clark or someone had moved from trains to the ranch house at Spiney McSwain, attacking as night fell and taking everything in the safe.

"What about Robert McSwain?" I said.

I was still thinking inside job. Robert McSwain could have set the whole thing up. He would have known about the safe, how to get into it. He might have taken the opportunity to get rid of the nagging mother. Stealing money from your own house seemed like a ruse anyhow. Maybe it had all been set up with the purpose of getting rid of Mrs. McSwain. It seemed like something to go on.

"It's not Robert McSwain," Jack said.

I wasn't so quick to give up my theory.

"You know that for a fact?" I said.

He walked over to me.

"It's good to see you again, Wilkie John. I apologize for being so tardy. The situation required that I postpone my travel."

I wanted to punch him in the jaw.

"I just wouldn't be so quick to take Robert off the suspect list," I said. "That's all."

Charles Stirling motioned for the same boy who took my horse the day before, and he grabbed Alice and started walking her away.

"Charles, I'm only staying for a few hours. Before sunrise, I'll be heading north," Gentleman Jack said. "And I suspect my friend here will be traveling with me."

He nodded at me. Of course, I didn't tell him that I had just been on my way north when he showed up. I wasn't sure I wanted to wait.

"I wasn't sitting around waiting for you to show up," I said. "I'm not sure I'm inclined to wait now."

Jack seemed sure of himself. I didn't like that he seemed so sure of me, too.

"Give me a couple hours' sleep, let Alice rest, we'll head toward Still Creek."

It was true that Alice would need rest. It was a hard ride from Spiney McSwain to Alameda.

"You've heard about the body," I said.

Gentleman Jack walked toward the ranch house like he owned it.

"I know about the body," he said. "I suspect when we find it, we'll find it to be none other than Robert McSwain."

Now that was something I wasn't expecting.

I left the Alameda Ranch headed due north, which split the two large hills that made up most of the ranch itself.

CHAPTER SIXTEEN

Back on the trail with Gentleman Jack, I felt like I was going forward and back at the same time. We traded information, what we had learned since we split up, and, for a while, nothing was said about the split itself.

"Robert McSwain left the same day you did. Maybe before," Jack said. "He was going to the Still Creek Ranch. He was convinced they killed some of his cattle a couple weeks ago. He had the whole scenario cooked up in his head. He thought they sent the kid to the house to look around or something, and then she was going to meet Pete Rondell and he was going to attack them."

I could see how Robert might think such a thing.

"Think there's any truth to it?" I said.

There was still the inconvenient matter of the body in the desert. I tried to remember the face, at least the part of it that was still a face. I wondered if anyone had ever taken a photograph of Pete

Rondell. He seemed to be well known. Surely, someone had. I had been a photographer's assistant in San Antonio. Everybody wanted a photograph of themselves.

"Somebody sure attacked them last night," Gentleman Jack said.

If there was a photograph out there I could find, I was fairly confident I could identify the man we had burned up only a few days before.

"You were there when it happened?" I said.

I was trying to think and not look like I was thinking at all. It's a trick I'm pretty good at.

"I was asleep," he said. "It was after dark."

If what he said was true, the attackers knew who their target was. They were attacking in the dark, so they must have known the way the house was laid out. And they very likely wouldn't have known there was an extra guest sleeping in the back. Or wouldn't have cared.

Jack told the story of how he'd been awakened in the night by the sound of gunfire. How he first thought it might be Robert shooting at a wolf or coyote. Then he heard the scuffling and voices. By the time he got to the front of the house, the intruders were gone. Mrs. McSwain was on the floor in her husband's old reading room, a room of books, dust, and the safe. The safe was opened and empty. She had two bullets through the chest.

"Was she still alive when you found her? Was she able to say anything?" I said.

I remembered her sitting outside, shelling peas. It was hard to think of her dying like that.

"Yeah, she did," he said.

He didn't seem inclined to go any further.

"She tell you who did it?" I said.

He didn't answer right away.

"Maybe."

"Maybe?"

"Yeah, she called out her son's name three times."

Somewhere in my mind, I thought of Sister Mary Constance, back in San Antonio, teaching Ira and me and a bunch of other grubby little kids about someone denying Jesus three times before the cock crowed. I don't know why that memory came up. Mrs. McSwain was in no way the mother of Jesus, and I was fairly positive the man so full of denial was not named Robert.

"You think?" I said.

I didn't have to say anything more. I knew what he was thinking.

"Well, she was dying," Gentleman Jack said. "She was probably wanting to see her son."

I admitted that was a possibility. But there were others.

"She could have been trying to tell you something," I said.

I was trying to get far enough back from everything that I could take in the complete picture. That was the picture of the train, the people on the train, the dead body in the desert two miles south of the robbery, the little girl Bess, and the Spiney McSwain Ranch, Robert, and his now-dead mother. At the same time, I was trying to look close enough to see each detail, each small thread that might tie one thing to another, and hopefully all things to each other. It was giving me a headache.

"What are the chances Robert McSwain could be our Phantom Bill?" I said.

I remembered Robert talking about gambling in Austin. Maybe he had stacked up debts there and was robbing trains to pay them off. That didn't make sense. In that case, I thought, he would have robbed the safe first and not last. When it's something like that, you tend to rob the people you love before you rob the people you hate.

"I don't think Robert McSwain had the guts to rob the Pacific Railroad four times," Jack said. "And if he had the guts, I don't think he had the brains to actually get away with it that many times."

I couldn't find disagreement with any of that, so I let the conversation be for a while. We had stopped midafternoon, when the sun was at its most brutal, and snacked on lamb jerky and biscuits from the Alameda kitchen. While I tried to read a few pages from *Middlemarch*, Jack decided it was time to tell his version of buying the Texas ranch from a rank stranger in New Orleans.

"The fellow who owned this land had gone to New Orleans for a week and decided he wasn't coming back."

So Gentleman Jack had paid the man enough to start a new life there in the Crescent City, and Jack came west to do likewise. Most of the story was close enough to Stirling's to pass muster, and it was moderately more entertaining than George Eliot's tale of English life, so I got little to no reading done.

It only took another hour of riding before we reached Still Creek, and when we rounded a corner and stared upon it, I thought no creek had ever been better named. It looked like mirror glass twisting its way down through the rocky banks. I immediately began searching for the body, but we were still a good ten miles downstream of it. We did run into yet another Pinkerton coming down the far bank, and by talking with him, learned that the body was still waiting to be moved and was on the far side of the creek.

"It's not a pretty sight," he said.

He looked about my age, far from home, and not happy about it. Jack told him there was a ranch several hours to the southwest that would take him in and give him a warm meal. He seemed happy to hear it.

"There's a little ranch back up the creek a ways, too, all colored folks," the boy said.

He said it like Gentleman Jack either wasn't sitting right there or wasn't colored himself, and he looked kind of surprised colored folks would even know how to ranch. I wondered who he thought ran all the ranches for all those years under slavery. That was the thing about those Pinkertons. They wanted to act all high and mighty, but they seemed to have a more troubling view of things than anybody I knew.

"Oh please, don' tell massah that, suh," Gentleman Jack said.

Of course, Jack was making fun of the poor idiot across the creek, but I was relieved when the idiot didn't hear him. We crossed the creek a few miles upstream, and the rocky hills gradually gave way to a greener flatland I hadn't seen in a while. In fact, we saw where the body had been found from a good ways away, and it reminded me of watching Jack jump up and down and wave his hat when he found the other body. There was a man sitting on a black horse and a flag or some sort of material had been draped over the body. I didn't see any vultures overhead.

"Why don't you let me do the talking?" I said as we approached the soldier, whom I could identify as U.S. Army.

I was still a little leery of Jack's attitude. More than that, I had been in the army and knew how they thought, how they talked. If that wasn't enough, I thought the Texas Ranger card might help us out again.

"Okay," he said.

We hadn't gone five lengths before he un-okayed everything.

"Good afternoon, soldier!"

The soldier rested his right hand on his rifle. You could see his whole body tense up. Or maybe it was just me.

"You from the ranch?" the soldier said.

I don't know what gets into Gentleman Jack's head sometimes. I think he thinks life is all just a game. You buy sheep ranches from strangers because nobody would do that, and you answer questions wrong just to see where it gets you.

"Yes, sir, I sure am, and I'm bringing this man in to help stand guard."

As much as I wanted to strangle him, I also had to restrain myself from hooting in laughter. The soldier must have wondered why I was grinning like a mule eating briars. Nonetheless, he pulled his horse back from the path, giving us room to pass. Maybe I was emboldened by Jack's big mouth, but, as we passed the small tent that served to protect the body, I decided if I didn't make a move, I would regret it later. I dismounted and stepped toward the spot where a tattered flag and an army canvas kept the poor man's embarrass-ment concealed. I pulled up a flap and peered inside. He had obviously been pulled out of the water, as he had bloated up like a dead carp. Still, he had both eyes, and I saw enough to know what I wasn't looking at. I pulled the covers back over him and let him continue his nap.

"Y'all made an identification on this man yet?" I said.

The soldier had seen my badge. I made sure of that. It may have been the only thing that kept him from dismounting his own horse and stopping me.

"No, sir," he said. "No one from the ranch could put a name to him. We sent someone down to the Alameda Ranch to see if they knew."

I washed my hands in the creek and returned to Little Cuss, who was eyeing the soldier's horse with something that looked like a cross between jeal-ousy and plain old suspicion.

"They won't know," I said. "I might be able to help with that, though."

We got back on the trail, which slowly meandered away from Still Creek and suddenly, the ranch came into view. Much smaller than Alameda and set into a flat, grassy land, the only thing they had in common, from that distance, was the smell. Gentleman Jack waited as long as he could stand it before saying anything.

"What did you see?"

I was still too angry to give him an answer that easily.

"Looked like a dead man," I said.

In little moments like that, Jack's hat looked less like something to attract attention and more like it was meant to hide something. He must have known that some people made fun of it. He must have known that I was one of them.

"You told that soldier you could identify," he said. "So let me rephrase the question: *Who* did you see?"

Looking at the scene before me, I was fairly sure the Still Creek Ranch had once been a cotton field. Most likely, some of its herdsmen had kin who had been slaves right there in that same location. That made the place heroic in a way.

"I told him I could help identify," I said. "I don't know for sure who it was, but I know who it wasn't."

That didn't have to sink in too deep.

"It wasn't Robert McSwain, then," Jack said.

It wasn't a question, so I didn't feel the need to answer it. No, it wasn't Robert McSwain. As much as I had hoped it was. It was a man similar in age.

Similar in build, depending on how much the creek water messed with him.

"That colored fella down there in the desert died on a dried-up creek bed. The water that would have saved him wasn't there," I said. "This one here fell in a creek and drowned there or, if he was lucky, died before he ever hit the water."

I wasn't sure where I was going, but Gentleman Jack got the gist of it.

"Life is ironic," he said.

Soon enough, we could make out people and even individual sheep ahead of us. There was only one ranch house, a long wooden house with a porch running the length of it. Looked like at least a dozen little children standing on the porch eyeing us as we approached. I scanned them as best I could but didn't see Bess. There was a man riding to meet us on a mule. You could tell it was a mule by the way he bounced along. Nothing rides like a mule. He was waving his straw hat as he got closer.

"Wonder if he's trying to shoo us off," I said.

If we looked like turkey vultures from where he sat, I couldn't have much blamed him.

CHAPTER SEVENTEEN

Still Creek Ranch was under the control of Lewis Absher. He was a colored man, but he had never been a slave. He came to Texas from Philadelphia with the purpose of buying a cotton plantation and making a working sheep ranch out of it. And that is exactly what he did, hiring on as many of the former plantation slaves as he could locate to help run it. He was a handsome man, with a little bit of an exotic West Indies look about him. I liked him a great deal. Gentleman Jack did not.

Lewis had quickly agreed to meeting with us, although he was a little hesitant at first. I thought he was nervous because of me being a Texas Ranger or maybe of me being white. He put that thought to rest.

"I have no issue with the Texas Rangers. Y'all have been my friend," he said. "I'll admit I'm not used to a colored man and a white man traveling together the way you do. It makes me suspicious."

If he had known more, it would have raised his suspicions even more, so I didn't mention the part about Gentleman Jack trying to hang me in the middle of Fort Worth. I should have. Soon enough, I was able to convince Lewis that Jack Delaney was not in trouble with the law and was actually there to help me deal with colored sheep ranchers like himself.

"We're a small ranch compared to Alameda," he said. "They've got sixty, maybe seventy thousand sheep down there. We have ten. But we only had six last year."

Gentleman Jack had to make sure Lewis knew Alameda had once been his.

"Alameda was mine for about a year," he said. "I think we had ten thousand sheep that year. I set it up to grow and then got out of the way. I had bigger things in mind."

Bigger things than the seventy-thousand-sheep Alameda Ranch? Not even his ego was that big. Even so, our meeting started off on a less-than-satisfactory note.

"I know you want to speak with the little girl who was on the train," Lewis said. "I'm afraid that cannot be done."

It wasn't what I wanted to hear. I wondered if our whole trip had been a waste. Not to mention, I had come a long way and was ready to get off Little Cuss. Waiting for a *Y'all come up to the house* or something. Lewis didn't seem interested.

"Something happen to the girl?" Jack said.

It hadn't occurred to me. I immediately felt uneasy.

"No, and I wanted to see to it nothing did," Lewis said. "It's a miracle the man who robbed that train didn't shoot her and Pete, too."

That was true, unless he knew them and knew not to. I say that, because that's exactly what I thought when he said it. I didn't say it back to him, but I thought it. It's how a Texas Ranger has to think.

"You know where they are?" I said.

I was pretty sure I knew where one of them was. I wanted to compare my cards to Lewis Absher's.

"Bess Harper is in Dallas," he said. "Way I hear it, Pete Rondell should be up there soon, if he ain't already."

Dallas gave my heart a stir. I had no great feelings for the town, one way or another, but it plopped right up next to Fort Worth, and there was a part of me that wouldn't mind seeing that place—and a couple of the women in it—again.

"Where did you get word on Pete?" Gentleman Jack said. "Last we understood, he was where-abouts unknown."

Of course, I was thinking that could have been a completely other colored man that we found out in the desert. There was no way I could have made an identification. I had never heard of the man before.

"Man come down from Dallas to get Bess, her uncle," Lewis Absher said. "He said it. Said it was the understanding up thataway."

We were still sitting on our horses. I wanted to

get down, to get into some shade and maybe have a drink or something. Lewis sat there on his old flop-eared mule, so comfortable-like I began to wonder if he slept on him, too. I kept looking at Gentleman Jack, who never budged. Don't get me wrong. I wasn't done with the conversation. It was clear Lewis had heard things we hadn't. Who knew if some of it might be true? Some of it was bound to be.

"What all do you know about the whole situation?" I said. "Why Bess was on the train to begin with and why Pete Rondell was there with her."

We knew so little about everything, he was bound to shed a little light.

"Want me to start from the start?" Lewis said.

"Start from the start," Gentleman Jack said.

Lewis took a swig from a brown bottle that might have been whiskey and might have been water. If I was a betting man, I'd have gone with the first.

"We been getting hit hard. Dead sheep. First it was two or three, here and there, and we made little of it. Then one of my herdsmen got shot at. We figured out, someone was sitting up in the trees by the river and picking 'em off. I didn't want no trouble. But I don't have that many herdsmen, and they're all like blood to me. I can't lose one."

"Did you get any kind of look who was doing it?" Gentleman Jack said.

There was a tone in his voice that reminded me of the day in Fort Worth when he tried me for crimes I hadn't even thought of committing.

"First off, I thought it was some of Charles Stirling's bunch," Lewis said. "I thought maybe he didn't like me grazing sheep so close to his."

I tried picturing him doing it, and much as I didn't want to, I could see it.

"Then one of Stirling's boys come up here and told me, they been getting the same thing down there. Just a few at first, and then a few more."

My mind flashed back to Mrs. McSwain and what she had told me about the wars. The battles between the cattle barons and the sheepherders. It looked like we were getting dragged into it, slowly but surely.

"You think it was someone from the Spiney Mc-Swain Ranch?" I said.

Lewis Absher looked like I had punched him in the throat and took the words out of his mouth.

"Y-y-yessir," he said.

It felt like we had dug our way from the Alameda all the way to the Still Creek Ranch and our shovel had just clanked against treasure.

"So how does the train robbery fit in?" Gentleman Jack said.

Always trying to steer the conversation. Never content to just ride the train.

"We were sending Bess Harper to Amarillo, to meet her cousins and stay there for a spell," Lewis said. "Her father, Ishum Harper, was killed three months ago, and, ever since, things been a little scary round these parts. Bess don't belong here no more."

"What about the mother?" I said.

Where was she, and why hadn't Bess either gone with her or gone to her?

"Ishum's wife passed when the baby was small. Bess ain't got no mother or father now."

You could tell the man cared for the little girl. It occurred to me that he made a good sheepherder. He had done the same thing Jesus had done in that Bible story.

"What I don't understand is why, knowing what you know, you would put this Pete Rondell character on the train with her," Gentleman Jack said.

He wasn't wrong to think it.

"Them white men wouldn't know Pete from a goose," Lewis said. "Only we know Pete Rondell."

The last sentence was spoken looking directly at Gentleman Jack, and there was a nodded agreement there that I had no part in. I had no argument, as I had never heard of Pete Rondell until a few days before.

"We were going to put one of Bess's cousins on the train with her," Lewis said. "But Bess doesn't care for him. Pete reminds her of her father, I think. And Pete wanted to go to Amarillo and check on the situation there."

I'm sometimes surprised at my own reaction to conversations like this. I've shot people full of holes just to have a job digging their graves, and yet, I could muster up feelings for these names and faces I didn't even know. I asked myself a lot of questions. Did Bess remind me of a childhood friend, Ginny Hay, who had walked me to school every morning, even though she wasn't allowed to walk through the door? Did she remember me of Sunny at the Black Elephant, who told me of growing up in a place called Waterproof, Louisiana, that flooded so bad, she got moved to Fort Worth where she became a whore? I had questions. I didn't have answers.

"Can you tell me about Pete Rondell?" I said.

It seemed almost polite to ask, since Gentleman Jack and Lewis had both agreed that white folks didn't know. I didn't want to appear snooty.

"Pete Rondell come down here from Memphis," Lewis Absher said. "I ain't never been there, but they tell me that's in Tennessee, and they tell me that's in the United States. You ever been to Memphis?"

Turned out Gentleman Jack had, or at least he said he had. I hadn't, but I did know it to be in Tennessee.

"Pete Rondell and his brother Joe Rondell come down here with helping the colored folks on their mind. This was after the War between the States, you understand. And lately, Pete's been trying to help settle down this war broke out between the cattle ranches and the sheep ranches. Pete Rondell is a good, good man."

"He's been staying here on the Still Creek Ranch?" I said.

It felt like we were finally zeroing in where we needed to zero in.

"Yes, sir, he was. Until the train. I'm not sure where he is, but the word has it, he's on his way to Dallas."

If Bess was in Dallas and Pete Rondell was on his way, it did seem like something worth considering.

"I want to know one thing," Gentleman Jack said. "How many heads of cattle, how many sheep, and how many men have been killed in this little war between the sheepherders and the folks over at Spiney McSwain?"

I wanted to mention that he hadn't asked for one thing, but three things. But I held my tongue.

"We've lost over a thousand sheep," Lewis said. "Just one man, but there's been threats, and they've shot at us a few times."

"It's just a matter of time until more of you get killed," I said. "The McSwain family could surround you and squeeze the living hell out of you, if they wanted to."

Lewis didn't argue that point.

"What were the circumstances of Bess's father getting killed?"

More lawyerly talk from Gentleman Jack. I think he just truly liked to hear those big words coming out of his mouth.

"Ishum Harper," Lewis said. "He was herding on the south part of the ranch. The sheep were grazing. We don't know how many people came up on him. We could see tracks of at least four horses, probably five. They took him back to their place and hung him from a tall tree in front of their house. Leastways, that's what we've been told."

There wasn't a tall tree in front of the Spiney McSwain Ranch. But there was one in the back, and it looked like it would make a good hanging tree.

"Sure it was the McSwains'?" Gentleman Jack said.

Sometimes details get mismanaged, I reminded him. I didn't bring up specific instances in our past. I saved him that punishment. Sometimes, I added, trees even get cut down.

"You get the body back for a proper burial?" I asked.

He shook his head.

"I expect they set it on fire. No telling what they done with him."

I thought of Robert. I could picture it happening.

"You've told Bess about it?" I said.

Lewis's head never quit shaking.

"Couldn't do it. She thinks he went off to do something big. Thought he might even be in Amarillo."

"One thousand sheep?" Gentleman Jack said. "How many head of cattle have they lost in this thing?"

He thought for a moment.

"I've heard a hundred," he said. "And they all up in arms over a hundred."

That was a number I wasn't expecting. I wanted to go back to the Alameda Ranch and talk to Charles Stirling some more. I wanted to go back to the Spiney McSwain Ranch and finish the job there. Kill Mrs. McSwain's son of a bitch son. I wanted to go back to the desert and undo what we had done with the colored man's body out there. I wanted to go to Dallas. Check up on Bess Harper. See if Pete Rondell did show up.

Finally Lewis decided we were safe enough for

his hospitality. We were invited back to the house and instructed that there was ample space in a building out back for us to bunk down for the night. We were given salt pork and coffee and tattered blankets to make beds. It felt good to lie down. Talking to Gentleman Jack after we settled in, I presented a new possibility.

"You know, we have a new piece of the puzzle, and it's turning the picture into something bigger. That body out in the desert could be Mr. Harper. Bess's father."

Gentleman Jack wasn't buying it.

"You think they hung him and then carried him out into the desert to be eaten by turkey buzzards?" he said. "Turkey buzzards will come to you."

"But would you want them to?" I said.

Truth was, we didn't know what happened to Ishum Harper after he left Still Creek Ranch. What we didn't know far outweighed what we did know. Wasn't anything wrong with that. You always start out that way. And we knew more now than we did before visiting Lewis and the Still Creek Ranch. I went to bed that night thinking a trip to Dallas might not only be in the cards. It might be the next card to play.

We slept that night under a slatted roof that let in half the starlight. I lay there on my bedroll looking up, so as not to see Jack lying less than ten feet away, when the first drop hit me square in the eye. A little summer storm passed over, and the roof let half of it in, but I didn't mind.

"You gonna tell me what happened out there, chasing that light around in the desert?" I said.

He took so long to answer, I thought maybe he was trying to fool me into thinking he was asleep. Of course, I knew better. He snored loud as a steam engine.

"I rode all around," he said, "but I couldn't catch it. Soon as I got close, it seemed to sense me and either shoot up into the sky or just disappear in front of me."

I didn't know whether to believe him or not, so I fell asleep.

CHAPTER EIGHTEEN

Sometime in the dead of the night I awoke from a dream with an itch to saddle up and ride out ahead of Gentleman Jack. I'm naturally a loner, so I travel best when it's just Little Cuss and me. He's my best company. When I say *ride out ahead*, I'm meaning timewise. I wasn't sure which direction Jack would end up going. I was pretty sure it would be toward Dallas. We both agreed we needed to find Bess and, hopefully, this Pete Rondell fella. I felt sure Jack would think I was going that way and would follow me there. Meanwhile, I was going to circle back to the south again.

Maybe the dream had pushed me to move on. In the dream, I had been back in Mobeetie, where I had once lived, relatively happy and at peace, with Greer. There was talk of buying a small ranch of our own, maybe raising and selling horses. Maybe Still Creek was what brought the memory back up. But the man with the envelope came crawling into it, as he had before, reminding me of unfinished business. I needed to find out who he was and why he had an envelope with my father's name scribbled on it. I wasn't sure what Charles Stirling could tell me, if anything, but, the more I thought about it, the more I knew I needed to find out. If he knew Jack Delaney before he called himself a gentleman, maybe he had something for me to go on. Some way of connecting the different pieces.

My idea was to go back to the Alameda Ranch and spend a little more time with Charles, then get back to Dallas a day behind Gentleman Jack. He would get to Bess before me, but that served little purpose for him compared to me talking to Charles Stirling. It was a good trade-off.

With Jack still snoring away, I set off in a slightly different direction than the one we had taken to the Still Creek Ranch. I did this to get around the soldier guarding the body in the water. We heard the body had either been moved later in the day after we passed or was about to be moved, but Lewis also heard that extra Pinkertons were coming up to the scene to look for clues to the murder. I didn't like the idea of explaining myself to them, and I didn't want them to be able to tell Jack that I had passed through, if he happened to run into them.

There was a moon in the sky, smaller but still enough to give a little light. My old Kiowa Apache friend Long Gun had once told me that the early people grew frightened when they saw the moon getting smaller and smaller every night, because they thought it was being ground away to nothing as it made its way through the sky. I didn't believe him. I said even early people must have noticed that it came back again every month. They would notice cycles.

I don't think he was right about that, but I could see how a dumb person might think such a thing. I was thinking on this when I heard a dog bark between me and the creek. I knew immediately that I was in potential trouble. If the ground had better footing I might have tried to outrun the dog and whoever might be with it, but we were in the heaviest undergrowth along the creekside. I pulled my rifle and listened to the barking get closer.

"Put your hands where I can see them. You make any sudden moves, you'll be dead before you hit the ground."

It sounded like a kid. Like a nervous kid. That was about the last thing I wanted to run into. I raised my hands, but I kept a grip on the rifle.

"Throw the gun on the ground," the voice said.

I couldn't see him, but it was plain he was seeing me.

"I'd rather not do that," I said.

He fired off a shot that whistled over my head, and I dropped the gun at my side. I had the Peacemaker in my saddlebag, but there was no way of getting at it. I sat and waited for him to approach. What I eventually saw, coming at me on foot, was maybe the scariest thing I could have run up against. A kid who looked a hell of a lot like me.

Except if I had been him, I probably would have shot me.

"I'm with the United States Army, Private Silas Hadley. I'm detaining you on suspicion of misbehavior. Are you aware that you are on private property?"

I was deeply regretting the fact that I had dropped the rifle.

"I'm a guest of Still Creek Ranch," I said.

Private Hadley was now close enough that I could look him in the eye. I had seen more joy in the eye of the dead man in the river.

"If you will, please dismount your horse there," he said. "I will remand you to my superior, and he will take it from there."

He kept his gun trained on me the entire way, through the trees to where the creek bottom marked the end of Lewis Absher's property and the beginning of a long walk, first escorted by the young kid and then by someone who was quite the surprise. Even in the half-light, I recognized his face even while he stood several lengths away and discussed the situation with Hadley and another soldier.

"I think I know you," I said.

He was walking toward me, and he stopped for a moment to study me. He didn't seem to return the thought.

"What is your name, son?" he said.

I don't particularly like it when people call me that. Only one man had the right to do it, and he never had much opportunity. This was not the man to step into my father's shoes.

"I'm Wilkie John Liquorish," I said. "And you're Lieutenant Zephaniah Swoop."

To say I was happy to see him might have been an overstatement, but it was nice to see a familiar face. I'll just explain the situation, I thought, and he will let me be on my way.

"You the fella looking for Phantom Bill," he said.

A few of the men standing around Swoop snorted and craned their necks to get a gander at me. Private Hadley was standing to the side, my rifle slung across his back and his on his shoulder.

"Looks like you just found yourself a whole bunch of trouble," Lieutenant Swoop said.

Me and Little Cuss came to a stop there in the clearing south of Still Creek but still a three-hour ride from Alameda. I looked to the east and saw the first bony fingers of a new day reaching out from the darkness and thought about Gentleman Jack. He was probably getting ready to hit the trail north, cussing me for leaving him behind. Was I any different from him, chasing lights across the desert? Maybe not as much as I wanted to think.

"I wasn't trying to cause any trouble, Lieutenant," I said. "I was on my way to the Alameda Ranch to meet with Charles Stirling."

I knew Swoop would know Stirling.

"Well, see now, that's very interesting, son," he said, "because we've had us a real problem with people such as yourself coming into the area just to stir up trouble and maybe make a little coin while they're at it. You wouldn't happen to know anything about that, would you?"

I thought about the two guys I had run into on my first trip to the Alameda Ranch. The old guy and his mute son. I had cussed them for the same thing I was being accused of now.

"I've run into a few like that, yes, sir," I said.

He held a lantern up to my face and nodded, as if what he was seeing was in agreement with some thought or belief or suspicion inside of him.

"When I look at you, Wilkie John, and I look at one of those people, you know what? I have a lot of trouble telling one from the other. What am I supposed to do about that?"

I thought about Hadley and how he looked like me.

"We all look a lot alike," I said.

Lieutenant did something I wasn't expecting. He reached behind his back and produced a pair of iron cuffs and asked me to place my hands into them. I held my hands out flat in front of him, holding the left one on top of the right. As soon as he made his move to cuff that hand, I balled my right hand into a fist and came straight up, clocking him under the chin and raising his whole body, briefly, off the ground. He fell back with a shudder, and I jumped on Little Cuss, kicking at Hadley and another young soldier as I did. Little Cuss and me lit out across the creek and went straight for the trees with part of a company from the U.S. Army in tow. It was a hell of a chase. I had one advantage and they had another. On my side, there wasn't another horse for miles as fast as Little Cuss. He was a mustang, and he had just enough wild blood in him, when you let him loose, he would outrun any other animal on four legs. On their side, they had rifles, and they weren't shy about using them. Thankfully, none of them were used to shooting on the fly, and they had no way of knowing which way Little Cuss was going to cut and run. None of them got close enough to scare me.

I had learned a few things from my old friend Long Gun, and one of the most useful was how to outrun pursuers. Soon as I got out of eyesight of the soldiers, I changed course, heading straight into the desert and not in the direction of the Alameda Ranch. I knew they wouldn't expect me to do that. Once I made that change, I circled back around to where I was actually behind Lieutenant Swoop and his boys. They separated ten miles north of the ranch, with Swoop leading half of them toward Alameda and Hadley taking the other half into the desert, in the general direction of the train robbery. I wanted to talk to Charles Stirling, but not that bad. I followed Hadley at a healthy distance. None of them ever thought to look back. If they had, they wouldn't have seen me anyway.

I was half expecting them to hang a right and go toward Spiney McSwain Ranch, and they did slow down for a few minutes and talk it over. I could see Hadley pointing in the distance, and he might have been arguing to go west to the cattle ranch, but, if he did, he was outvoted. Soon enough, they took off again, heading straight into the heart of the desert. The sun was rising over the eastern horizon, and the heat was rising with it. I knew they would give out and turn back soon. I slowed down and bided my time.

Before turning back, they must have seen the great expanse before them and realized I wasn't any part of it. They came back north at half speed, their horses already tired from the chase. Little Cuss was still full of piss and vinegar. When he saw them coming, you could feel him tense up. Not out of fear. Little Cuss knew no fear. He wanted to meet them head-on. I reined him in, pulled the Peacemaker from my saddlebag, and took long and careful aim. I pulled the trigger once, twice, three times and reloaded while they reeled in confusion. I got off six more shots while they shot wild all around me and then took off in all directions. The attack caught them completely unaware, and it was over inside of a minute and a half. Four bodies lay wounded in the morning sun, their horses standing around looking confused. I took their canteens, watered the horses, and picked out the best of the bunch, a young Appaloosa mule with markings that reminded me of a female mule named Bird I had once known.

"I'll send somebody out here for y'all," I said. "Just try to hang on. If the turkey vultures spot you, flap your arms and make as much noise as you can."

"Who the hell are you?" one of them said.

It wasn't Hadley. He was nursing a clipped wing. There had been so many bullets flying for a few seconds, I didn't know if I got him or one of his own men did.

"Just call me Phantom Bill," I said.

Phantom Bill the Texas Ranger was on the job, and he was not to be detained. At last, I was on my way back to the Alameda Ranch.

I walked out of the desert with Little Cuss on one side and this new Bird on the other. If I ran into Swoop and he wanted more trouble, I was ready for that, too, having confiscated a healthy supply of bullets and a nice rifle that one of the soldiers had dropped when he took off running.

CHAPTER NINETEEN

I made one useful observation on my first visit to the Alameda Ranch, and it came in handy when I approached its entrance for the second time. I knew that Charles Stirling was in the habit of riding the fence line every evening from where the eastern hillside gave way to the flatland all the way to where it began to rise into the hills again on the west end of the property. I had found him in mid-ride on the previous occasion, and he told me it was his favorite time of the day. A time he could get away from his wife and family and all the workers there on the ranch and be alone with his thoughts. Just him and the land, like it had been when he first came to the area.

I realized I could sit and wait a long time for him to come by the same spot I found him before, and so I decided to enter the gate and ride east along the fence. Hopefully, that way I would run into him coming westward and have a chance to speak with him again before he got to the house. I wasn't sure I wanted to chance meeting Lieutenant Swoop and his boys at the kitchen table.

None of that was worth fretting over, for when I approached the front entrance, much to my dismay, it was a Pinkerton on horseback who met me. Too late to turn back, I gritted my teeth and rode straight at him.

"Those are two beautiful horses you have there, stranger," he said.

I was happy to be called a stranger. Maybe it meant he didn't know who I was or what I had been doing for the last several hours.

"I'm with the Texas Rangers," I said, "and I'm looking for Charles Stirling."

I made sure he saw the badge.

"Mr. Stirling is in the middle of a meeting," the detective said. "You'll have to either pass a message to him or come back."

One thing I could do was think on my feet. Even when I was on Little Cuss.

"I'm supposed to take part in the meeting," I said. "I represent the Rangers."

The detective hemmed and hawed, looking back at the ranch house like some kind of signal was going to flash from the window.

"Well, since it's the Rangers . . ." he said.

He didn't exactly finish the thought, but he pulled his horse around and motioned for me to follow and I did. Riding the quarter mile across from the gate to the porch, there was as much silence as there had been friendly conversation before. That was fine and dandy with me, because it gave me time to think. If they had a detective sitting at the front gate, it stood to reason that the meeting involved, to some extent, the Pinkertons. If it involved the Pinkertons, it was probably about the cattle and sheep wars. Or maybe it was about the Pacific Railway murders. New information could have been discovered. Maybe a suspect had been captured.

The ride in seemed shorter than before, and soon enough, we were at the front porch. I tied Little Cuss and the new Bird up next to the detective's horse and tromped up the steps to the front door. The detective made a motion for me to stand back. He knocked lightly at the door and then slid it open and stuck his head through.

"You got a man out here, says he's here to represent the Rangers."

I heard a scuffling but couldn't really make anything out of it. In a minute, Charles Stirling's head popped through the door and took a look at his late-arriving guest.

"Wilkie John Liquorman?" he said.

I didn't feel like it was the time and place to correct him. He seemed happy to meet me, so I would be whoever he wanted me to be.

"Sorry I'm late to the party," I said.

He widened the opening enough to accommodate his entire frame, which stepped out onto the porch and slapped me on the back like we were old friends.

"Thank you, Henry."

He nodded at the detective, who got on his

horse and rode away, never to be seen again, by me, anyhow. I was mildly surprised when Charles brought me into the big dining room, which held a twenty-foot-long banquet table which was over half-filled with men and boys, some obviously Pinkertons, two colored men whom I took to be from the Still Creek Ranch, and a scattering of scruffy young army boys. I felt right at home.

"Everybody, this is Wilkie John Liquorman from the Texas Rangers," Charles said, "and I can vouch for him. You may treat him just the way you would anyone else in this room."

There was a rush of voices and a few people even applauded, and I almost felt like taking a bow as I walked across the room and took a seat on the far side of the table. I appreciated the warm welcome, especially coming after a pretty hard day, but what I was really interested in was this meeting. What was it about? Or who.

Charles walked to the end of the table nearest the door, and, standing right over me, addressed the room.

"Bennet, I believe you were about to speak on the subject."

At the far end of the table, a Pinkerton stood and appeared to read most of his words from a piece of paper. I couldn't tell if it was a telegram or what, but it seemed official.

"We have no proof that Robert McSwain was involved in the recent robbery and death at the Spiney McSwain Ranch. We have not been able to locate Mr. McSwain since that time. Neither do we have any proof or indication that the robbery and death were perpetrated by any member or members of surrounding ranches. Any speculation that it had anything to do with the so-called Cattle-Sheep Wars is just that."

The room fell silent. I wondered if everyone in the room followed what the man was saying.

"Is just what?" one of them said, answering my question.

Bennet sat back down and seemed satisfied with leaving the question unanswered.

"I think he meant to say that it was all just speculative," Charles said.

That didn't help matters any.

"Speculative to what?" another man wanted to know.

Bennet finally stood again.

"It means there's no proof that it had anything to do with the war between the cattle and the sheep."

Charles Stirling got tickled at that.

"I don't think the war is between the cattle and the sheep, although it might be better if it was."

I wasn't so sure about that. Seemed to me that the cattle would have a very natural edge in one-on-one competition, but then again, I had seen a few angry sheep in my time, and I had to admit, one or two of them together could probably take a cow down pretty fast.

"All I know, most of the people working the Spiney McSwain Ranch think Robert done it," one of the Pinkertons said. "That goes a long way in my book."

I found the discussion interesting. Obviously, Stirling thought otherwise.

"I could really give a rot who killed that old lady," he said. "I know for damn certain somebody over there had their finger on the trigger at the train robbery. They're responsible for killing Mrs. Foucault—or whatever her name is—and the Foucault son, who was heir to the Pacific Railway. As long as you people are wasting your resources on the old lady at Spiney McSwain, I'm not going to have much use for you around here."

It was a lot to digest, but I wanted more.

"What was the motive in killing the lady and the boy?" I said.

I didn't address Charles, but I was assuming he would answer. Instead, he looked at Bennet.

"Mr. Foucault was the major financier of the railway. He still owns half of the stock. He's put a lot of effort into stopping the robberies. He had Pinkertons on two thirds of the trains. Three fourths, even. And they were supposed to be on this one. Foucault believed in the safety of his trains, and he was desperate to show the other stockholders that he could provide safe travel from California to Gulfport and back. But Foucault wasn't stupid. He would not have put his wife and son on a train with no protection."

One of the Pinkertons was quick to point out, no one knew if the Pinkertons were ever told to be on the train or had any idea that it was even there to be on.

"So it was a message to Mr. Foucault in California?" I said.

Charles Stirling nodded.

"It would appear so."

"And she was on her way back home to California?" one of the young soldiers said.

I had been watching them from the corner of my eye, making sure they weren't looking at me funny, watching for signs that any of them recognized me. Surely, none had been on Still Creek that morning. The morning seemed days away by that point. And I had been there, so that meant they could have been, too.

"Yes," the detective said. "She had been in New Orleans for a month."

Charles pulled up a chair and sat down to light up a cigar. We all sat and waited for somebody to say something. Finally, he looked up and grinned.

"I rode that same damn train back from New Orleans ten days ago. The train is safe."

I liked the sound of that. It meant that he still had business in New Orleans. Maybe he would know something about Gentleman Jack's dealings there. I was ready for the meeting to be called to a close.

"You got stock in the railroad, Charles?" the detective said.

"No, Detective Salter," he said, "but I do have stock in people being able to ride through this area without being shot by somebody with an ax to grind. And I'm still not convinced it isn't somebody at Spiney McSwain."

That was the moment I finally realized the man at the end of the table was my old friend, Pinkerton detective Bennet Salter, who, without his hat, didn't look like himself.

"Bennet Salter!" I said.

He looked startled that I called him out.

"I know you?" he said.

"Lonetree Mountain," I said. "I was with a tall colored man, dressed like he was going to a ball."

Charles Stirling reared back in his chair and let out a laugh and a puff of smoke.

"Gotta be Jack Delaney."

Later, when the meeting finally dispersed, I was able to take Charles Stirling aside for a few minutes. A few of the Pinkertons were staying in rooms at the ranch, but everyone else had ridden away. We were sitting on the long front porch, looking out at the stars.

"Gentleman Jack Delaney came here from New Orleans," I said. "I know he came here and started this ranch with you, but, at some point, he decided to locate me and try me for crimes I didn't commit. Now, there may have been crimes I was guilty of, but they weren't the ones he wanted me hung for. And he did hang me, but, the fates knew better and saved my life."

Charles was listening closely but stopped me at this point.

"But didn't the two of you just take off together from here?"

It was hard to explain. I admitted that much. I couldn't even explain it to myself. I wanted to be close to him, because I had to be close to bring him down. And I wanted to be close enough to figure him out, so when I took him down, he would know that I knew why. But that was all hard to put into words.

"There was another man who was trying to find me in Mobeetie," I said, ignoring his question and hoping he would figure it out for himself. "He had something he was trying to deliver to me, and it had my father's New Orleans address on it. He disappeared. And I wonder if Jack had something to do with that, too."

Charles didn't seem fazed by my story.

"I think you're grasping at straws here, Wilkie John. I don't see it."

I decided I was going about things the wrong way. I looked for another way in.

"You have connections still to New Orleans," I said. "Do you know what connections Jack has?"

"He lived there at one time, but it was long ago," Charles said. "I don't know that he has any connection there anymore."

My visit hadn't been a total disaster. I had learned a few important details concerning the train robbery and shooting, but I hadn't got anything that I came for.

"You don't know how he might have had any connection to my father in New Orleans?" I said.

He stubbed his cigar out, which I took as a sign that he'd had just about enough talking for one night.

"I suppose there's a way, Wilkie John. Jack Delaney worked at finding people. Maybe he found your father, or maybe someone wanted him to. Maybe he had some reason to find you. I guess he must have. I wish I could help you, but I don't know what that reason was."

I thanked him for his help, and I meant it. Charles was willing to listen to me, and I do believe, if he had answers, he wouldn't have kept them to himself. He walked me partway across his great front lawn, and before we shook hands, he gave it one last go.

"I'm not going to tell you Jack Delaney's a great man. I'm sure you know him too well to buy that. It may be that he's hiding his cards. He does have a habit of it. Be careful. Keep an eye on him."

I left the ranch and turned north. It was getting dark, but I liked to stay on the run through the night, when the wolves and coyotes were out and about. I would make up good ground and then sleep in the early part of the day, from the first hint of daylight until the sun got high enough overhead to beat down on me and wake me. Charles Stirling had offered me a nice bed for the night, but I wanted to get as far away from the area as I could. I didn't like the way I felt. I didn't like the way the day had gone. I was hoping a change of scenery would do me some good. Maybe I would even look up Madam Pearlie at the Black Elephant in Fort Worth. Of course, that started me thinking about Sunny.

CHAPTER TWENTY

Meridian, Texas, was a ghost town. There were people living there, but they were outnumbered by the ghosts. And I knew one of them too well. My brother, Ira, had died on the prairie, and I buried him in Meridian, marked by a grave without his name or the date that he died. I wasn't even sure of the date. 1882. Summertime. Was it July? It didn't matter. A year had passed since then, and I was still on the right side of the ground, although I wasn't sure why or for how much longer.

More than anything, I had lived a reckless life. I had lived most of it as a boy put into a man's world too early. Ira was older than me by a few years, so he became the father figure in the house, but then he became like our real father and disappeared. I was the one who stayed and did my best to help Mama. A mama's boy, they call it. I wasn't that so much as I was a person of responsibility. I got things done when they had to get done.

In a funny way, that's exactly what set me on the

road I was on. I depended on nobody else to get things done. If that meant shooting somebody who was deserving of it, I didn't wait for the sheriff. Sometimes the sheriff was just deserving of it, too.

Being back in Meridian reminded me of it all and made me reflect on my life. I got to missing Ira and wishing he could see me being a Texas Ranger. He would have laughed at that, but he would have been proud.

I got the idea to go out to where I had buried him. It seemed like the right thing to do. I remembered how my childhood was full of old people paying respects to the dead heroes and saints of San Antonio. I had always put my father, who died before I was born, in that company. For years, I almost convinced myself that he had died in the siege at the Alamo. As if that were even possible.

I rode to the area where I buried Ira Lee. I knew it well enough that when it came into view, a wave of panic rolled over me. It was almost like I was back there, with the cows dying, and our cook Jacobo and Ira both dead. I rode past the spot he was buried without realizing it, because the headstone was gone. I made two more passes in the area, one on foot, but whatever sign there had been that Ira was buried there had been pulled up. Maybe by wolves, maybe by somebody. I sat down in the dirt, as near to where I had thought he was buried, and cried. I usually turn that kind of thing into anger, but I didn't have the energy to do that. I slept there on that spot that night, and I dreamed of Ira.

In the dream, he was riding left flank on the cattle drive again, and I was following the bell cow.

"Keep that cow going straight," he was saying. "She's getting off track."

His voice seemed as real and natural as if it had never been hushed.

"If you don't like the way I'm doing it, why don't you get up here and take over," I said.

I don't think I ever said such a thing to him in real life, but it sounded true.

"You're doing fine," he said. "Just keep her moving."

I covered myself up with my bedroll and lay there thinking. It seemed to me almost like Ira's spirit had seeped up through the ground into my head. I don't think I would have moved if all the heavens had opened up on me.

When dawn came, I was up and at 'em, feeling refreshed. I built a fire and warmed up the last bit of lamb jerky I had in my saddlebag and thought of Charles Stirling. He still had that music in his voice that let you know he had come a long way to be where he was. Still, he reminded me more of Gentleman Jack than I wanted to admit, and I wasn't sure if that was to Jack's credit or not. My thoughts about Jack were even more convoluted. I hated the man, but I looked up to him, and not just because he was almost seven foot.

I stretched my bedroll out over Bird, thinking the morning sun would dry it out as we continued north. While I was doing that, I noticed a mule and wagon and a group of colored folk approaching from the south. I grabbed the rifle, in case of trouble, and waited for them.

"How are you doing, sir?"

It looked like a family. A man and his wife, two boys, and a little girl in the wagon. The mule looked like it had seen better days, and a dog walked all around it, seeming to trust that it wouldn't get stepped on or maybe not caring.

"Where are y'all headed off to?" I said.

You didn't see that many families going through places like Meridian. I wondered if maybe they had been banished from someplace. Maybe one of them had the fever or flu or something. I was keeping my distance, just in case.

"We headed up the road here to a little place called Froglip," the man said.

I thought I heard wrong, but, no, he said there was a community of colored people living just south of Walnut in a place called Froglip.

"Place down on Bosque River, sir," he said. "Way I heard, it's so low down in the bottoms there, they said it was low as a frog's lip. I think you white folks call it Low Point."

I had to admit, the white name wasn't nearly as memorable.

"What's going on down in Froglip today?" I said.

They laughed and all shook their heads at one another.

I sometimes have to remind myself, when people like that talk to me the way they do, they're looking at me and just seeing the badge. I forget it's there half the time. They don't. That affects the way they talk and what they say, too. Sometimes they say as little as possible. They want to stay on the right side of the law.

It was the child in the wagon, who turned out to also be a boy, who steered the direction of discourse.

"We going to see the Phantom."

The mother called him Riley and told him to hush up, but he had already given me enough to go on.

"You talking about old Phantom Bill?" I said.

He was the only phantom I knew of. If there were others, I wanted to know.

"You know how kids are," the father said. "He just hears something, it don't mean nothing, but he can't tell no difference."

One of the older boys took the opportunity to step in.

"Yeah, Riley, you don't know nothing."

I let them pass and told them to say hello to Froglip for me, but it sure did get me to thinking, and this thinking stayed with me halfway to south Dallas, a trip of four days riding Little Cuss one day and Bird the next.

Word was that Pete Rondell was supposed to show up in Dallas. It was part of the reason I was going there. But the more I thought about it, the more convinced I became that those people were traveling to Froglip to see the very same Pete Rondell. And maybe or maybe not, Pete Rondell could be moving from community to community as Phantom Bill or the Phantom. A secret name to keep certain people guessing. A name to tell kids so they wouldn't spoil the secret. I became convinced that I had been fooled by the colored family in Meridian. I stopped and had a drink while I debated with myself.

By the time I got to Glen Rose, I knew I had made a mistake. I should have ridden into Froglip and checked it out. But by then, I was overdue for a drink. The bar in Glen Rose was called the Whiskey Rose in keeping with the town's theme. I tied up my horses and went in, hoping the bar wouldn't be too busy or disorderly. I wasn't there as a Ranger. I was there to have a drink and move on. I wasn't much of a drinker. I preferred a sarsaparilla to whiskey or beer, so I ordered that and paid a nickel extra for a headache powder, not because I had a headache but because the last time I had the powder, it had left me feeling invigorated and ready to continue on my way, something I could stand feeling again at the Whiskey Rose.

Turned out there were only a few men in the bar and the only one that paid me any attention was the man behind the bar. He reminded me of someone I had seen around San Antonio, but when I asked him, he said he had never been there.

"I run into a colored family back in Meridian," I said. "Said they were on their way to see Phantom Bill."

He poured himself a little glass of whiskey and drank it down in one gulp.

"I had someone in here the other day telling

me Phantom Bill was none other than Governor Ireland," the barkeep said.

"Oxcart John?" I said.

The idea of it was amusing. I didn't know much about the governor, but I knew he was up to his eyeballs in trouble with the state's cattle ranchers. If it wasn't war between them and the sheep-herders, it was war between the free grazers and the fence builders. Texas was big, but it wasn't big enough for everybody to be neighborly. Everyone was grabbing for land, and if you had what they needed, they didn't mind taking it.

"I don't know when the governor would have the time to ride out into the desert and hold up a train," the barkeep said, "but I'll be damned if he didn't almost convince me of it while he was sitting there."

I didn't claim it as my own theory, but I decided to put mine on the table and see what happened.

"I heard somebody say it was that Pete Rondell character. You know, the one organizing the sheep-herders in their battles with the cattle ranchers. They say he's trying to make it look like the cattle people are behind it. Robert McSwain or some-body."

He thought about that for a minute.

"I've never heard of this Pete whoever you're talking about, but do know of McSwain. He's a good man, from what little I know. I do know he puts a lot of people to work and treats 'em all decent-like."

I didn't have any argument there. I had been on

the Spiney McSwain Ranch. No one at the ranch was suffering under Robert McSwain, except maybe his mother.

"Some are saying he was involved in the killing of his mother," I said.

I was starting to feel a little hot under the collar. Sometimes, in the past, that led to problems.

"People kill people because they either hate 'em with passion or they love 'em with passion," the barkeep said. "I don't see a man killing his old seventy-year-old mother like that. From what I've heard, he didn't need her dead to get to the family fortune. That was already his."

He made decent enough points. I didn't feel like I did. I needed to study a little longer on it. Thankfully, I still had a couple days before I would see anything looking like Dallas. I hated the thought of skipping past Fort Worth on my way to do it, but I knew Gentleman Jack would already be there. Might already be there even as I sat in the Whiskey Rose in Glen Rose. I paid up for my sarsaparilla and headed for the door.

A man sitting close to the door caught my attention.

"Hey, partner," he said, "you not a fence cutter, are you?"

I had cut some posts to make fences before, but that was about the extent of it.

"No, you?" I said.

He looked offended.

"Fence cutters are ruining this state," he said. "There's just a matter of time before these ranchers get enough of it and meet force with force. They's really gonna be some cutting going on when that happens."

His friend slammed his glass of whiskey down.

"I'll tell you what. There's a bunch of people walking around that needs to be locked up and throw away the key. Problem is, they're all walking around in clear daylight, and you can't tell which is which. I might drink a bottle of whiskey with you today, and you might be out cutting my damn fence posts down tonight while I'm asleep."

He was right about that. You couldn't tell the good from the bad by looking at them. They might be a fence cutter and they might be a sheepherder cutting the throats of cattle in the night. You might be the man who shot a baby in the face right in front of its mom, and you might be a bounty hunter with some kind of secret motive. Chances are, nobody would know it to look at you. It's what made being an outlaw an easy ticket to wealth and fame and being a lawman a hard row to hoe.

We were in the hottest hot of summer and in the middle of a sizable drought to boot. It felt to me like everyone was on edge, and the whole place was about to shoot up in flames. I was hoping to find a little bit of normal in the wild streets of Dallas and Fort Worth. If I didn't, I had half a mind to keep riding north into Indian Territory.

CHAPTER TWENTY-ONE

Thing about south Dallas, the way it laid out on the flatland above Waxahachie, you could see it a long time before it got wind of you. I wasn't a fan of Dallas, for the most part, but I was looking forward to it this time. I'd had enough of sheep and cows and phantoms and angry ranchers. I was ready for some more proper entertainment.

The real reason for coming to Dallas, of course, was to pay a visit to Bess Harper and find out what we could find out about the Pacific Railway train robbery and killing. I still wanted to know what happened to Pete Rondell when she started west for the Spiney McSwain Ranch. I wanted to know any- and everything she could tell me about the man who shot the lady and the little boy. I wanted to know a lot.

I wasn't sure at that point if I wanted to meet back up with Gentleman Jack Delaney or not, but I assumed it would happen. I began to plot against him at this point, almost as a mental exercise to pass the time. There were only so many times I could go over the list of questions I had for Bess Harper. Or the reasons I thought Gentleman Jack was setting me up. I began to set about in my mind the act of turning the tables.

I knew, right off the top, I had one thing going for me. I was a Texas Ranger. He wasn't. And that was a second thing. I was riding Bird, the second Bird, because Little Cuss was still having trouble with his hooves. The hard ground hadn't been kind to them, especially the front ones. Bird, on the other hand, was in fine shape and seemed to enjoy me riding her more than she did just tagging along behind us. And so there we came, Bird with me riding and Little Cuss out to our left, just far enough to feel his own independence and just close enough to feel safe.

It would be a good thing that I showed up in Dallas behind Gentleman Jack. I would ride in with word that the Phantom had robbed another train and had escaped into the rocky hills south of the San Saba, out beyond Cookie's hideaway. The Pinkertons, I would say, had him located and were waiting for backup from the U.S. Army. I would tell him I knew where the Phantom—or Manley Clark, or whoever—was hiding out. By the time I painted the picture, so would Gentleman Jack.

We would take off for the spot, of course. I knew Jack wouldn't be able to say no to that. He would want to leave at once. When we got out into that very worst part of the desert, I could pick my moment, turn on him, and kill him. It would be over quickly, probably too quickly. Maybe he wouldn't even see it coming, but I wanted him to see that. I decided I would make sure of it.

I wasn't sure whether I would burn the body like we had the colored man or just leave it for the turkey buzzards. I decided I preferred the second option. It would be a bit of poetic justice. Irony. He would be like the little lamb whose shepherd never came. Nobody would ever know what became of Gentleman Jack.

I wasn't thrilled with that last bit. I toyed with the idea of shooting him down and then bringing him in as the actual culprit. The Phantom himself. The idea had its good points. There were even reasons to wonder. He had been in the general area at the time of the killing, hadn't he? He had come riding up Lonetree Mountain from the south. He would have had to travel at top speed to get there when he did, but could he have done it? If he knew he had to, yes.

I thought about what the man in the Glen Rose bar said. People kill out of passion. The woman had been traveling from New Orleans. Jack also had ties to New Orleans. Maybe there was a history there. Maybe that's precisely why she had been dallying in the Crescent City. Would Gentleman Jack be stupid enough to have an affair with the king of the Pacific Railway's wife? Again, I decided the answer was likely to be yes.

I had never been to New Orleans, but I figured I needed to go, and the sooner the better. The Texas & Pacific left Dallas for Shreveport, and I was pretty sure it went on from there to New Orleans. I could go down and scout things out. Poke around in Jack's nests, see what I stirred up. I could find out if there was a connection between him and the railroad man's wife. And while I was there, I would find out if there was a connection between Jack and my father. Maybe I could find out who the man was that crawled into tiny Wheeler, Texas, carrying an envelope with my father's name on it.

That's how a plan to kill Gentleman Jack in the desert took a turn and became a plan to travel to New Orleans. It was a shorter distance from one point to the next than from Glen Rose to Dallas. By the time south Dallas showed itself as a smudge on the horizon, I had begun weighing the pluses and minuses of just shooting Jack in the streets of Dallas ahead of the train's exit for Shreveport. To my mind, I couldn't think of another person I had ever disliked more than Jack. In my past life, if I thought I disliked you, you would be dead before the dislike got to be a real problem. I certainly wouldn't have let you try to kill me and live to tell about it, much less team up with you later and go into business together.

The second day since leaving Glen Rose was coming to an end with the lights of Dallas still just a faraway promise. I knew I could push the horses and get there late in the night, but all good people would be in bed asleep. That certainly meant Bess Harper and her family. I stopped and made a fire and warmed up some supper. Later, I made a bed underneath the stars and lay on my side so I could see the distant city. I couldn't hear any sounds from it. Only wolves and coyotes and night birds.

The lights on the horizon reminded me of nothing so much as the light Gentleman Jack had taken off after in the desert south of Lonetree Mountain. Appropriate, I thought, on two different counts. For one, I wondered if the light had mesmerized men enough to chase after it. Even as I lay there in the cool evening wind, there were hundreds, maybe thousands of men there chasing after something. Some after happiness or excitement, maybe something they couldn't even name. Maybe instead of trying to rope it, that thing had roped them and was pulling them along. I had almost felt that way at times. On the second count, I knew Gentleman Jack was out there in those very lights, probably in some bar or bawdy house, spending time, money, and energy on things that would be gone in the morning. He was always the one chasing lights. It was his weakness, and it was a weakness I aimed to take advantage of before all was said and done.

I fell asleep looking at the lights of Dallas, maybe eight, ten miles in the distance. I could have chased them down that night, but I didn't. I would save that for the next day, when the sun overhead would dim their allure and make their magic less effective.

The next morning, I couldn't even see anything there on the horizon. It seemed to have packed up and moved along. A trick of my tired mind, a ghost

of a town. I packed up and headed in the direction
where it had been. I knew it would be there.

And it was. I came riding into town still in the
early part of the day, before the heat collected
itself. The first thing I saw was the Sabine & East
Texas Railroad pulling in from the east, dropping
off people, mostly men, mostly workers coming to
town looking for jobs. Right behind it came the
Texas & New Orleans Railroad. Part of me wanted
to stop and see what it would cost to ride to New
Orleans, but the light of day had tempered me on
that notion, and I continued on. I might wind up
in New Orleans someday but now wasn't the time
for it. I had other things to do.

Interestingly enough, my desire to kill Jack Delaney had not dimmed in the day. In fact, I went
along with a certainty, as if the question of it had
been answered and only the when and how remained. It wasn't an angry reality that pushed me
forward. It brought more of a calm to me. It made
me question the man in the Glen Rose bar who insisted that murder came from passion, whether it
be love or hate. There was no passion in me for it,
I told myself. Just an understanding that it needed
doing.

I had a map with me that was supposed to lead
me to the house on Dallas's south side where
Bess Harper was staying with her family. I took
Cockrell Street past the Masonic cemetery, took a
right on Commerce and followed it past the post
office. There I took a left on Preston, crossed the
Texas & Pacific Railroad line, and found my way to

Gaston Avenue. The fourth house on the left looked similar to every other house I had passed, as if the same man had built them all, one at a time, as he worked his way along Gaston. Its front porch swing was hanging empty, the muffled sounds of life barely contained by its thin walls. I tied Little Cuss and Bird Two to a post and knocked at the door. The sounds inside fell hush, and there was the brief sensation of both sides trying hard to hear the other. That soon gave way to an opening door and a family of faces peering out at me. I didn't expect to see Gentleman Jack amongst them, and on that detail he did not let me down.

"This the family of Bess Harper?" I said.

There was no answer forthcoming, and I was beginning to think I had miscounted houses or misread street signs or something.

"I've come a long way," I said.

I heard someone back in another room say I hadn't come any longer of a way than they had. I could understand that woman's spirit. She reminded me of Madam Pearlie at the Black Elephant. I wanted it to be her. Maybe I knew only then that I would have to go and pay the Black El a visit.

A large-set lady pushed her way to the door and frowned. I guess she was disappointed in what she saw.

"You one of these pink detectives?"

I showed her my badge.

"Ain't no Pinkerton, ma'am. I am a Texas Ranger."

I'm not sure she was listening to me.

"You a cattle ranch owner?"

I told her I was nothing of the sort. She backed up and invited me into the house, not with a hug or handshake but with a motion that told everyone else in the room to step back and give me a path. The walls were filled with photographs, so many photographs I thought of my very first real job, as a photographer's assistant back in San Antonio. It might also have been the first private home I ever saw with a piano in it.

As my eyes adjusted to the low inside light, I could see a ring of family members around me, and if I'd had time to study it, I might have been able to place each one of them with a corresponding photograph on the wall.

"I was lucky enough to have met young Bess Harper down in San Saba," I said. "I'm trying to find the man who killed the wife and son of the Pacific Railway owner. I believe Bess might be able to give me some information that would help bring him to justice."

No one smiled. The old lady was still giving me a hard look-over.

"You one of them lawyers. We done had one come by yesterday," she said.

I told her I wasn't a lawyer and I didn't appreciate where she was going. That at least got a chuckle out of the man sitting over to my right. I took him to be her husband, but I didn't want to make an assumption right back at them.

"Lawyers are wanting to talk to her?" I said.

The man was holding a little girl on his lap, but I could tell it wasn't Bess. At least, I was pretty sure.

"Robert McSwain threatened to take the Pacific Railway to court and have her as his star witness when those railroad people come around," he said. "That's when we had her brought up here."

I didn't like lawyers any more than I liked those "pink detectives," but I hadn't seen any around Spiney McSwain Ranch or either of the sheep ranches.

"Why were lawyers snooping around the Spiney McSwain Ranch?" I said.

We were getting off the subject, but I was intrigued.

"They said they have proof someone from the ranch there had did it," the lady said.

"Robert McSwain knew they was onto him, and so did that poor mama of his," the man said. "I imagine that's why he killed her and hit the road."

I had to find out who killed the two people on the train. I also needed to find out who killed Ishum Harper, Bess's father. Who the man in the desert was. Who the man in the river close to Still Creek was. And who killed Mrs. McSwain, if it wasn't her own son himself. You could almost lose Phantom Bill in the confusion. I began to wonder if Phantom Bill wasn't the answer to all of the questions.

CHAPTER TWENTY-TWO

Bess Harper wanted to put on a piano recital, and if that was the price for talking to her about what happened on the train, I would have listened to every sonata Beethoven ever wrote. As it turned out, the concert mostly consisted of "Camptown Races" and "Way Down upon the Swanee," both of which I first heard in a brothel although I didn't mention it.

I liked Bess and was surprised to find she liked me as well. She gave no indication that she remembered me from our short visit at the Spiney McSwain Ranch. The whole family stuck around and rooted her on through the musical portion of the meeting, singing along on "Way Down upon the Swanee" until she made it through the main verse and a chorus. After that, they all seemed to find better things to do, and soon it was only me, Bess, and the grandmother of the house, who I learned was named Winny. Winny seemed concerned that I be kept in check as I talked to Bess, and I was happy enough to get the opportunity. I wasn't going to jeopardize it by arguing with her.

"Bess, I just want to ask you a few questions about the day you went on the train ride with your friend Mr. Pete," I said. "Do you remember that day?"

She was still sitting at the piano bench, but Winny had shut the top down on the keys to help the little girl focus on our conversation.

"We got stopped by the bad man," Bess said.

She spoke the words matter-of-factly, not as if she was traumatized by the memory.

"That's right," I said, "and I'm going to make that bad man pay."

I stopped myself, thinking maybe I shouldn't start talking about what I planned to do to him. Winny seemed glad to see me hold back.

"Mr. Pete walked to that house with me, but then he told me to walk ahead and he would see me later, only he never did see me later."

Winny sat right over her, nodding as the words came out. It was obvious they had been over the story a few times, and she was there partly to make sure it all came out the way it was supposed to. I didn't mind this so much, as long as I felt like it was the kid telling the story and not being coached.

"Do you have any idea where Mr. Pete was going when he turned around?"

She looked at Winny and shrugged.

"He was going to pick up Mr. Cry Baby."

The path of a Texas Ranger can lead you into

some weeds and crevices. You know it can lead you into danger. It's the other places that surprise you.

"Mr. Cry Baby," I said.

She acted like it was Winny asking the questions and not me. I was willing to deal with that.

"You know who Mr. Cry Baby is," she said, and by "you" she meant Winny and not me.

"Mr. Cry Baby was her pet lamb."

Winny looked at me and whispered, "Mr. Cry Baby was a girl."

I wanted to ask more. Why had they left Mr. Cry Baby the girl lamb behind? Why was he going back to get her? Winny shook her head *no* and made a face that said, *I will tell you later about Mr. Cry Baby.* I moved along.

"Do you remember when the bad man stopped the train you were riding in with Mr. Pete?"

Bess looked at Winny and nodded her head. She did remember that.

"Can you tell me what you remember?"

She looked at the floor. Her manner of delivery suggested she was reading it off the floor. Evidence showed otherwise.

"We were riding, then the train was shaking and making a noise, then we stopped, so I sat and held Mr. Cry Baby and Mr. Pete went to look."

I couldn't help seeing it through this girl's eyes. Her words, the way she said them, put me there. I felt like I was Mr. Cry Baby. Not because I was crying, because I felt like I was right there with her.

"Did he come back and tell you anything?" I said.

"No, he didn't do that, I didn't see Mr. Pete until I was past the trees where the house was," she said.

I was trying my best to put this all together in my mind, making this puzzle from the pieces she gave me, trying to see the big picture.

Why did she leave the train? How did she carry Cry Baby? When did she finally let him go? Did she hope he would follow? Did she say she would try to come back for him? Did she know where she was going? How did she know the way?

As she answered my questions, I wished I had something to write her words down on. I was trying to commit each word to memory, so I could go back over them later. Not that I would share them with Gentleman Jack. I remember thinking that even as she was talking about Mr. Pete and the blood.

"How did you get to the trees where you could see the house?" I said.

Again, she looked at Winny, who would repeat the question and nod her head until a response came.

"The man with the blue face showed me where to go."

Winny turned to me.

"We couldn't figure out what she meant by 'the man with the blue face.' My husband thinks he had some type of cloth or material covering his face."

I wanted to know if Winny thought so, too.

"What do you mean, 'the man with the blue face'?" I said.

"He had a blue face when he talked," Bess said.

Did ghosts have blue faces? Did they turn blue when they talked? I had more questions than ever, but I knew the way to the truth was straight ahead. I plowed on.

"When he talked, what did he say?"

She thought about that for a while, even with Winny's urging. I was beginning to worry that she had completely forgotten that part.

"The first thing he said was to give him Mr. Cry Baby and my bag. Then he said where did I stay at and what was I on the train for."

She looked like she wanted to cry. Part of me wanted to stop. The other part won out.

"What did you tell him then?" I said.

She actually looked at me when she answered. It was the first time.

"I told him I was riding to Amarillo."

She had trouble with pronouncing the town and looked to Winny for guidance. I couldn't blame her. I didn't know Amarillo from Adam when I was five. Or fifteen.

"Can you tell me more about the man with the blue face?" I said. "Did he look or dress funny?"

He had a blue face. Of course he looked funny, but I wanted to know more. I was starting to think maybe he was a Comanche or possibly a Tonkawa. Both were known to paint their faces. Both dressed distinctively. Not like white folks and not like the colored folks, either.

Bess leaned in toward Winny and whispered her answer.

"He looked like him."

She was saying the man looked like me. I was almost ready to abandon the Indian idea.

"Was he an Indian?" I said.

"Does she know what an Indian looks like?" I said to Winny.

Winny talked to her about Indians, what they looked like and what they did, places Bess might have seen them. I set that idea aside, at least temporarily. All we got was one shake of the head after the other.

"I heard him talking loud and shooting his gun," she said.

Again, she was looking right into my eyes. The combination of childlike innocence and adult words was startling.

"Did you hear any of the words he was shouting?"

It was a long shot, but any shot was a shot worth taking.

"He talked funny," she said.

My Comanche idea was still barely alive.

"He spoke another language, maybe?" I said.

I wasn't sure if a five-year-old even knew there were such things as other languages. I was pretty sure I thought we all spoke English. I remember hearing people speak Spanish in the market, but I thought they were just using words I hadn't learned yet.

"Was the man speaking words you didn't know?"

She nodded her head *yes* and then shook it *no.* Maybe some of the words, I thought.

"He said 'I love you.'"

She didn't know who he said he loved. She said it wasn't her, because it was when she was hiding at the bottom of the car with Mr. Cry Baby. He hadn't seen her yet, most likely had no idea she was there.

"He told Mr. Pete 'I love you,'" she said.

I wasn't so sure I bought that. She hadn't seen Pete again until much later, so I wasn't sure Pete was involved in any conversations with the killer. Most likely, he had slipped around the back of the train and was planning to stop the robbery. I assumed he thought that was all it was.

Bess didn't have any more to add to the conversation, so I spent a few minutes asking her how she liked living in Dallas, and she said she liked it, but she missed all the sheep.

"There aren't as many sheep here in Dallas," I said, "but there are a lot of people."

Me and Winny both agreed that she would make a bunch of new friends in the town, and she would learn to like it even more. I hoped I wasn't lying. I was trying to imagine her as a young Sunny, my friend from the Black Elephant. That worked to a certain extent, but thinking of Sunny put more adult thoughts in my head, and that kind of put an end to that endeavor.

I thanked Winny and her family. They turned out to be welcoming hosts, and they wished me well. He husband walked me out to the street and

pointed out the most direct way of getting to Fort
Worth.

"I hope you catch the son of a bitch who did
this," he said.

I assured him I wouldn't stop until I did.

"That girl has bad dreams. She can't get through
a night without waking us up."

I hated to hear it, but it did bring up more questions.

"Is there anything she says about the dreams?"

He said it was mostly just crying and thinking
she heard gunshots when there weren't any.

"She don't say much to me," he said. "She tells
my wife the same thing she told you. He was a man
with a blue face, and he talked funny."

She seemed sure enough of those two things.

"I think it was the same man been robbing them
trains down there, and I think he had a rag over his
face so you couldn't see him."

I had to admit, it sounded right to me. As I left,
he stammered for a bit and left me with one last
thought, which seemed to be real important to him.

"I guess you know, Ishum Harper was my little
brother. He was four years younger than me, and I
always took care of him while we was growing up."

His words reminded me of me and Ira Lee. I
wanted to tell him so, but I lost my chance. The
words that came next washed that right on downstream.

"We was both owned by Mr. Bill Don Bryant.
Mr. Bill Don was what we called him. After the war,
Ishum went with our mother. They didn't travel

far. Found the Still Creek ranch not ten miles from where we was slaves, working cotton fields all day. Me, I wanted to get as far away from that place as I could. Guess Dallas was as far away as I could, at least at the time."

I didn't know what to tell the man. An apology seemed like not enough and too much at the same time.

"I just been thinking," he said, "if I had been down there, maybe this whole thing might not have happened."

I did know how to answer that.

"Bad things happen everywhere," I said. "Just keep Bess and your family safe here. That's the best anybody can ask of anybody."

I left the man standing at the gate of his home in a neighborhood where colored people made more than I probably ever would. Still, for all of that, he had to watch his back. Dallas was his home, but he wasn't welcome on most of its streets, and he never knew when things would turn against him and his family. We did have one thing in common that the difference in our skin couldn't do anything about. We had lost brothers. I knew what it was like to wonder if I might have done something to save Ira Lee. It was something I lived with. Even on a good day, the thought might come back. Any little thing could remind me. The way someone said something. The way they smiled. I got to live on and do things Ira would never do, but those little reminders were the price I paid for it.

I had thrown myself at Fort Worth the last time I arrived in the town, as a way of shaking off the death of my brother and the disastrous end of the cattle drive. This time, I would return to the Black El as a changed man. Much better prepared for what I would meet. Of course, Gentleman Jack was still out there somewhere, and there was no telling when he would show up or what he would do. He wouldn't be able to do the things he'd done the last time, though. I was ready if he tried. I was ready even if he didn't. This time, I had the upper hand.

CHAPTER TWENTY-THREE

You could take a train to Fort Worth. A lot of people did. You could sit and study it and see the way life worked. Men would ride over there if they had jobs. It would take two or three hours, but that was faster than Little Cuss or Bird could do it by a considerable sight. Other men would hitch rides in freight cars. They often went farther, sometimes riding all the way out to California.

As a Texas Ranger, I could have ridden to Fort Worth if I had wanted. But I would have had to get Little Cuss and Bird shipped over, too. It was easier to ride Little Cuss, even if it took a day to get there. It was at this time I decided to hold on to Bird. My original plan had been to sell her in Dallas. There were people arriving there daily without anything at all, and a good horse would fetch a healthy price. Bird was a beautiful part Appaloosa and fit as a fiddle. After laughing at Willie Gee for riding a mule he named Bird, I don't know why I decided

to name this one Bird, too. There was something I
liked about it in hindsight, though. This earth-
bound pack animal named after a creature that
could fly the heavens and look down on us all. So
this new little mule had taken on the name, and it
had stuck. In so doing, she had stuck on me, and I
decided not to let go of her. Bird and Little Cuss
and me hit the trail for Fort Worth, moving fast
enough to arrive late in the night. Late in the night
was when the Black Elephant was at its best.

The trip into Fort Worth was uneventful except
for the fact that I was entering from a direction I
had never entered from before. So I had new things
to look at and a new perspective when the town
finally came into view. I had grown up in San Antonio, and I had made a home in Mobeetie with
Greer, but Fort Worth felt more like it fit me than
any place I had been. And this in spite—and maybe
a little bit because of—it almost became my end.

I had time to think on the trip, and for once I
wasn't thinking about ways to kill Gentleman Jack,
although I had begun to wonder where he was.
Mainly I was thinking about Sunny. Sunny had
been my friend in the darkest days when Jack was
trying me for the deaths of hundreds of head of
cattle and almost that many people in Wichita
Falls. She had nursed me back to health after Jack
stretched my neck to its very limit and left me lying
in the dirt under the gallows like a prostitute's
petticoat. I watched Sunny leave the Black El to go
and be another man's bride, and I was thinking
that might have been the single worst mistake of

my life, at least until the day I paired back up with
Gentleman Jack. Now, riding into Fort Worth, I
felt I had undone the mistake with Jack. At least,
I was well on the way to doing so. I didn't know if I
could undo the one with Sunny. I wasn't even sure
if I should.

The Black Elephant was sitting right in the same
place I had left it the year before, at Main and
Fourth, but it seemed different. The blocks
seemed shorter, the buildings smaller, but THE
BLACK EL still faced one direction, EPHANT SALOON
the other.

I wasn't sure what kind of reception I would get.
It had been a year. I hoped Madam Pearlie Tutt
would remember me, and in a good way. Even if
she did, it might not mean much to her. She had
certainly seen a lot of faces since mine. I decided
to walk in and take a table, order a sarsaparilla
from the one-eyed barkeep whose name I couldn't
recall, and quietly observe things. I tied Little Cuss
and Bird up and wandered in, underneath the
veranda full of women who called down at me.

"Hey, white boy, come on in here."

It was one of the few places a colored girl could
safely call out to a white man without fear for
her own safety. Pearlie made sure her girls were
protected. She didn't put up with shenanigans.
Girls were waiting just inside the front room,
where they would escort men to either the waiting
room or the bar, depending on which sin you wanted
to indulge. As much as I might have enjoyed picking a girl from the evening's lineup and climbing

the spiral staircase, I wanted nothing more than a seat at one of the tables, not a poker table, and a drink, not a whiskey.

"Will you look who the wind blew in."

I knew the voice. It wasn't the one I was hoping for. I looked up and saw Gentleman Jack sliding across the room like a bad memory. He had a drink in each hand. I wondered if he had been waiting for me.

"Where you been, Jack?"

Seeing him back in the Black El brought back a full dose of bad feelings. It was like finding your sworn enemy in bed with your best girl. If Sunny had been on his arm, I would have shot him dead right then and there.

"I figured out who killed the Pacific Railway lady and her son," I said. "And I know where Manley Clark is holed up."

Neither of those things was true, but he didn't know it. The look of surprise was worth it.

"I tried to talk to that damn kid yesterday," he said. "They won't let anybody near her."

He had been the lawyer they were talking about. That didn't surprise me. Jack knew how to mesmerize people, but if they knew they were being mesmerized, his charm didn't wear well. I could imagine Bess's uncle. I could see his reaction to someone like Gentleman Jack. It made me laugh.

"Would you like a drink, sir?"

The one-eyed bartender looked at me and

squinted, like he knew me but couldn't name me, either.

"You remember me?" I said. "I'm Wilkie John Liquorish."

He grinned and shook my hand.

"Course I remember you. I'm Black Price, still at your service."

Black Price. Yes, of course.

"You still take a sarsaparilla?"

A good barkeep remembers his customers. A great one remembers their drink of choice. I ordered one and turned away from Gentleman Jack, leaving him with both hands full.

Finding an empty table, I sat down. I was surprised that Jack followed.

"It just so happens I talked to Bess Harper this morning, Jack," I said. "For a kid, she was more helpful than you might have imagined."

Jack sat down across from me, and my return to the Black Elephant became something very different from what I had imagined.

"Wilkie John, I thought we were in this thing together," he said.

He picked up one of his whiskeys and downed it in one long swig. Then he picked up the other. I tried to recall how dapper, even otherworldly, he had looked to me the year before. Even as he dragged me around the town and watched the gallows go up in its very heart, I had been transfixed by him, unable to look away. Now he seemed sad, like he was trying too hard. The suit needed a cleaning.

"Only person I was ever together with was my wife, Greer," I said. "Maybe you remember her."

It was a line I had practiced until I got it perfect. The delivery was quick and it sunk in deep, but I saw no guilt in his eyes. Just a dull, tired anger.

"You know where Manley is?" he said.

Black Price showed up with a bottle of sarsaparilla and left it on the table.

"On the house, sir," he said.

I nodded my appreciation and took a swig.

"The Rangers want me to do it, Jack," I said. "I'll take Bird and Little Cuss, and I don't expect we'll need any assistance."

"Would you like for me to get Madam Pearlie, sir?" Black Price said.

I turned my attention away from Jack.

"Is she in the house?" I said.

Black Price hadn't grown another eye back, but he did have a new pair of eyeglasses, and it amused me to see the glass was only in the one that had the matching eyeball. I suppose with one eye having to do all the work, it had grown tired, too.

"Oh yes, sir," Black Price said. "She's upstairs. Miss Sunny is here again, too."

For all my attempt to look tough in front of Gentleman Jack, I suddenly felt weak in the knees as a schoolboy in front of his first heartthrob.

"I thought Miss Sunny got married," I said.

Black Price came closer and leaned down.

"Her husband is missing and presumed dead.

Seems he had another wife in Dallas who found out about Sunny and was none too happy about it."

I remembered the man. Hampton Balfour. A real unlikable man. I had no tear to shed for him, but I did worry about Sunny.

"She killed Mr. Balfour?" I said.

I had almost done the same thing a time or two. I was almost jealous.

"Not Sunny," Black Price said. "His Dallas wife either killed him or run him off good. Ain't nobody seen or heard from him since then."

I couldn't imagine anyone would be looking very hard for him.

"By 'nobody,' you mean Sunny, I guess."

Black Price nodded.

"The bank come out and took their home back. Sunny come back here. First off, Madam Pearlie just give her her old room back and she lived up there. After three or four months of no Hampton Balfour, old habits come back. Sunny started working for Madam Pearlie again."

Sometimes I get to thinking people are like books. If I'm reading *Twenty Thousand Leagues Under the Sea*, and I finish it and start on *Middlemarch*, I think *Twenty Thousand Leagues* is done, over, no longer relevant. In reality it's still there being what it was for me, only now for somebody else. That's the magic of books. I guess it's the magic of people, too. When I left Sunny, she kept right on doing the things Sunny does, only for somebody else. And like a book, some of the things weren't always so good.

"Jack, I'm about to walk up those stairs and find Madam Pearlie. After that, I'm going to find Sunny. And if you sit here and wait for me to come back down, I'll just warn you. You may be waiting for a considerable time."

I downed the last of my sarsaparilla and stood up.

"When you get ready to head back down south, you come get me," Jack said. "And don't bring anybody else with you. Like you said, you don't need nobody."

Of course, he was trying to turn my words against me. What he was saying was not to bring Sunny. Maybe he was feeling a little on the jealous side. I was about to make a beeline for the stairs when I heard a commotion at the top and looked up to see the madam herself, looking all dressed up to the nines. She looked at me like I was the ghost of Hampton Balfour himself.

"I can't believe my eyes!" she said.

No, she wouldn't have come running down the stairs for Balfour. I, of course, played it off.

"Yes, it is Gentleman Jack Delaney, back here in your fine establishment."

She waved him off just like I knew she would.

"Wilkie John," she said. "I was beginning to think I wouldn't never see you around here again."

She spread her arms wide and came at me at pretty close to full strength. I braced myself and grinned.

"Pearlie," I said.

She wrapped me up tight and planted a wet kiss on my cheek.

"I got somebody upstairs you gotta see," she said.

I pretended like I didn't have a clue. I wanted to hear her tell me all about it. Most of all, I wanted to see Sunny. Finally, I felt like I was back home. I knew I was supposed to go back south. I knew I was luring Jack back down into the desert, into a trap. I knew what I was planning to do. All of a sudden, I just didn't want to do it anymore.

CHAPTER TWENTY-FOUR

The last time I left Fort Worth, I left watching Sunny all but betrothed to Hampton Balfour. I had helped arrange their union. In my mind, it was the only way I could kill her off. If she was married to a man I could barely stand to look at, she was easier to ride away from. And that worked up to a point. That point being when I rode back into town. I found out there were other things to deal with as well.

"Wilkie John, you gotta listen and understand this," Madam Pearlie said. "Half the people around here think Hampton Balfour was killed by his other wife in Dallas. She's in jail in Dallas right now because of it. But the other half—and that half may be more than half—think Wilkie John Liquorish done it. So you gotta watch yourself."

This was all relayed to me on the second floor of the Black Elephant. On our way to the room at the end of the hall. The room that had once been

Pearlie's herself, until she moved downstairs and gave it to me. Before Sunny had taken it over. She knocked on the door.

"Sunny, you ready for a guest?" Madam Pearlie said.

She might have knocked on that door a hundred times. Might have asked Sunny if she was ready to entertain a guest almost as often. It was nothing to Sunny to come to the door in her best manner and greet whatever guest downstairs had taken a particular like to her. There were many who did.

"Welcome to the Black El."

She got that far before she abandoned the usual script. She stood there for what seemed like such a long silence, I was beginning to wonder if she was trying to remember who I was. I finally let her off the hook.

"It's your old friend Wilkie John," I said.

I had made an initial step into the doorway. Enough that Madam Pearlie was now behind me. I felt her nudge me slightly and then give me a more firm shove. I looked back and saw for the first time that Gentleman Jack was standing a few steps behind Pearlie. For some reason, that struck me as odd. The door was pushed to, and I made one more somewhat nervous step forward. Sunny took the next step, took my hand in hers, and the door seemed to close itself behind me.

To many of the men coming into the Black Elephant, the touch of her hand might have meant the world. I could easily imagine a man on his first trip up those stairs losing all his composure in

such a moment. Knowing that she would take any
mother's son in hand and it would be no different,
the effect was not unlike a slap in the face.

"Sunny, it's great to see you," I said.

She glanced up into my eyes and I saw only the
blankest of expressions.

"I will have to give you a short bath if you plan
to lie down in the bed with me," she said.

I was familiar enough with the procedure.

"That won't be necessary," I said.

I looked for some sign of disappointment in her
eyes. Finding none, I pulled my jacket off and
hung it over the same coatrack I'd hung it over
dozens of times before. Its response was similar.

"Would you like a chair?" she said.

She wasn't unkind. To the contrary, she sounded
happy. It was just a professional kind of happiness
and not a personal one. I took the chair and sat
down, turning it backward so that my legs straddled
the back and my arms rested on it.

"You aren't happy to see me," I said.

I expected tears. Laughter. Even anger. If she
had been mad that I left her with Mr. Balfour, I
could have understood that. Hell, even if she was
mad because she thought I had killed the bastard.
What I wasn't expecting was a sincere lack of any
detectable emotion.

"No, I am happy," she said.

My thought was, she didn't want me complaining to Madam Pearlie. Madam Pearlie would dock
her pay. Not that I would have complained. I knew
better than to do that. I sat in the chair and told

her stories of things that had happened in the year since I had seen her last. I told her about Gentleman Jack asking me to help him hunt down Phantom Bill. Just as I had done the year before, I opened up and told her things I wouldn't have told anyone else. Not even Madam Pearlie. I talked about my doubts. Why I began to think it wasn't smart for me to continue on with Gentleman Jack. How I had separated from him and gone to Dallas. How the little girl there had reminded me of Sunny's stories of living in Waterproof, Louisiana. I thought maybe those stories would provoke a response in her, but she listened passively and said nothing. I asked her questions about her life. She answered briefly but always holding back more than she gave.

"We lived in a nice part of town.

"I enjoyed my days.

"I learned to do many household chores.

"Some of them, I do here for Pearlie."

She spoke quietly, as if she suspected someone was in the hall with their ear to the door. I finally told her how I had come back to the Black Elephant just to see her, and how it was there that I had run into Gentleman Jack again. It was at that point that an idea popped into my head.

"You knew he was here, didn't you?"

To avoid looking at me, she busied herself straightening the pieces of a bed that we weren't putting to any use.

"I've seen him, yes."

I'm not an unobservant man. She didn't have to

say more to say enough. It was clear enough in my mind that he had been up to her room, maybe more than once. I knew her job. I knew everything it entailed. I wondered if I had stumbled onto the reason for her behavior. Unfortunately, once I stumbled, I kept going.

"You have feelings for him?"

I thought I knew the answer. It had to be *no*. That didn't seem possible. Her silence wasn't helpful. I left her room soon afterward. Not before paying my fare and a little extra. Not before reaching out and stroking her cheek, pushing her hair back. I felt like I had come a long way to look at the moon, only to find a sky full of rain. I walked back out and smiled at Madam Pearlie and Gentleman Jack, who were sitting together at the bar, drinking some concoction from Black Price. It was the hardest smile I've ever smiled in all my life.

That night, in a hotel room two blocks away, something even more confounding and unexpected happened. As I lay on a low bed that wasn't much more than a flat rock compared to the big feather beds in the Black El, I opened up the Colt, which I normally kept two bullets in, and filled it the rest of the way up. I would be lying if I said I didn't think about shooting my own self, because I did, but not with any fervor. I was more interested in shooting Gentleman Jack, but even he was escaping the brunt of my wrath. I had his demise planned out in the desert, and I didn't want to cheat him of that. But I did consider putting Sunny out of her misery and, to be fair, mine to boot.

"You were right, you old coot," I said.

There wasn't anyone in the room but me, but I was talking to that old man in the Glen Rose bar. He got it right. Passion was the finger that pulled the trigger. I was feeling like the man who stepped up to that train and, maybe I would take the bags of money—if there were bags of money—but it wasn't what I came for. I wanted to return to the Black Elephant, march up the stairs, walk down to the end of the hall, knock on the door, open the door, and shoot Sunny Balfour in a way that would stick in Gentleman Jack's mind for the rest of his days, as short as they might be.

I told that sorry old coot from the Whiskey Rose bar that things were fixing to change. I was fixing to change. There would be no more sitting around on a rock of a bed, thinking myself crazy. I wasn't going to let the Texas Ranger badge on my coat keep me from doing what had to be done. The badge was the reason for it. I was sworn to execute justice. Gentleman Jack only thought he was sworn to do so.

I thought about leaving my coat in the dingy little hotel room. That way, I wouldn't sully anything with that Ranger badge. But I convinced myself it was the reason I had to do what I had to do so I went, with the badge and my hat and my Colt, full of fire and ready to burn. I felt like everyone I passed on that walk back to the Black Elephant could surely see I was trouble coming.

Somewhere along the way, something shifted inside me. It was so deep down even I didn't see any evidence of it on the surface, but underneath, where my subconscious had been fooling with this whole situation of the train killing, and the killing of Mrs. McSwain, and the killing of Ishum Harper, the killing of Gentleman Jack Delaney in the desert below San Saba, and now the killing of the one person I wanted the very least and most of all to kill, Sunny Balfour, the weight of these things pulled something apart and it broke.

"Wilkie John," Black Price said. "Back for more."

He may not have seen it right away, but he did see it. I could tell when he did because he reached down under the bar where his rifle lay.

"Don't do it," I said. "I do not want to have to kill you."

There was a commotion coming from the kitchen and Madam Pearlie came barreling through the door into the main room, where the card tables and pool tables made for insufficient hiding places. People scrambled left and right, but I had already seen Gentleman Jack at the back of the room. And, as much as I thought I wanted to climb those stairs and shoot Sunny right in the face, I never even set foot on the first step.

"Jack," I said.

He was sitting at a poker table, lighting a cigar and watching it burn. He didn't bother looking up.

"Mr. Liquorish."

It was the first time I ever recalled him calling me that.

"You're from New Orleans," I said.

If he had any clue I was crazy for stomping into
the saloon the way I did, those four words might
have just sealed the deal. They had to have been
the last four he would have gambled on.

"I wasn't born there," he said, "but yes, I have
lived there."

I had the Colt in my hand. I wasn't pointing it at
him, but it was pretty close. He knew I could get off
a shot if I wanted to. It must have made the discussion even more perplexing. But I had been thinking, in my subconscious, where all of my best
thinking gets done. I was following my instincts. It
was a desperate thing, but I knew, in that despera-
tion, I was onto something.

"You knew Mrs. Foucault," I said.

I didn't like asking Gentleman Jack questions. I
didn't want yes and no answers. I wanted something more.

"I might have known who she was," he said.

He put the cigar down and leaned forward in
his chair. He seemed to be intrigued about where
the question was going.

"Because you go back to New Orleans pretty
regular," I said.

He sighed a long, deflated kind of sigh.

"There's where you lose me, Wilkie," he said. "I
used to go back, but not so much anymore."

I didn't let up. Not at all.

"Because you had a woman back there who stood
you up and left to go back to her husband?"

He laughed, and I lifted the Colt up enough to

put his privates in my scope. I thought he would simmer back down in a hurry, but he didn't.

"No, Wilkie, it's more a case of not wanting to get into some high-stakes game and walking away with deeds to sheep ranches and such."

"You're doing the same thing here," I said.

He pointed to a stack of chips.

"This is small change, Wilkie. I have a much bigger reputation down there."

Right there, standing at the back end of the Black El gambling room, with my Colt pointing at Gentleman Jack's jewels, and with my every intention of causing murder and mayhem, it dawned on me. It was like a light suddenly got switched on, and I could see. I knew who had killed Mrs. Foucault and her child. Maybe Gentleman Jack was beginning to see it, too. I don't know. In my great excitement, I didn't give him the chance. I did something I should not have done. It was something I would almost immediately regret.

"Jack, I know who killed the lady and her kid."

He raised his hands in mock surrender.

"You got me, son," Jack said. "It was I, Phantom Bill."

I knew when he was lying, which was actually at least half the time.

"No, it wasn't you," I said. "It was Charles Stirling."

He laughed at the preposterousness of it, but that laugh did simmer down right quick. And I was no longer holding the Colt on him.

CHAPTER TWENTY-FIVE

Gentleman Jack and I made plans to leave Fort Worth the next morning. I was in no mood to stick around, and if half the things I thought were going on were truly going on, I didn't want to leave Gentleman Jack behind when I unstuck. To be fair, however rattled I was about the situation with Sunny, I was enthusiastic about heading back toward the Alameda Ranch. I wasn't exactly sure what I was going to do when I got there, but I knew I had a four- or five-day ride to figure that part out. The way I looked at it, if I let Jack come along and be part of the Charles Stirling arrest, it would set him up that much better when we turned our sights on Manley Pardon Clark in the desert to the south.

"I'm just saying, you're putting all your eggs into one basket here, Wilkie."

I had gone over everything with Gentleman Jack before, and I already knew I made a mistake. I should never have said word one about my great insight. I should have kept my mouth shut and left the next day by myself. But I wanted him to know I had solved the mystery. I wanted to dangle it in front of him. Now I was stuck with the consequences.

"When I asked Bess to describe the man on the train to me, she kept saying he sounded funny, he sounded funny," I said. "So I immediately think it's an Indian, even a Mexican, maybe."

It hadn't occurred to me she could be talking about Stirling.

"He does sound kind of funny," Gentleman Jack said.

"So do you, Jack."

He did. Either by hook or by crook, he polished up a pretty good Creole accent, although he didn't have a drop of Creole blood in him, far as I could tell. That's why I first pointed the finger at Gentleman Jack. I suppose there was a part of me that wanted it to be him, but I did consider him to be a real candidate for the funny-talking award.

"But you didn't really think it was me, did you?" he said. "I will lose a little trust in you if you did, but I will lose a great deal more respect."

I had thought for sure it was Gentleman Jack, right up until he laughed at me and said no, it wasn't. I could almost always tell when Jack was lying, and at that point, I was fairly sure he wasn't. I changed horses in midstream. It was something I knew how to do, so I just did it.

Even so, I knew I was now right. The puzzle pieces were coming together, and they told me so. Jack couldn't deny what I was seeing.

"Maybe you don't go back to New Orleans," I said, "but does Charles Stirling?"

We were having one last drink at the Black Elephant before leaving town, and everyone in the bar was trying to act like they weren't paying us any attention. The words got out fast, though. Of course, they knew Jack had tried me for murder and sentenced me to hang. That had all happened in the shadow of the Black El. Now they were watching the two of us pair up to go out and get the Pacific Railway killer. It was a story that reached the ears of the *Fort Worth Chief*, who promptly sent a young female writer around to ask us a few questions. What had it been like to live down there where the killing was going on? Did we know the killer? What was his motive? Did we plan to bring him back in, dead or alive? Which did we prefer?

I enjoyed our moment of recognition more than Jack did. That's because the girl, whose name turned out to be Lucy Beeman, took a liking to me and preferred my more expansive answers to his more biting ones. As a result, the story in the *Chief* referred to us as the colorful Texas Ranger Wilkie John Liquorish, and his consort, the colored bounty hunter Jack Delaney. I wouldn't find a copy of it for several months, and reading back on the events from a hotel lobby in Austin would be a particularly interesting endeavor.

"She didn't write down a single thing I said," Gentleman Jack said.

We weren't even out of town for good before he

started the bellyaching. He was looking to make a long ride even longer.

"She was intimidated by how tall you are," I said.

By that, I meant she was intimidated by that silly Lincoln hat he insisted on wearing, but I didn't want to make things harder on myself. At least, not so soon.

"By how colored I am, you mean," he said.

It was much easier for a man like myself to talk to a colored woman like Sunny than it was for him to talk to a white woman. Fort Worth was still a divided town. There were few white men to be found in a place like the Black Elephant and even fewer colored men permitted in the White Elephant, even if Jack Delaney was one of that number.

"Just be glad I invited you along," I said.

The first day, we made it only as far as Johnson County, riding through part of the night and then sleeping the early hours away until the sun got high and hot enough to rouse us. The second day, we made a pass on the west side of Glen Rose, and I made no move to stop there, not even mentioning the Whiskey Rose to Gentleman Jack. It didn't seem like the kind of place that would be welcoming to him, nor to me if I was with him.

That night, we moved into a long stretch of Cherokee Indian country, and we could see smoke from a couple of different camps south of us. I didn't want to stop for the night, feeling that, with a decent amount of moonlight, we could make better time by pushing on.

"If we're gonna keep going, we should go west," Jack said. "Hit the Harris Trail toward Concho."

He was right. It would bypass the Cherokees, but it would also bypass the Alameda Ranch and everywhere we were going. I had a better idea.

"If we go right through that pass in front of us," I said, "we'll go right between the two camps. We'd be a good ten miles from the eastern one, at least five from the other."

I reminded him that, as long as we saw smoke rising from the camps, it meant they were there. I didn't see any reason we couldn't slip right through between them and be that much closer to where we were going in the morning. We didn't stop and talk it over, and that's the main reason I got my way. Me and Little Cuss never slowed down, and with Bird following right behind, Jack could only decide whether to follow or break off on his own. I had nothing to lose.

We did pass closer to the west camp than I estimated. At one point in the middle of that night, we could hear a few of them shooting at coyotes up in the hills to our right.

"I hope they don't mistake us for a band of coyotes," Jack said.

But that was as close as he ever got to complaining, probably because he didn't want them to overhear him.

We rode right through the night and made it to an old abandoned army fort just a couple hours past sunup. Jack had sworn it was there, right around the bend, for most of those two hours, and when he was finally proven right, I was possibly happier than he was. We watered the horses, used what was left of an old cooking area to cook up some stew, and, with our bellies full, settled down to sleep for a few hours. When I awoke a few hours later, I thought rain was pelting down on me.

"Wilkie John," Gentleman Jack said, "wake the devil up."

I blinked my eyes to life and grimaced. Standing over me and tossing handfuls of sand down into my face was a Cherokee Indian. He looked amused, either by my state of sleep or by my confusion on being roused from it.

"*Kago eets di?*"

Jack was lying up against his saddlebags, his fingers stretched but coming up short of his rifle. He looked like half an inch of fuse on a long stick of dynamite.

"*Kago eets di?*"

I recognized a word, part of a word, something there. I went through my memory, trying to grab something from my days with Long Gun, the Kiowa Indian who knew Apache, Comanche, and Tonkawa. He was so much more useful than Gentleman Jack.

"*Kago?*" I said.

He pointed at me. I pointed at myself and answered.

"I'm a Texas Ranger. I'm going to San Saba."

"*Kago eets di?*"

I tried again.

"I'm a Texas Ranger."

It was all I could think of. I showed him my badge. I knew a lot of Cherokee had dealt with Texas Rangers. They provided scouts for us on occasion.

"You just asking to get us scalped?" Gentleman Jack said.

"Jack, if he wanted to scalp us, I'm not sure he would have taken the trouble of waking us up first," I said.

The Indian had a gun and a knife on him and had his hand on neither. He also had a young squaw and a papoose. The squaw was watching carefully.

"He asks who you are."

I was surprised to hear her speak English. She sounded more American than Cherokee. She must have read my thoughts right off my face.

"I'm Flora Miller Pathkiller," she said. "I was born in Saint Louis. This is our daughter."

The Indian never took his eyes off me. I held my hands out in front of me, to let him know I meant no harm. I could've gone to my Colt in less than a second.

"I'm Wilkie John Liquorish," I said. "I'm in pursuit of the man who killed two people on the Pacific Railroad line south of San Saba."

The Indian continued to speak, but this time, I couldn't make out any of the sounds. I stood quietly, hoping his white squaw would translate.

"He says we were told you would be traveling

with a dark-skinned man with a hat such as this,"
she said. She nodded at Gentleman Jack. "Your
name is Jack Delaney."

"What is this about?" Jack said.

I studied his face for a sign. I could see no great
fear, no great curiosity, either. It was more of an annoyance. The man pointed at Jack and said something in Cherokee, and I wished again that I'd had
Long Gun with me.

"There was a very sick man calling for you,"
Flora Miller said. "He will pay you to follow us."

I wasn't sure if I had the time, but I was intrigued enough to ask questions.

"How did you find us here?" I said.

The man pointed to the ground and spoke.
Flora listened and then explained.

"Tahlequah Pathkiller says you were not difficult
to find. We followed you from Glen Rose and we
even carry a crying infant."

"We're a little busy at the moment," Gentleman
Jack said. "What does this man need with us?"

Flora moved up next to her partner. She was
dressed in a deerskin skirt and moccasins, and with
her hair braided in their typical manner, it would
have been hard to identify her as an Anglo.

"We've been told to bring you by whatever
means necessary," she said.

Tahlequah Pathkiller took one step in Jack's
direction, and Jack had had enough. He pulled his
pistol from beneath his longcoat and shot twice.
The thunder of the gun sent the baby into full cry.

The Indian fell back without a sound. Flora fell next to him, not struck by a bullet but by sheer panic.

"We need to be on our way, Wilkie John," Gentleman Jack said.

He was going for mean, but I wasn't buying it. He sounded more desperate to me.

"This man is still alive," I said.

I could see he was bleeding from his upper torso. I wanted to get a closer look. If it was in the chest, it wouldn't be worth the trouble. The closest doctor was at least a day away.

The second shot rang out from about two feet over my left ear, and, at first, I thought we were under attack from more Cherokees. We were as good as dead. I rolled down and moved up against the Indian. I'm not going to lie. I was fully prepared to use his body as cover. Looking up, I found only Jack, sitting there on Alice like nothing had happened.

"Now he's not," Jack said.

Flora Pathkiller had a small pistol in her hand, but it was shaking so bad, I don't think she could have hit Alice, standing five feet away.

"You don't want to do that," I said.

She clutched the baby close to her.

"You ought not to have done that," she said, looking at Jack.

She didn't have Jack's sympathies.

"He ought not to have done what he did," Jack said.

Even I wasn't entirely sure what that might have been. I considered, for a moment, maybe I had found my time and place to kill Gentleman Jack. I could have done it then and there and walked away with never a question asked. I chose not to.

She pointed the gun right in Jack's face and then in mine. She didn't trust either of us, and why should she? That was worrisome. I knew if she was going to kill Jack, she would have just done it. Every second that went by without her doing so, the chances went up that I would end up getting shot.

"Lady, you shoot me, I'm gonna have to shoot you back," I said. "Even if you hit me, I'm liable to put one bullet in you. That don't leave nobody but wolves and Jack here to take care of that baby."

I wondered if my last moment of light was going to be that white-skinned Cherokee squaw and her dark-skinned baby.

"What's the baby's name?" I said.

I was trying to make some kind of connection. I glanced over at the Indian who was now as dead as any Indian I'd ever seen.

"Minnie," Flora Pathkiller said.

"Minnie Pathkiller," I said.

We told her we would help wrap the Indian's body up. We would help her get him onto his horse and ready for the ride either to Stephenville, or back to Glen Rose, the area they seemed to come from. I promised her I would come back and find her there. I would help her out however I was

able. I could give her money. And I would go and
see the man who wanted to see me.

"First of all, I have to go take care of some
business," I said. "You have to let me do that. May
take me a month, but I'll do it, and I'll come back."

Why she would listen to a man whose partner
had just shot and killed her husband, I don't know.
She didn't have many options. She still had the
gun, so I guess she still could have taken a shot at
me. There had been enough shooting and death
for that day, though. It hung over the rest of the
day like a darkness that didn't want to lift. I showed
her where the two Cherokee camps had been, and
she named each of them. One was friendly and the
other, not as much, she said. She left headed west,
to a tribe who knew her, who would take her in and
help her take care of Tahlequah's body. I sat and
watched her ride away, her partner's horse silently
carrying its owner away from the place where he
had met his end.

Sometime during all of this, Gentleman Jack
moved along. He seemed troubled, like he was
itching to get as far away as he could, as fast as he
could. From what had happened or from me, I
didn't know. I made no move to stop him. I figured
I would catch up to him soon enough. I was in no
hurry. I was tired and didn't want to face the trail
again so soon.

I made a place on the ground and slept in
between two Cherokee tribes, right next to the
spot where one of their men died. The wind was
cool and blew the day's heat from my skin, but it

couldn't blow the thoughts from my mind. I lay there for hours, thinking about Greer and her family. Thinking about Sunny. Thinking about Gentleman Jack and Charles Stirling and the path that lay ahead. I fell asleep thinking of ways to kill and reasons to do it.

CHAPTER TWENTY-SIX

I would have been fine going the rest of the way without Gentleman Jack. When I ran back into him a day later, I wasn't particularly thrilled. He seemed preoccupied, like he wanted to be alone with his thoughts, and that wasn't normal for Jack. We rode through the night again, and we stopped for sleep before sunrise. It became apparent that he'd suffered an injury. I knew Flora Pathkiller hadn't hit him with anything. Hadn't even got a shot off.

"What the hell happened to you?" I said.

He was unwrapping a bloody bandage and replacing it with cloth from his bedroll. It didn't look like a bullet wound. This looked like he had been run over by Alice or maybe a stagecoach.

"It happened a while back," Jack said. "Just flares up from time to time when I don't keep it clean."

I told him there would be a doctor at the Alameda Ranch. He should have it looked at.

"Ain't nothing but an animal doctor down there," he said. "I don't wanna get poked on by no animal doctor."

Seemed like foolishness to me.

"I would rather get fixed up by an animal doctor than die and end up buried on a sheep farm," I said. "But suit yourself."

We lay there for long enough without talking, We decided to take turns sleeping for the rest of the trip, so I took out *Middlemarch* and read. It was slow, but I didn't dislike it. It was nothing like anything I had ever known, and I counted that as a good thing. After reading several pages with no interruption, I assumed Jack was asleep.

"What do you think happens when a man dies?"

There wasn't a whole lot of dark left in the sky, and I didn't want the sun to come up on my answer. All the same, it wasn't a question easily tossed off.

"A man like Tahlequah Pathkiller?" I said.

I wondered if it was wearing on him, killing the man right in front of his squaw and child. In a way, it made him no different from Charles Stirling killing the lady and her son. Maybe Jack was trying to come to terms with that same thought.

"Any man," he said. "What do you think happens?"

I wasn't a religious man. I never had been. A lot of people were religious in San Antonio when I was there. People like Sister Mary Constance, who had been influential on me, but I had even seen through her rules and regulations.

"What were you doing before you were born?" I said.

I thought maybe he would get the point and not press the issue. He wouldn't let it go.

"I don't reckon I was doing anything," he said. "I wasn't anywhere."

I looked up into the brightness of the rising sun. The north star was right where it always was, even if I could no longer find it in the sky. Orion was, too. That was where I found my belief. I had faith in the sky. Faith in the stars. I liked the night better because you could see them, but I knew they were always there.

"That's right," I said. "And that's where I expect you'll be when you die."

That wasn't an easy answer to live with. It would be nice to think of Pathkiller chasing a buffalo through the happy hunting ground or whatever. It absolved you of a little guilt. Otherwise, you robbed him of everything.

He didn't say any more, and soon he fell into a fitful sleep. I sat and listened to him fight dream after dream, reading when it suited me and waiting until I could wake him and take a few hours' sleep myself.

I thought about shooting him in his sleep a time or two, or slitting his throat. I questioned my own resolve. I would have done it ten times over in my wilder days and never thought twice about it. I told myself somebody like Gentleman Jack deserved a greater death than that, but I wasn't even sure what I meant by that.

The following night, we went through the same motions, riding till dawn was an hour or so away and then finding suitable cover to sleep. This time, he had that light on the plains in his mind. Something I had almost forgotten about. I was settling down for sleep. It was Jack wanting to talk.

"You saw that light out there on the plain south of San Saba, didn't you, Wilkie John?"

Was he questioning what it meant or was he questioning his own sanity?

"I saw it, Jack."

I wanted to tell him to look at Orion next time he wanted to contemplate lights in the night. Those lights up there were pretty magic. Far as I knew, people overlooked them all the damn time. Off chasing lights in the city or lights in the desert, when we're surrounded by lights at all times, even in the day, when you can't see them. It's a fool's errand. Like the guy who chased after windmills.

"Every time I would get close, it would move on me," he said. "Like it was playing a game."

That was more a game I was willing to play.

"You ever think, maybe it could be some kind of connection with Phantom Bill?" I said.

The hair on my arm stood on end, just thinking about it.

"I thought Charles Stirling was Phantom Bill," Gentleman Jack said.

Gentleman Jack may have drifted off to sleep thinking Charles Stirling was Phantom Bill, because I didn't feel like explaining the difference, and soon he was snoring away. I didn't have it in me to read from my book so I lay there and went over the difference between the Pacific Railway killer and Phantom Bill in my own mind, just to make sure I still believed it.

I had never been convinced that Manley Pardon Clark was Phantom Bill, and I damn sure knew he hadn't killed Mrs. Foucault and her son. Even if he was the Phantom, there was no reason to move from looting Pacific Railway of bank money to killing women and children who put up no resistance. Charles Stirling had been going back and forth between the Alameda Ranch and New Orleans for a long time, and Mrs. Foucault had been doing the same thing. My theory was, Foucault finally caught wind of it and was bringing her back. Stirling didn't like it.

Then I had another idea. Lying there, looking up at the sky and listening to Jack's whistling nose, it occurred to me. What if Foucault was the person driving the train? No, not the literal train. What if he was the one behind the killing? He would have known better than anyone, which of the trains had Pinkerton detectives on them. He might have let that information out on purpose. He might have set Stirling up for it, or it might not have been Stirling at all. I lay for a good while thinking about that last possibility.

That night, I brought it up to Gentleman Jack.

"What if Charles Stirling didn't kill the lady and her boy?"

He stopped Alice dead in her tracks and turned around.

"That mean I can go back to Fort Worth?"

He knew I wasn't going to beg him to continue with me. Probably the only reason he did.

"I'm just saying. I thought of another possibility."

That made him laugh. Something he didn't do much of anymore.

"Possibilities are like womenfolk," he said.

I didn't want to ask, but I couldn't help myself.

"Always promising, never following through?" I said.

I wasn't particularly fond of my response. Greer had followed through. Maybe Sunny hadn't. But she hadn't really made any promises.

"No," Gentleman Jack said. "There's always another one."

I shot a big old rabbit sitting just off the trail earlier in the day, and so when we stopped, we cooked it for supper. It was the best meal I'd had since Fort Worth, and it came at a good time. We were getting close enough to Alameda to arrive early the next morning, and I was in some need of one more night with the star field.

"Talking about possibilities being like women," I said, "there does come a time you have to choose one and go with it, you know."

I wasn't interested in women at the moment. Finally, I really began piecing together the different possibilities concerning the day of the train robbery, and I was surprised which ones held up and which ones didn't. First in sequence, though, I fell asleep while I was on watch. It's not like me to do that, but the book was getting boring, and a thin layer of clouds kept all but the sturdiest of stars from getting through to my position. I fell into a dream, and it felt so real to me, I didn't think it was a dream at all. In the dream, I was accusing Gentleman Jack of something bad. It seemed like murder, but I know what it was. I was accusing him of sleeping with Sunny when he knew she was my special girl. In the dream, I placed my gun at his chest and told him to prove he had a heart beating inside of it.

"Prove you have one, and I won't shoot you," I said.

He moaned and complained about how was he supposed to prove something like that, and I said that was his problem and not mine. He said he loved his mama, and I said everybody loved their mama, even the devil himself. I finally told him, "I hope you don't have one, because if you don't, these bullets might pass right through you and leave only holes for the wind to whistle through." I shot him three times. The crack of the third shot woke me from my sleep.

"Jack, you hear that?"

I wasn't sure if he was awake, but I didn't know how anyone could've slept through it.

"Rifle shot," he said.

There was no opportunity to hide ourselves. Any move we made might have been overheard by whoever was out there. The horses snorted and kicked around, meanwhile I grabbed the Colt and held my breath.

"An Indian," Jack said.

I wasn't sure how he knew that, but I didn't

argue. Probably Flora Pathkiller, I thought, circling back around to make us pay for Jack's misdeed. If so, I hoped she remembered I wasn't the guilty party. We waited and waited, but we never heard anything else. I finally told him it was his turn to sit and watch while I slept.

"How do you know it was an Indian?" I said.

He answered more loudly than I felt necessary.

"Hell, I could hear him singing two miles back, Wilkie John," he said. "He was riding straight for that camp we saw yesterday. If he'd come up the trail, he would've ridden right into us."

A white man or even a Mexican would have taken the trail. Only an Indian would have ignored it.

"Oh, and you've been sleeping for a while now," he said.

As a Texas Ranger, I'm sworn to help conduct criminal investigations and apprehend criminals. Because I take those duties halfway serious, I'm always working through those different possibilities. When I'm not actively working through them, they're still there in the back of my mind. And every so often, one will come up for air. When they do, it can be a wondrous thing, like the whale surfacing in front of Captain Ahab.

"Jack," I said.

It was habit. Once again, something big came to me, and I wanted to share. Wanted to show off. This time, it wasn't all I wanted.

"What, Wilkie John?"

I didn't say a damn thing, just lay there like a

rock. Pretty soon, he huffed and rolled over on his side. I watched his back heave with his breathing until it slowed down and turned into a snore, his body never relaxing its tension, like part of him was still listening for that Indian to start singing again. I lay there doing pretty much the same thing and worked on plans for his demise.

CHAPTER TWENTY-SEVEN

I'm seldom wrong about Gentleman Jack Delaney. When I think bad of him, he never lets me down, and I make it a habit not to think good of him. When I started putting things together that night before we reached the Alameda Ranch, I knew I was on the right track, just as well as I knew we were on the path that led to Charles Stirling's place. And the fact that the ranch had once belonged to none other than Gentleman Jack himself just made my realization that much fuller and more appropriate.

If the Indian hadn't passed our encampment in the night, I'm not sure when I would have come to the conclusion that I came to that early morning, but, once again, I knew it was true because when I looked at Gentleman Jack, I saw the very worst in my own self staring back at me. Jack had broken camp and gone out ahead, not to get away from anything but to chase her down and keep her from getting away. I wanted to turn back and go looking for Flora Miller Pathkiller and her Minnie

Pathkiller, to see if maybe they were okay. But I knew they weren't. I was willing to bet the wound in Jack's side had been her. She was the kind to go down fighting. I was pretty sure of it.

Working backward from what I knew to what I didn't know to what I knew again, which was a system I had learned years before from a soldier in San Antonio, trails and paths had finally begun to connect up in my mind. Tahlequah and Flora had been following me. That was the part I knew. I heard that much straight from their own mouths. And I knew it was me they were following, because Flora had mentioned that she knew it was me because she knew I would be traveling with the big guy in the Lincoln hat. In other words, she wasn't really looking for both of us. And she wanted to take me to somebody who wanted to talk to me.

Now, people want to talk to Texas Rangers all the damn time. Usually they have some particular wrong they want you to right, but sometimes they just want to shake your hand, or they want you to shake their son's hand, so they can say they shook the hand of a Texas Ranger. It's not my favorite part of the job, but I understand it, and I've come to enjoy it more, especially when Jack is around. But I think this person had something important to tell me, and I started wondering if it had to do with the man who had crawled into Wheeler, Texas, the previous year with the envelope with my father's name on it. That had happened just months before Gentleman Jack came on the scene with his plan to swing me at the end of a rope. If Jack had known that much, it just might have given him reason to shoot Tahlequah Pathkiller the way I was pretty sure he had. Jack didn't care for Indians, but he didn't make it a habit of shooting them dead, either.

"That Indian that come through here," I said. "I wonder if he might have been looking for somebody."

Jack was shaving himself with a straight razor and, always to my amusement, trying to catch his reflection in a piece of silver he carried in his pocket. I was letting my beard grow, although it didn't seem to know it, only taking a wispy form right around my chin.

"Could be," he said. "He seemed to be headed in the direction of that camp."

He pointed to the northwest with his razor.

"Yeah," I said. "I just hope nothing happened to Flora Pathkiller. We should have escorted her to Stephenville."

I watched his face, which stretched out and winced, but only because the razor was pulling across it.

"She's practically one of them now," he said. "I wouldn't spend much worry on her. She'll have herself another chief in no time."

I pictured the razor pushing into his flesh and slicing across his jawline, down into the neck. If I had thought there was a chance I could wrestle it from him, I might have done so. But I had let too many opportunities pass by, waiting for that big moment.

"You killed her, didn't you, Jack?"

I knew he did. I wanted him to know I knew. It didn't matter if he admitted it or not. I also knew that it would give me an upper hand in the next day or two, as we approached Charles Stirling and, later, Manley Clark in the southern desert.

Jack raised up like a rabbit that just heard the bark of a coyote.

"No, son, I did not kill her," he said, "and I am damn sick of the accusations. Either we're a team, and we're going down to get this train killer, or we're not, and I'm moving on by myself. But if I move on by myself, you will not be following me, and you will not be following Flora Miller Killer or whatever her name is."

It was a voice I had seemingly raised up from the dead. He paced as he said it, just as he had on the gallows in Fort Worth. All he was lacking was the crowd and a rope.

"Keep your guns holstered, Jack," I said. "I was just yakking. Way I figure it, you kill her and that baby, I should have never even known. Except that Indian passed through and got me thinking. You take me off down in the desert hunting for Manley Clark, you probably try to kill me, too. Tell 'em Manley did it. Tell 'em Phantom Bill did it."

I laughed like it was all a joke, but I knew it was no joke. So did Jack. I had just laid every card out on the table. My hand was itching for the Colt. Jack knew that, too.

I don't know what Jack was thinking, but he must have felt a little like a trapped coyote, because he said nothing. But it was like everything in our history had been simmering away and then finally came to a boil right out there on the path to the Alameda Ranch. All plans for the future were put on hold. He went for his rifle. He reached for it with his left hand, which isn't even his shooting hand. Maybe he was going to shoot me and maybe it was just reflexive. Defensive. Maybe he was just looking for something to hold on to. I shot at his hand and missed high, just a warning. He could have pulled back. He should have. That first shot gave him time to grab the stock and swing around for a shot. I caught him in the side of the head with either the second or the third shot. I know, because I shot that damned hat off his head. I saw his head snap back and to the right, and it sounded like it popped open when he hit the ground.

"I wasn't going to shoot," he said.

You want to know how it felt to finally shoot that son of a gun? It felt terrible and it felt great. The terrible part of it kept me from celebrating and shooting him again, and the great part kept me from feeling sorry for him.

"And I'm here to say you didn't," I said.

I was standing over him, and I have to say, he was looking a little peaked. Blood loss will do that. I started to tell him I had enough shells left to finish the job. But I wanted the buzzards to do that. And I wanted him to still be alive when they smelled blood and came pecking around. So I left him holding the side of his head to keep his brains from spilling out. I don't know if he knew how much was seeping out between his fingers. He didn't seem to know a whole lot at that point. He watched me saddle up Little Cuss, but he said no more. It was like he was having to concentrate to make sense of normal things like a horse and a tree and me riding away and leaving him there to die. I headed out, feeling a hunger in my stomach that I didn't want to quench. I would ride on and use it to propel me into Alameda and Mr. Stirling. Nothing goes to plan.

CHAPTER TWENTY-EIGHT

When I saw the Alameda Ranch come into view, I was riding on Bird and feeling like me and Little Cuss were both on our last legs. Little Cuss was acting jumpy, and I wasn't sure what was causing it, but I kept telling him the smith at the ranch would fix him back up again in no time. Me, I wasn't so sure about. I felt like Gentleman Jack had put me in a bad place, left me with no good options. I hadn't wanted what happened to happen when and where it did. It threw me off.

I was still unsure how I wanted to approach Charles Stirling. I was sure the sooner, the better. The longer I had to be nice, the more awkward it would be. I decided I had to approach him, not as Wilkie John Liquorish who chatted with him about all manner of things on the previous visit, but as a Texas Ranger, doing his job. I could act disappointed in him, but I couldn't look weak or unsure of myself. And I would shoot to kill if I had to.

I circled around the Alameda property so as to

come at it from the entrance. I decided it made no
sense to sneak up on him. I would ride in like I had
both other times, as if nothing was different.

"Oh yes," I would say. "There is a little matter
that we need to clear up."

Hopefully, he would be alone and we could
handle things between the two of us, get things
under control before they had time to spiral away
from me. I would take him to Llano, where I would
turn him over to Rangers there. They would trans-
port him to Austin, where he would stand trial for
the murder of Mrs. Foucault and the Foucault son.
It wouldn't be pretty.

All of these things seemed well thought out and
logical. That's what worried me. I knew things
wouldn't all go to plan. I tried to look for other
plans, contingencies. The first one came up before
I got within eyesight of the front gate. It presented
itself in the shape of Charles Stirling, sitting on his
big black stallion at the front gate with three horse-
less wagons backing him up. I stopped in my
tracks, got off Bird, and loaded my rifle and went
through plans in my mind. I didn't want to have to
shoot Stirling. It seemed like a bad thing coming
so soon after shooting Jack. I considered camping
out south of the ranch and approaching the next
morning. I considered every option I could think
of, up to and briefly including shooting him from
a distance, leaving him to rot like I had left Gentleman Jack. I worried my standards weren't up to
Ranger standards. I decided to bite the bullet and
move on in. Just as I did, the first few shots rang

out, and, all of a sudden, it seemed like the whole mountain came alive with gunfire. I ducked down between Little Cuss and Bird.

First thought was, Charles Stirling had spotted me and was shooting at me. Didn't take long to dissuade me of that notion, for no gun ever fired could unload so many bullets in such a space of time. And a few of them were coming from the direction of the ranch, but, as became apparent, many more were coming from directly behind me. I was caught in a cross fire, and, far as I could tell, neither side knew I was there.

I thought I had stumbled into the final battle between the sheep ranchers and the cattle barons, so I was astounded when, not too much later, I began to hear the war whoops and cries of the Tonkawa Indians up above me in the hills. That was bad news, because the Tonkawa were fierce fighters, and they certainly didn't mind breaking a few rules while they were at it.

I could spot three different places where the gunfire and noise were coming from, but I couldn't see enough to get anything but a blind shot off. Of course, doing that would let them know my location, if they didn't already know it. I placed no trust in any God that would look down on all of this mess and not send a mighty storm to blow the totality of it away, but I nonetheless decided to keep my powder dry.

I could see Charles Stirling occasionally moving from one wagon to another, and I could see him reach into one, now and again. It appeared that he had stored up a stack of rifles there. This had been a planned attack. He was defending Alameda. I was in a quandary. I had grown up hearing of the brave exploits of Congressman David Crockett and Lieutenant Colonel William Travis. How they defended the Alamo Mission against the forces of General Santa Anna, even knowing they were greatly outnumbered and sure to be overpowered. Now I had to decide whether to try to work my way to Stirling and help him defend the ranch, only to turn around and arrest him on murder charges, or let things go the way they would. I didn't like staying where I was. It would only be a matter of time before one of the Indians either spotted me or walked right up on me. It would be assumed I was with Alameda, and I would be done a lot worse than Gentleman Jack was done. I decided to make the first move.

There was one group of Indians closest to my position, and I was most worried about them. They would see any move I made into the opening, and it was a good quarter mile to the front gate of the ranch. My best chance of getting to Stirling would be to make my way back east, try to cross the fence line somewhere, and make my way into position from the back. That would not only make it much harder for the Tonkawa to pick me off, it would hopefully keep Stirling from getting jumpy and shooting me before I got to him.

Making that move had its risks. The obvious one was being discovered as I moved east below. The other one was time. It would take the better part of the afternoon to get all the way around. I began to look at a compromise. If I could make my way around to the east side of the hill, there didn't seem to be anybody in place up there. They had left that position completely open, and I could see why. Nobody would be coming in from that direction unless the New Orleans Greys decided to reband and join the fray. Either that or Phantom Bill.

If I could make it to that position, I could come in toward the front gate, signal my arrival in time for Stirling to make way for me. In an ironic sense, he would let the Trojan horse into the ranch. If he let me in, that is. If he started shooting, I would be easy pickings. A little lost lamb surrounded by wolves.

Getting down the side of the hill proved to be more time-consuming than I had thought. Undergrowth was hard to cut through and threatened to swallow us up a few times, and Bird was timid about walking where she couldn't see her feet on the ground. I had to move a couple of fallen trees as well. It was easier than going up to get around them, and going down meant leaving yourself wide open for a bullet. We did finally make it to a place where we could get at least halfway to the gate before being seen by the Indians. They were still firing away at intervals, during which I could assume only that they were reloading. The gunfire was no longer directly overhead, though, so Little Cuss and Bird were happier. That made me happier.

I made double sure my rifle was loaded and that the Colt was, too. I thought about riding Bird.

Mules are faster than people think they are, and they're jumpy as hell. I thought maybe I'd be harder to hit on her, but I ultimately went with Little Cuss. He was faster than the wind, and he loved to cut loose.

I studied the pattern of the shootings as we moved, so, by the time we were in position, I had a pretty good idea of what they were doing. The gunshots were coming from two main areas, and they were either running people back and forth between the two spots or refreshing troops to wear Stirling down. If they were wearing him down, they were wearing him down for something, and I guessed it might be coming at, or sometime after, nightfall. I didn't have a lot of time. I waited until the next round of fire closest to us settled down and made my move. I told Bird to try and keep up, and we were off and running.

Charles Stirling saw us coming pretty quick. He was watching for somebody to try to sneak in from the side. He had his gun up and was waiting for me to get closer to take a shot. Thankfully, he recognized me before he did.

"I noticed it was Little Cuss before I saw that it was you," he said. "You're damn lucky the McSwains didn't get ya."

Considering the circumstances, I thought it better to wait before trying to put the man under arrest. I surely wasn't ready to ride him out of there.

"That ain't the McSwains," I said. "You got a fair amount of Tonkawas out there in the hills. They're bunkered down in two places."

He pointed out exactly where they were.

"They've hired a bunch of them, but it's the McSwains," he said. "The bunch straight up the hill there is Robert and whoever he's banded together. The other bunch to the west is just holding the valley down where we can't get out. I figure they've got some people coming around that side, probably after dark. At that point, I'm not sure what I can do."

He had it figured pretty good.

"How many people you got protecting the ranch?" I said.

My thoughts were, at nightfall, we drop back to the ranch and protect from there. It gave up ground, but it gave us a lot better protection. The three wagons wouldn't stand a minute once the Tonkawas came through the gate.

"The ranch is emptied out," he said. "Everybody gone except the sheep. All the herders, all the workers, the cooks, everything. We knew they were coming. I have my spies, some maybe right up there among them."

If he hadn't been such a bad guy, there was a lot to like about Stirling.

"So why are you still here?" I said.

A few rounds went off in the hills, and I could hear them kick up dirt and grass in the field not too far beyond our cover. He never answered me, but continued as if I had never asked anything.

"I figure when they come around the side, they're gonna leave that east valley wide open for at least a short spell," Stirling said, pointing in the direction I'd come in from. "When they do, I'm gonna let 'em have it."

He laughed loud enough it seemed the McSwains or the Tonkawas, or whoever they were, could have heard it. If they did, they must have thought he was either fearless or completely crazy.

"What you got in mind?" I said.

"I'm letting them have the place. I'm letting all the sheep out and making a beeline for the desert."

I thought he was completely crazy.

"That's a hell of a lot of sheep," I said.

"Fifty thousand," he said. "That ought to slow them down a little bit."

I couldn't see him walking away from the biggest sheep ranch in Texas like he was walking away from a bad meal. Something wasn't adding up. I knew things it could be. I wondered if it was time to step forward and really ruin the evening for him.

"Why would you want to step away from the ranch like that?" I said.

A single rifle shot cracked from the hills, and he rolled his eyes in response.

"If they attack the ranch, that requires a legal response," I said. "I am here in my job as a Texas Ranger. I can tell you right now, I will bring anyone to justice who does anything to your property."

I was getting farther off track, but it seemed like a promising way back to where I needed to go, if I could manage to guide it.

"Don't you think for a minute I'm walking away for good," he said, "but there comes a time to get out while the getting is good, as I've heard said around here. I don't mind dying on my own property, but not at the hands of a bunch of cattle barons who've just decided they don't want my kind around anymore."

As I listened to Charles Stirling talk, I was watching a haze fall over the land behind us, and, as the sun hit the tops of the trees, it would soon be getting hazier. We both smelled smoke at about the same time, but I think I understood first what it was we were smelling. Stirling was correct in thinking the group to the west would circle around to the back of the ranch. That they had done. What I first thought to be a glint of light from the sun turned out to be something much more ominous.

"Mr. Stirling, I do believe they've set one of the ranch houses on fire."

There was a real sense of panic and, for me, it wasn't so much that the houses might be going up in flames. The fact of the matter also meant we had people targeting us from two sides, and those damn wagons weren't going to hold from both sides, even if we jumped into them and stayed down.

"I'd say we have four, maybe five minutes to open the gates and let the sheep out," he said.

He was already in motion, his rifle up to his shoulder and ready to provide cover. He was pointing at the main gates, which I already knew from the previous visits. I had never seen fifty thousand sheep all in one place. On the previous visit, it had been explained to me that they were grazed in an elaborately arranged order, in twelve different groups and in twelve locations. I doubt they had even seen one another all together at one time, either. They must have sensed the specialness of the situation, and, with the smoke beginning to waft its way back to them, they were getting louder and more restless as we made our way to them.

I could see flames coming from at least two of the buildings on the west end of the ranch, and I knew the Tonkawa were using arrows to light them up. They would be coming in behind the arrows. Stirling was correct again. We had minutes.

"I think I have a way to get you out of here successfully," I said.

He didn't slow down. I wasn't sure if he was paying me any heed, and I couldn't blame him. We got to the first gate, and I quickly saw that it was the first of many, an elaborate, expansive system of gates that kept fifty thousand sheep all where they needed to be. Only they were keeping them where they didn't need to be.

"I have to go through and open up each gate, one after the other," he said.

I looked back at the hillside behind the ranch houses.

"You don't have time," I said.

He didn't argue.

"You've gotta help."

He pointed out how many gates there were, where they were located, where the locks were, and how to switch them open and push the gates.

"You do half, and I'll do half," he said. "And then what's your idea for getting us out?"

I had no time to worry or wonder.

"You're gonna be trampled to death by either sheep or Tonkawa if you hang around," I said. "Meet me back here, and I'll take you out safely."

There was a look on his face that reminded me of relief, but it wasn't your normal look of relief. I had seen it before, but it had been on the faces of men who were just about to die. Men who knew they'd run to the end of the trail and had nowhere else to turn.

"You came here to arrest me, didn't you?" he said.

He was a perceptive man. Perceptive almost to a fault.

"You need me to take you in, Charles," I said.

He looked at his ranch houses, smoking and starting to burn, and then looked at the hills.

"I've gotta take care of these sheep."

He went one way, and I went the other, releasing the locks on a dozen gates, flinging the doors wide open and waving my hat like I had once seen Jack Delaney wave his to scare away vultures. It seemed like hell had busted wide open that night, and I was prepared to ride the devil himself out of the flames, if I had to. Even so, I had a hard time thinking of Charles Stirling as a devil. I tried picturing him as the man with the funny voice who shot a small kid to death in his mother's arms and then shot the mother a few seconds later. I knew damn well he did it. People will do things you don't expect of them. Lots of times, they're grand, heroic things. But not always. People are puzzles. That's what makes solving crimes so hard. You have to solve people first.

When I got back to the central position, I didn't see Charles Stirling anywhere. I looked for him along the row of gates, but I knew I wouldn't find him there. The sheep were loose and running for safer pastures, and so was Charles. I would chase him down. Out of this hell and through a hundred more, if I had to. It was what I lived for, and, if necessary, it was what I would die for.

I wasn't going to die at the hands of a family of rich cattle barons and their hired hands, though. That was something I wasn't prepared to do. I would come back for them another day.

CHAPTER TWENTY-NINE

Moving into that desert was like spilling out of a frying pan straight into the grease fire. I followed Charles Stirling's trail west past Cookie's hideout and then north toward Fort Concho. It wasn't a move I was expecting, even if I knew he would do something to try to shake me off. I rode into Concho and, seeing no trace of Stirling, was happy to at least see my friend Lieutenant Swoop.

"You're about the last thing I expected to see round these parts, Liquorish."

I counted it a positive thing that he remembered my name. He didn't seem as thrilled to see me.

"I'm in pursuit of the man who killed the Foucaults," I said. "He came this way, probably a couple, three hours ago."

He didn't salute, but he snapped to attention in a damn hurry.

"The Foucaults?" he said.

We quickly gained a crowd. I pulled Little Cuss back. Something felt wrong. Maybe he sensed the same thing. Lieutenant Swoop brushed away the soldiers in his immediate vicinity. A couple of Pinkertons were harder to get rid of.

"I'm not at liberty to share with the general hoi polloi," I said.

I looked at the detectives and shrugged, like if it were up to me I might do it. It must have hurt their pride to be lumped into the multitudes like that. Which was the only reason I did it. Swoop told them to make themselves scarce, and they went at it, but not without some pouting and stomping around. When they moved away, they did so sideways, with one foot in my direction, like they were dancing away, and with eyes fixed on some invisible partner in between. I waited. When I was comfortable that only Swoop's ears could hear, I leaned forward.

"You seen Charles Stirling?"

I heard one of the Pinkertons half suppress a snicker.

"This all some kind of joke, I fail to see the humor, son," Swoop said.

I assured him I wasn't in any joking mood. I started telling him about the siege at the Alameda Ranch the previous night.

"I haven't slept since," I said.

He didn't want to hear it.

"We've heard all about it. We've got a battalion headed that way from San Antonio right now."

I wondered what good it would do. I had my doubts as to what they would find. Maybe a bunch of sheep. Maybe not even that.

"Did Charles Stirling tell you himself?" I said.

I could see Pinkertons from the corner of my eye. If their detective work was so subtle, I wondered how they had ever gotten such a stellar reputation. I glared at them until they saw I was onto them, and they danced away again.

"Stirling was here, headed to San Antonio," Swoop said. "He left orders to arrest you, if you showed up here."

I didn't see what power he had to do such a thing. He was a rich man, though, and that brought a power that couldn't be underestimated.

"On what charges?"

He had the look of a man who knew he was being fooled with but didn't know by whom.

"Murder of the wife and heir of John Daniel Foucault," he said.

I could see it was going to be another long day. I got down from Little Cuss and walked toward the detectives.

"Gentlemen, I have a question. Any of you know if a lieutenant in the U.S. Army has the authority to put a Texas Ranger under arrest?"

Swoop wasn't expecting that kind of talk from a kid like me, and he didn't much like it.

"I never said you were under arrest," he said.

I had made my point. He made his. I wasn't through, though.

"I would like to know what evidence you have. I would also like to know what my motive was."

Most of the Pinkertons were moving away from

the scene by that point. Only one, a young man about my own age, caught my eye.

"Mr. Stirling was here. He said he was going hunting."

Swoop, by this point, had walked up right behind me.

"Stirling was chasing the train robber," he said. "Are you aware there was another robbery on the train line, yesterday morning?"

I hadn't been aware, but it never hurts to look more informed than you are.

"Yeah, I know that much," I said. "What do you know?"

He looked to one of the detectives. I guess it was the lead detective, if detectives have such things. Who knows how the Pinkertons work?

"They're reporting five grand taken," the lead detective said. "In actuality, it was ten grand. No real description, no shots fired, no injuries."

"Stirling is friends with John Daniel Foucault," another detective said.

I guess they thought he was going after the money for his good friend. I didn't have the time or inclination to set them straight. Part of me wanted to find the train conductor from the latest holdup and ask if he had heard the man's voice. If he sounded funny in any way. I was pretty sure what the answer would be.

"This is Phantom Bill, Manley Clark that held up the train," I said. "This is positively not the same man that stopped the one east of San Saba and killed the lady."

The Pinkertons nodded in agreement. They had reached the same conclusion.

"Now, gentlemen, you do realize that you just let that killer leave Fort Concho," I said. "If you're gonna arrest me for something, go ahead and do it. If you're not, I aim to be in pursuit of that particular man."

"But that's Charles Stirling, Foucault's friend," that one detective said.

I just shook my head. I think Swoop did, too.

"I could jail you if I wanted," he said. "I got another man here. His story pretty much backs you up. Far as I can see, you're free to go."

That intrigued me. I wasn't in too big of a hurry to find out whose story had saved me from being arrested by a U.S. Army lieutenant.

"He's over at the med tent, getting patched up," one of the Pinkertons said.

I stomped across Concho to the hospital and took a gander inside. It looked like an old man, and I didn't recognize him until I heard his voice.

"Wilkie John Liquor."

I almost fell over.

"Jack," I said. "I thought you were dead."

The nurse came running and held his bandaged head steady. I wondered if she thought it might roll off.

"I guess it's a good damn thing you did think that," he said.

The nurse shushed him from saying anything else and told me she would have me kicked out of the camp if I interfered with her work. I told her she was the second person who had made such a boast since I had arrived, and I was beginning to take offense.

"What's the medical report on this gentleman?" I said.

She asked me if I knew him, and I said I did, like a brother. Cain and Abel. I might not believe in the Bible, but I've read it. In fact, that's pretty much the reason I don't believe. She took the point.

"He says he was cleaning his rifle and it went off," she said. "He's lost his left ear. No hearing in it at all. But he'll be fine. In fact, we're planning to release him in the morning."

I went about my business, but not before finding out a little bit more from Lieutenant Swoop. Swoop said Charles Stirling had come into camp to report his ranch being burned down by Robert McSwain and a ragtag army he had put together out of friends, family, and a band of Tonkawa Indians.

"They don't like where he's grazing his sheep, but he says he has just as much right to that land as they do," Swoop said. "They put up fence posts, Stirling cuts 'em down. That's what's causing the trouble. He says the fences don't belong there, and, by the law, he's right."

Everyone knew that was what caused the trouble. Fences. What they needed was someone with an idea of how to end it. I wasn't that someone.

"So which direction was he going?" I asked.

I wanted to get as far as I could, whatever the direction, after sunset. Me and Little Cuss and Bird

would travel through most of the night. We might
catch Stirling that first night. I didn't see him as
someone who could outrun me. If he couldn't
outrun me, he would have to outfox me. I didn't see
that happening, either.

"We have information that Manley Pardon Clark
is hiding in the hills southwest of here. It's brutal
out there. Hotter than the devil's crotch," Swoop
said. "Nobody can last out there unless, say, they
got a camp or something. I'm willing to bet if Stirling tracks Clark's Phantom ass down, he's gonna
track down more money than God and his angels
got time to count."

Just what Stirling needed. Then again, if he had
plans to head on toward Mexico, it really might be.
I knew the hills Swoop was talking about. I'd never
been into them before. You only went that way when
you were going to Mexico. Chihuahua. When you
were running from something.

"And that's the place Stirling said he was
headed?" I said.

Two or three of the detectives looked at me like
I was crazy.

"No way Charles Stirling is Phantom Bill," they
said, pretty much in lockstep.

I wasn't implying any such thing. I just had my
doubts why he was headed in that direction. I
made arrangements for Bird to stay at Fort
Concho for a few days, while me and Little Cuss
went hunting for phantoms. Not as quickly as I
wanted, but soon enough, we were back on our
way, and in a slightly different direction than I
had planned, going straight south until we hit the

railroad tracks and then making a westward turn
right into the sun.

Stirling was making no effort to cover his tracks.
He was taking what I had always heard called the
Spanish Trail. The only trouble came when the
desert would take the trail over and it would get
lost in the big picture. Sometimes I would lose
track and almost give up, only to pick him up
somewhere farther along. Then we got into the
rocks. That was where it finally broke down completely. Distance is deceptive out there. There's
little to judge by. A rock formation in the distance
looks like a signpost, but it might be twenty miles
ahead instead of five. You never knew until you got
there. You could lose yourself pretty easy. A great
place to hide out in.

I spotted Charles on his black stallion on the
morning of the second day in the desert. I already
knew I was in trouble. The sun had already taken a
lot out of me, and I didn't have enough water. I
considered turning back for reinforcements, but
I knew I would lose him. I decided to continue on,
deal with him, and then return to Concho. Again,
I miscalculated distances, the heat, the effect on
Little Cuss.

If Stirling hadn't encountered the same problems, I wouldn't have caught him. As it was, I didn't
do so until after sunset that second day. I was in no
shape to take a prisoner. He was in worse shape
than me. He was on all fours, vomiting up the
supper I had watched him heat up and then eat a

few bites of. He never saw me approach, never knew I was there until I spoke.

"Where in the world are you going, Charles?"

He turned to look at me and fell onto his side, rolling in the sick. A majestic-looking man when he rode the fence line of the Alameda, he was a pale ghost of himself under the white-hot West Texas sun.

"What are you doing out here, Wilkie John?"

He seemed confused. As if maybe I had just been out there beating my clothes against rocks and happened to see him crawl by.

"I'm here to take you in, Charles," I said.

He didn't seem to grasp my meaning.

"I'll be just fine," he said. "I just need some rest. I'll be back on my feet by sunup."

I had the Colt in hand, loaded and ready. I had no desire to use it, but I thought it might be useful if he saw it. It seemed to do the trick.

"You mean to shoot me with that?" he said.

I shook my head *no.*

"I don't mean to do any such thing," I said, "unless you mean to make me."

He tried to move himself into a sitting position. The effort it took let me know there would be no fight coming from him. Whatever fight he had still in him was all inside his head.

"I come from the Highlands of Scotland, you know," he said. "I have no intention of dying in a godforsaken place like this."

I didn't know if that was his way of saying there would be no fight or if he was saying there would be. You couldn't be sure with him. I wasn't taking a chance.

"It's no place for a man to die," I said.

If he had a pistol on him, I couldn't see it. He had a rifle with a shortened barrel lying next to him. I would have had to pick it up and put it in his hands for him. I didn't make any offer to.

"I have a few questions I need to ask you, Charles, and I need to hear an honest answer from you. I'm not gonna ask if you killed Mrs. Foucault or that little boy. We both know you did it. I need you to own up to it, if it's the last thing you do. You don't want to shut your eyes on this world with that weight on you. What I want to know is why the hell you had to shoot the boy."

He licked at his lips and pulled them apart, trying to get something to come out. I was afraid he was going to vomit up again.

"That little boy was the heir to the Pacific fortune," he said.

It wasn't what I wanted to hear. I wanted to hear something every Tom, Dick, and Harry didn't already know.

"No reason to kill him," I said.

Stirling fell back into the rocks and grunted as the wind pushed out of him. If he'd had any water inside him, he might have shed one tear there. As it was, he was as dry as the land around him.

"Was that your boy?" I said.

The sound that came out of him was somewhere between a cry and a bellow. It came abruptly and with a force that surprised me. I pulled the Colt up and pointed it right at his head. He looked up at me, and a stillness came over him. At least, I thought it did. Maybe the stillness came over me. Or maybe it was over everything out there. All I know is, in that small stillness, all I could see was Gentleman Jack Delaney sitting in the dirt with that hat blowing off his head. I couldn't shoot the man.

"Get up."

He scurried around and tried to collect himself, whimpering as if getting his fat, rich backside off the earth was going to take the last bit of life he had in him. He said nothing, and, soon enough, he was on his feet, even if he was a little wobbly.

"Just go on and get it over with," he said.

That's exactly what I intended on.

"Empty your pockets, Mr. Stirling," I said.

The look on his face amused me. He wasn't sure whether I was going to kill him or just take his gold pocket watch. He handed it to me, along with a few worthless trinkets. Matches. Mexican coins.

"It's been in my family for a long time," he said. "Take everything I've got, and I'll never tell a soul. Just let me keep the watch."

I brought the butt end of the Colt down on the watch's glass, shattering it against my palm and sending the hour hand flying. The seconds kept ticking.

"Empty your back pockets," I said.

He pulled that blue cloth out like it was nothing, and, in a way, it meant no more than that box of matches. Unless a match in that box had been used to burn down the house where his mistress lived. The mistress that was leaving him to go back across country to her husband.

I almost killed him. I decided to save the bullet.

"Take off running, sir," I said.

He glanced around and looked back at me. He reminded me of a dog when you tell them to go fetch a stick or something. There was something comical in it.

"Run?" he said. "Which way?"

You could look in any direction, and it all looked the same. Except for the one I was in.

"Take your pick," I said. "Come at me or run away. Don't make me no difference."

He stood there for a good minute, seemed like. I finally pointed each of the ways out to him with the barrel of my Colt. He turned tail and took off in the opposite direction, then turned south. I don't know that you could call it running, but he was kicking up a lot of dust.

I'm not sure what would make a man kill his own flesh and blood to keep that flesh and blood from attaining something that was denied him. You can call it greed or selfishness, and I'm sure both of those things are part of it. It must be some-thing bigger than that, too. Something that's probably hard to live with. Charles Stirling was trying to get away to a place where he could live with himself, but I think he had gone just about far enough to see that it would remain out of his grasp. Maybe he was even beginning to understand that grasping for it was wrong.

I don't know if he was a good man who went

wrong. Maybe so. Maybe Robert McSwain even had
a role to play in that. Or maybe he was a bad man
who did a few good things, just on accident. Surely
even the devil himself told a few good jokes, made
a few people laugh, if even for a short spell. All I
know is he didn't run because he was a bad man,
and he didn't run because he had done horrible
things. He ran because I had a gun pointed at his
head, and he believed I might shoot it. That's all
that mattered. Maybe that makes me a bad man,
but I didn't feel one iota of bad about it. And it
wasn't the badge on my coat that made me feel
that way.

I don't believe in heaven and its pearly gates,
but I understand why some people need to. And I
admit, if there was such a place, I hope, when
Charles Stirling finally ran up to it, there was a
little boy sitting at the gate who decided whether
he got in or not. I don't care if he was sitting with
his mama or not. And I don't care if he let the son
of a bitch in or not, either. Because if Charles Stirling had to go through that process to make it in,
believe me, it was hell either way.

CHAPTER THIRTY

So this is where the story finally catches back up to me in that godless desert, almost dying of too much light and not enough shade. Too much rock and not enough river. I was actually on my way out of the damn desert when I decided to follow a line of hills farther south. My thinking was, there was probably at least a creek or something somewhere down that way. It might even be where Phantom Bill was hanging out. I was right about one of them, wrong about the other. The night came soon enough, and I stopped before I got to the hills, knowing there were wolves and coyotes up in them. Even I could manage to avoid trouble every once in a while. I fell asleep with their distant howls mild assurance that danger wasn't near.

The next morning, I went on my way, a little revived but still feeling sluggish. I knew I needed water, but I hadn't seen any behind me, so I decided to keep going forward. That was the morning Little Cuss stepped on a rattler and went down hard. Knocked the breath out of both of us. I told him I was going for help, but I didn't think I would find it for either of us at that point. I think Little Cuss knew it.

I stumbled up on Manley Pardon Clark's horse within a shout of Little Cuss. He was in worse shape than either of us, all white bones and red meat. I was happy to see him, mostly because it explained the turkey vultures flying overhead. Maybe they had seen me and Little Cuss and were waiting around for dessert, but we weren't the main course that day. I was flapping my arms, trying to shoo them away, or to at least let them know I was still alive. Mostly I was looking for money. I was looking for money like it was water.

I knew it was Clark's horse because there were two U.S. Mail bags wrapped around the bones. They were as empty as the horse was. I continued on, trying to figure out which way a man might go from there, if his horse went down. At that point, me and the Phantom had become one and the same.

When Gentleman Jack appeared, I thought maybe I really was dead.

"What are you doing down there? Wake up, you fool."

I was deteriorating fast.

"I can't see a damn thing, Jack."

I remember being both surprised Jack and Alice had caught me so quickly and relieved. If he hadn't come along when he did, I would have been a matching set with Manley Pardon Clark.

"You sure it's him, Wilkie John?" Gentleman Jack said.

By that time, he had given me a long draw on his canteen, and my eyesight was beginning to filter back. We were sitting on the ground next to Little Cuss, and he was showing me right where the rattler had sunk his teeth into the horse's leg. It was all swole up, and Cuss didn't have any interest in putting weight on it.

"Y'all are two of a pair," Jack said.

I think Little Cuss might have resented it.

"What are you doing out here?" I said.

He didn't have a ready answer, which made me know he wasn't sure what he was doing, either. We were both chasing Phantom Bill, and we had caught him, but we'd caught him too late. If we'd been a little earlier, we might have even saved him.

We were sitting in the shade of hell's furnace, trying to get enough wind back in us to make the trip back to civilization, and I was far from assuming anything. I could close my eyes and will myself back to some better place. It was a momentary escape to Sunny's side or Greer's side, but it sure made it hard to open my eyes again, and, each time, I was revisited with a white blindness that only grudgingly let in a little light at a time. I got worried I was watching my life flash before my eyes. I had heard tell that people did that when they were dying. I resolved not to close my eyes again. If I died, I would die on my feet.

"I'm going," I said.

Maybe Gentleman Jack was fighting a similar

ghost, because he didn't answer me. Didn't ask where or how or anything. Didn't get up and follow, either. I walked back to the bones lying facedown in the sand and grabbed at the bags. They were empty. I knew that. Tossing them aside, I got down on my hands and knees and began digging. Not deep, just enough to know if there might be something hidden by the layer of sand that blew to and fro like waves on the surface of the ocean. I wasn't even looking for money. I was looking for personal effects, clothes, a hat, anything that might tell me something more about the man who lay there and wouldn't say anything.

Jack slept and I dug. By mapping out lines between points on the ground, rocks, or cactuses, and by shoveling dirt always to the left, I could keep track of where I had been, what I had done. I found more bones. The bones of a deer of some kind. The shell of an armadillo. When I found leather, I knew I was onto something, and I changed my direction accordingly. There, torn in a dozen directions, I found the remains of the dead man's clothes. I knew right away what had been eating at me. I took the skull from the body lying there in the dirt and wrapped it up in part of the cloth, keeping it separate from the rest. Running back to Jack with more energy than I would have suspected, I shouted into his good ear until he slowly woke up.

"Jack, those bones out there with the railway bag are not Manley Pardon Clark."

When he finally came to, he bolted up like a preacher on Sunday morning.

"They're Tom Pascal's boy," he said.

Indeed they were. I showed him the proof, an almost fully intact overcoat with a torn inseam, an interior pocket pulled away from the coat.

"Reach inside," I said.

I pushed the coat into his face. Jack pulled at a corner of the torn material and felt something inside. He pulled it out just as I had done a few minutes earlier.

"Part of a bank bag," he said.

It was hard to mistake it for anything else.

"Anything in it?" he said.

He was pulling at it, but there was nothing there to spill forth.

"It's empty," I said, "but Tom told me his son had a bank bag like it in his coat pocket when they met in Austin."

Jack looked at me like I was pulling too hard and the fabric was going to fray into thin air.

"I know, Jack, but what are the chances Manley Pardon Clark would also carry a bank bag in the pocket of his coat?"

"There is a chance," he said.

"Do you?" I said.

"Carry a bank bag? No."

Normal people don't do that. Point made, we were soon warming up coffee over a small, unenthused fire and trying to follow through on what it might mean if the bones in the desert did belong to William Pascal. Did it mean Tom Pascal had been right? That Manley Clark really was somewhere in Mexico drinking tequila and singing Spanish love songs?

"There was no money around the body," Gentleman Jack said.

I had dug up enough dirt to feel pretty confident of that.

"There was no body around the body, either," I said.

We talked our way through several different possibilities. Could Charles Stirling have been the Phantom all along? Neither of us bought that one. We did get sidetracked on the possibility that John Daniel Foucault had purposefully set the whole thing up. Gentleman Jack made the point that, if he'd wanted his wife dead for, say, sleeping around with someone like Charles Stirling, he might have planted that seed and watched it grow. I had to admit, there was something there. Did Foucault even suspect that the boy might not be his?

What we did know was Charles Stirling was somewhere out in the desert, possibly without his horse, and probably without a clue how to get to civilization in Mexico or Texas. We decided maybe we should go looking for him at sunup. Whether to rescue him or finish him off was yet to be determined.

Gentleman Jack got a little weepy that night, and went into a rather long winding soliloquy concerning the fact that he had almost killed me the past summer and I had come close to returning the favor this go-around. It not only made us squash, as he put it, it made us some kind of brothers. He tried to explain it like the Indians became blood brothers sometimes after battles. I had a hard time understanding him because we were both getting tired, and he was slurring his words more than he'd ever done while drinking whiskey at the Black Elephant. The Indian talk did get me to thinking about Flora Miller Pathkiller. I asked him about it point-blank. Seemed like the timing was good.

"Did you kill Flora Pathkiller after she left our camp?" I said.

I had been so convinced of it, but now it seemed silly and amateurish. I was trying to solve the murder of one woman and her son, and now I was accusing Jack of murdering a completely different woman and her child.

"What reason would I have to kill Flora Path-killer?" he asked.

My reasoning seemed convoluted. But life was often pretty convoluted. I figured it was as good of a time as any to give it a stab.

"You shot Tahlequah," I said.

In my mind, we were suddenly back in Fort Worth, and I was pacing back and forth across the front of the gallows, except this time, there was no rope. There was only me and my trusty Colt. I had shot his ear off, and I was aiming for the matching one if he didn't answer the question right.

"He made a move toward me," Jack said.

I didn't shoot him yet, but I could have. If I had, he wouldn't have heard the rest of the question.

"Tahlequah Pathkiller had come to take me to someone," I said. "Someone who had something very important to tell me. Here's what I think. I think you knew exactly what he was doing, and you aimed to stop it. In fact, I think you set him up, either with or without Flora's help. I think you either killed her or—maybe you didn't—maybe you just scared her real good. Maybe you threatened the life of that little papoose. Is that about the size of it?"

Gentleman Jack reached up, and I almost squeezed the trigger, but I didn't, because it wasn't his shooting hand. He went to pull his hat from his head, and, as he did, he brushed clumsily against the bandages. I could see blood pouring from what had been his left ear. He seemed totally oblivious to it. The hat fell into the dirt behind me.

"I can't understand a damn word you're saying."

I couldn't tell if he was joking or not, but he seemed to go deaf to the world around him right then and there. No matter what I said or did or threatened to do, he sat there cross-legged like an Indian and looked at me like an illiterate man might look at a book.

That's pretty much the way he looked at everything from that moment on. The following day, the side of his head was so swollen up, his hat must have been half a dozen sizes too small. I wrapped him up and tied him onto the back of Alice, and we made a long slow journey out of the desert, traveling mostly at night and resting in the heat of the day. Little Cuss would favor his right leg, and when he'd had enough, he would stop. I walked almost all of the time, so as to keep weight off him. A couple of times, I rode Alice, sitting in front of Jack and counting his heartbeats against my back. At night, I would talk. I would include Alice and Little Cuss in the conversation. Try to make Jack feel left out, get him to say something. I even tried reading *Middlemarch* to him.

"Our deeds still travel with us from afar, And what we have been makes us what we are" and *"Men outlive their love, but they don't outlive the consequences of their recklessness."*

I knew he would hate that one. When even that didn't stir him, I knew we were in trouble. I packed the book away, and on we went. Five days later, we rode into Camp Elizabeth, having missed Fort Concho several miles to the east.

"Who are you and where are you coming from?"

A young lieutenant met us coming into camp, and he was leading a group of soldiers that looked like they hadn't seen anybody but one another in a long time.

"I'm Wilkie John Liquorish of the Texas Rangers, and I'm coming from the pits of hell," I said. "And this here is Gentleman Jack Delaney."

They didn't seem to know me from Timbuktu. Not so with Jack.

"You mean that's Jack Delaney the colored bounty hunter from New Orleans?"

I agreed that he was.

One of the soldiers claimed to have never seen a colored man before and stepped through the

crowd to get a look. He didn't seem at all impressed.
A few seconds later, the lieutenant asked me if I
knew my friend was deceased.

"What do you mean, deceased?" I said.

He looked at me like maybe I wasn't so far off
from it myself. Of course, I knew what *deceased*
meant.

"How.long has he been dead?" he said.

I got down off Little Cuss and took a look.

"He was aliver than any of you will ever be, right
up until he wasn't," I said.

I sure hated to see him dead like that. I guess it
made me sad a little bit, but mostly it made me
mad. For all the plans I had made to kill the man,
I felt like I was robbed and he was, too. He wouldn't
have wanted to go out the way he did.

"It looks to be a bullet wound," one of the soldiers said.

By that point, it was plain to see I had come sail-
ing into some kind of hospital camp. Everyone
there seemed to be a doctor of some kind.

"You know how it happened?" somebody said.

They sat me down on a cot and began prodding
at me.

"How what happened?" I said.

I wondered if I had some kind of injury I didn't
know about.

"Looks like your friend got grazed by a bullet.
Probably led to an infection."

I thought about how big a couple of inches can
turn out to be.

"We killed Phantom Bill," I said.

Those soldiers whooped and hollered like we had just beat the devil himself. And, in a way, it felt like we really had. They took him off and did whatever you do to a body. I didn't want any part in that. He was dead and buried by the time the trumpet sounded the next morning. It was that quick, that easy. I washed my hands and, once again, rode away.

EPILOGUE

I was in Austin a week later, fully recovered from my time in the desert and telling crowd after crowd how I had sussed out Charles Stirling and solved the Foucault murders. John Daniel Foucault had reportedly gone into seclusion and wasn't taking visitors. I didn't see any reason to bring him into the story. Any thoughts that he had anything to do with the murders remained inside my head and never left.

I left Stirling running around in the desert, and that's what I told both the Rangers when I gave them my report and the audiences that poured into the Austin Opera House where I entertained audiences with the story, sharing the stage with a troupe of actors from North Carolina. I was surprised to find out that Gentleman Jack Delaney was known all across Texas, mostly for being one of the first successful colored bounty hunters paid to bring in white criminals. He was also known, whether it was true or not, to have been an ex-slave who purchased his own freedom. When I mentioned being somewhat skeptical of that part of the story, there were some boos and titters from the audience. I didn't keep that part in the act for long.

Everyone wanted to know about us killing the Phantom Bill, and I always took the skull from the torn jacket lining and held it high for everyone to see. If you've seen one skull, you've pretty well seen them all, but it never failed to cause a stir when William Pascal grinned out at everybody.

I continued to argue that William Pascal had been the man the Apache Mescaleros had first named Phantom Bill. Not everyone agreed, but that was fine by me. A little controversy helped sell tickets, and we sold out six shows that week in Austin.

The other big news of the week came from a Pink. Riding in from the north, he brought word from Still Creek Ranch. The body in the water had been identified as being Robert McSwain. I was surprised how many people in Austin knew about the war between the sheep and the cattle. I was even more surprised at how shocked they seemed. What in the world would a prominent gentleman like Robert McSwain be doing that close to a place like Still Creek? I talked to a deputy sheriff who thought McSwain was going to Still Creek to form an alliance against the bigger Alameda Ranch. He seemed to know what he was talking about. Someone else swore up and down it was all a trick.

Robert McSwain was long gone with the family fortune. Maybe it was him sitting on that senorita's lap and drinking tequila somewhere over the Rio Grande.

The theatrical troupe had a railway car on the Pacific line, and they were due to move to Fredericksburg for more shows. There was a Ranger fort out that way, and I considered riding along until we got there. I realized I wasn't cut out for the stage. Gentleman Jack would have eaten it up, but not me.

On my last day in Austin, a kid walked up to me on the street and said he was from Fort Worth.

"My auntie says my mama knows who you are," he said. "Would you sign this newspaper for her?"

He stuck a copy of the *Fort Worth Chief* in my hand.

"You know how to read this?" I said.

He said he didn't, but pointed out the article that was about me and even showed me my name in the first paragraph.

"Who is your mama?" I said.

I didn't expect to know her. Most of the ladies I knew in Fort Worth were in Hell's Half Acre and weren't exactly the motherly type.

"She's just a mama, sir," he said. As if I had asked a dumb question.

I signed the article *Thanks, Wilkie John Liquorish*, being sure to spell out my name clearly.

"She with you?" I said.

He studied what I had written carefully, like it

was some secret message known only to the two of us.

"Who?" he said.

"Your mama," I said. "Or how about your aunt."

He appeared to have walked up out of nowhere.

"Me and my baby brother come here to stay with my auntie and uncle, sir."

My curiosity was getting the best of me.

"What about your mama?"

He didn't answer questions as Bess had, quietly and with her head down. He answered like a soldier reporting to a commanding officer.

"She's not well, sir. Auntie says the doctor in Weatherford is making her better."

"You can't tell me your mama's name?"

He nodded.

"Oh sure, sir. My mama's name is Flora. And my name is Andy Miller, sir."

I handed the paper back to him.

"Andy, when you see your mama, you tell her I'm gonna look her up one of these days real soon," I said.

He turned to walk away into the crowd.

"Hey, Andy," I said. "You mind if I read that article real quick before you take off with it?"

The article was written by the girl writer the *Chief* had sent over to interview me and Gentleman Jack on the day we left Fort Worth not that long ago. Somehow it seemed a lot longer ago than it was. The article was short but to the point, and well written. They got my name right.

The *Fort Worth Chief* was able to speak
with Texas Ranger Wilkie John Liquorish
of Mobeetie, Texas, and his confederate,
the colored bounty hunter Gentleman Jack
Delaney. They are departing our city in
quick pursuit of the infamous Pacific
Railway killer who made a horrible blemish
when he shot to death the wife and small
son of railway owner John Daniel Foucault.
Foucault has reportedly offered a handsome
reward to anyone who can bring the guilty
party in to authorities, and Mr. Liquorish is
determined to do that. "I knew who he is,
and I know where to find him," Liquorish
said. According to the Ranger, it's not up to
him whether the killer is brought back in
dead or alive. "That's up to him. If he makes
me go that route, I will go that route." Asked
if he was up for the adventure, the colored
bounty hunter said yes.

Gentleman Jack Delaney would have got all up
in arms being called a confederate anything. That
gave me a good chuckle. He did get his one word
in, though, I thought. *Yes.* Yes, he was up for the adventure. Didn't anything else really need to be said
about that. Yes.

I caught the train out of Austin that afternoon.

"Where you headed?" the conductor said.

You could tell he was happy to have a Ranger riding with him.

"I'm going to Fort Worth," I said.

It wasn't exactly the same as going home, but it felt a lot like it.

THERE ARE A MILLION WAYS TO DIE
IN THE OLD WEST.
THIS IS ONE OF THEM.

For a young man of seventeen, Wilkie John Liquorish has lived one sorry life. From his ill-fated stint in the U.S. Army to a back-breaking job as a gravedigger, Wilkie just can't seem to catch a break. His latest gig—working a cattle drive from Mobeetie, Texas, to Fort Worth—is no exception. The food-poisoning death of a chuckwagon cook has everyone spooked, and the fear spreads like a disease. Wilkie barely makes it out alive. But when he shows up in Fort Worth, he has another kind of death waiting for him—in the unlikely form of Gentleman Jack Delaney . . .

A fancily dressed bounty hunter from New Orleans, Gentleman Jack is ready to nail and hang young Wilkie as soon he arrives in town. He claims the boy is the most wanted outlaw in Texas. If Wilkie can manage to outsmart, outrun, or outgun this not-so-gentle man, he just might go down in history. Or swing from a tree. Or both . . .

In Texas, every man has his price.

A WORLD OF HURT
A Wilkie John Western

Tim Bryant

"If you appreciate a good story and good writing, grab anything Tim Bryant writes and prepare to be hooked and fully entertained."
—Joe R. Lansdale

CHAPTER ONE

My name is Wilkie John Liquorish, and I'm here for to rob you," I said.

The trip from Mobeetie to Fort Worth was a fool's errand. It's an angry hot ocean of sand, full of snakes and scorpions, Tonkawas and Comanches and maybe even ghosts, and when you're herding eight hundred head of cattle, it's akin to swimming the Colorado with a bale of cotton under one arm and a pig under the other. By the time we got to Comanche, Texas, speaking of Comanches, our cattle were skin and bones, completely unsellable, and half our boys were jealous of them, because the boys were bones only.

I buried my brother Ira Lee in Meridian, and that was it for me. I had lost all my taste for cattle driving. Far as I could see, we were driving them straight into hell itself. I was ready to repent of that life. When I walked away from it, I walked from there clear to Fort Worth. It was slow and hot and lonesome. I walked mostly by night and slept by day, and, when I wasn't walking, I was riding a mule named Bird. Not my favorite way to go, but more about that later. In between all of these things, I became my own man. When I arrived on the edge of town, I had no past and no great future either. The sun meant nothing and the moon meant less. Hell's Half Acre opened its arms.

Three days after arriving, I pulled a robbery. I was dead hungry and didn't have any coin on me. Tubbs's General Store at Sixth and Main seemed to have plenty. I'd been watching long enough to know their banking schedule. Another man I couldn't identify would come in at four o'clock to spell Mr. Tubbs, and he would take the day's earnings down to the Fort Worth National Bank on Eighth and Main. Way I figured, 3:30 would be just about right. Any earlier, the pot would be smaller. Much later, you might run into that second fella and have more trouble on your hands.

"Well, my name is Bill Tubbs, young man, and I hate to tell you, but you're doing nothing of the kind," the man said.

He was standing behind the counter and seemed to be set on staying put. I was in a quandary. If I backed down now, my outlaw days would be over in a hail of laughter instead of bullets. They would most likely throw me in the hoosegow just for trying. They might feed me there, but in general the thought wasn't appealing.

"Don't reach for nothing but sky," I said.

I pulled Ira's .44 Colt out of my holster and waved it once. I knew I didn't have the luxury of time.

"You say your name is Liquorish?" Tubbs said.

I could tell by the way he said it, he was thinking of the candy. It isn't spelled that way, but I didn't have time for a spelling lesson.

"You're wasting my time," I said.

"No need to do anything hasty, Mr. Liquorish," he said. "That's an awful big gun you got."

There was something implied there, and it was something that didn't need saying. Being barely five foot tall and a hundred pounds when packed down with holsters, guns and ammo, I can tell when I'm being poked at.

"You saying I'm little," I said. "I get that. I get that a lot. But you know what? So's a bullet, and I got six of them right here."

I leveled the Colt good and steady at his face, taking in the waxed mustache, the sweat that glistened on his nose, and those eyes, blue as the Gulf of Mexico and every bit as full of crap, and I fired twice. Tubbs fell in a huff and a puff against a shelf full of flour and meal, a cloud of white rising around him like a quickly fading halo.

He left a trail of blood and flour across the back of the store as I dragged him into a mop closet, where I traded him for the mop and went to cleaning up. I pulled thirty dollars from the money box to cover expenses up until that point. Leaving more than that behind would show it wasn't personal and I wasn't greedy. I was just about to be on

my way when the front door opened. In walked the
High Sheriff of Hell's Half Acre.

"Bill not here?" he said.

I scanned the back of the counter and found an
old rag, which I quickly dried my hands on.

"Not at the moment, Sheriff."

The sheriff scooted across the floor at me, squint-
ing like he was looking into the sun. The man easily
made three of me, and none of the three looked
particularly friendly either.

"Who in tarnation are you?" he said.

"Wilkie John Liquorish, sir," I said.

He had a big Colt Navy Revolver. I knew what it
was because I had seen one like it on a sailor back
in my San Antonio days. I had offered the sailor
three head of cattle for it.

"What the hell am I going to do with three cows
on a ship?" the sailor said.

I regretted letting that damn gun get away.

The High Sheriff was a little slow on the draw.
Maybe he didn't see me being all that formidable.
If that's the case, it was a mistake. I shot him right
in the teeth. That brought out such a holler, I was
afraid the whole neighborhood was going to come
running. The next two shots shut him up real good.

The sheriff joined Bill in the mop closet. Seeing
as I only had one shot left, I decided it was closing
time. I locked up the store and grabbed three
boxes of bullets from the top shelf behind the
counter. Nobody laughed when I climbed the ladder
to get them. Nobody laughed when I crawled out
a back window and slipped into a side street, two

blocks away from the whorehouse where I was keeping a room. I was seventeen years of age, but the Madam there didn't believe it. In that instance, it was all for good, as she took pity on me and took me in. An hour after I turned Tubbs's General Store into one more crime scene in the middle of the most crime-infested town west of the Mississippi, I was sleeping like a baby in the Madam Pearlie's big feather bed, her best girl, a caramel-skinned redhead named Sunny, keeping watch over me.

Waking the next day and heading downstairs, I was surprised to hear the news being whispered from ear to ear to ear. Mr. Tubbs, the city commissioner who had muscled his way into the Acre with the plan to clean up its dirty image, had been gunned down in his own store. The High Sheriff, who had been using the store as police headquarters in enemy territory, was shot dead too. The Madam called for a day of celebration. Call girls were going for half price and so were the drinks.

CHAPTER TWO

I thought about taking credit for the killings, but it wouldn't have done me any good. It would've been taken as a plea for attention, which I had no need of, or, more likely, for a joke. Then I might have had to shoot somebody else. I could see it was a vicious cycle, and, anyway, I sure didn't want to shoot up the madam's establishment, a right genteel place called the Black Elephant Saloon. And yes, I had been instructed right from the get-go that there was a White Elephant Saloon on Main Street where I might better belong. But Madam Pearlie had welcomed me like a son and told me to pay no mind to any such talk, I belonged right where I was. I liked being the only white man in the Black Elephant. It made me feel important. And I liked Madam Pearlie.

It was during that half-priced celebration, while the Black Elephant's six girls lined up the men in the back and the bartender lined up the drinks at the bar, that I first met Gentleman Jack Delaney, whom Madam Pearlie said was known, to close friends and family, as Jack Rabbit. That was the only time I ever heard her refer to him in that manner. Others said Gentleman Jack had once been a slave on a plantation somewhere north of New Orleans. They said he managed to save up money from blacksmithing and bought up his own freedom a few years before the war. Then, somewhere along the line, he went into business as a bounty hunter.

"I'm here strictly on business," he said.

I thought maybe he was referring to the Tubbs store murders as they were being referred to in the *Fort Worth Chief*. It's what everyone was talking about, inside and outside the saloon, me included. We would sit around the Black Elephant half the day talking about who might have done it, how they could have pulled it off and got away. It was such great fun that, every once in a while, I'd have to remind myself that my latest thought on the matter wasn't at all how it had happened.

The barkeep, a one-eyed man from Missouri named Black Price Hardwick, was taking bets on who did it and whether they would ever be found out. Even Madam Pearlie got in on the action, which she said was unusual for her, putting a fifty-dollar banknote on the authorities never fingering anybody.

"If they was somebody here in the Acre, we'd already be knowing," she said. "Whoever it was that done it, they're already east of the Mississippi or else west of the Rockies."

I had heard of both of those places, but they seemed far away from me as the ocean and maybe farther. I had no plans on ever seeing either of them. To me, Fort Worth was far superior to Mobeetie and the God-forsaken desert that made up most of the stretch between. I was staying put, at least until more reasonable weather arrived.

Gentleman Jack had a room at the colored hotel right across the street, so we saw plenty of him. Each of his days, as he told it, began with a breakfast of six eggs, salt pork bacon, biscuits, and brown gravy, all delivered up to his room and eaten off of a silver tray. Then he had his beard trimmed by one of the hotel staff while he watched in that same silver tray. After that, he was on his way. He would gamble at one of the poker tables or one of the blackjack tables in our front room until the clock over the bar showed noon, smoking and swearing up a storm and collecting his winnings. He always seemed to win. Then he moseyed on a little after noon.

"I've got to get about my work," he would wink. "I'm strictly here for business."

I wasn't too naïve to know what a bounty hunter was. I'd run into a few of them in San Antone. Still, it was an occupation of mystery, and I didn't have the first clue how it all worked or how a person would become such a thing. It was partly out of natural inquisitiveness and partly out of suspicion that I decided to follow along after him. I'd heard enough talk from Madam Pearlie and others to pique my interest.

Hell's Half Acre wasn't so different from places in Mobeetie or San Antone. The biggest difference, San Antonio's Sporting District was mostly filled with military boys, and its girls spoke mostly Spanish. As a result, it was something between alarming and downright embarrassing to hear pale-skinned girls calling out from their ratty little cribs, telling you specifically what they could do for you and how little it would cost you. If you had to walk down a block, you might hear two or three of them calling out and then arguing amongst themselves, trying to undersell each other. It was all a guy could do to get to the other end of the block with his dignity intact.

With Feather Hill in Mobeetie, on the other hand, it was all a matter of scale. Whatever Mobeetie had, Fort Worth had fifty of. Fort Worth was an overabundance of abundance.

It was easy enough to follow Jack through a crowd though. He stood a good head taller than most of the men in the street, which meant he had two heads on me. He also wore, as a habit, a dark red top hat with a feather stuck in it—surely one he had purchased down in New Orleans—that made him tower even taller. I couldn't help but admire his ability to wind his way through the girls, who all called even louder to him, caught as in a spell by his appearance.

He was heading in the direction of Main Street, and I began to wonder if it was foolishness or fearlessness leading him there. A colored man might move among the white people on that street if he kept his head down and didn't call attention to himself. Neither proposition seemed likely with Jack. With each storefront he passed, it became more obvious that he had no plan to turn back. I considered calling out to him, just as a friendly warning. I stopped against a hitching post right square in front of Tubbs's General Store and watched him go.

He ducked into the back door of Mary Porter's house, the biggest, fanciest brothel in all of the Acre. It wasn't uncommon for well-bred colored men to enter through the big two-story house's back door, but I watched as his silhouette made its way from window shade to window shade, and, suddenly, out he stepped through the big red double doors in the front, stepping down from the wraparound porch and continuing on his way as if the whole house had been no more than a puddle to step through and then shake off.

Down Main Street he paraded, barely slowing down to doff his hat at a couple of the townspeople along the way. Finally, he removed his hat and ducked into a small building I had never taken notice of. I had just come off a disastrously star-crossed cattle drive, so I was dressed as the other ninety-nine percent of the crowd, and my white face, sunburned as it was, blended in well enough that I could walk right up to the old clapboard building built against and leaning noticeably toward the constable's office. I meant to make a pass-by, take a quick glance into the two big front glasses, and try to identify the proceedings within.

What fell on my eyes, I must admit, staggered me in my steps.

The man was dead. That was the first and foremost thing that sprang to my mind. There wasn't any question about that. He was dressed in a fine looking suit. The kind you have shipped in from St. Louis or somewhere via stagecoach. He had a derby on his head that seemed too small by a size and determined to sit just a little off center. The man's face seemed contorted into an expression that said, "I'd rather not have my photograph taken in this condition," but that's exactly what they seemed intent on doing.

One man stood behind the camera, his left hand on his hip and the other on the contraption that made the bulb flash. Another man had what looked like a woman's powder puff in his hand, dabbing at the dead man's cheeks and repeatedly trying to level out that devilish derby.

"What you staring at?"

There was a gentleman standing outside on the small porch, and it took a moment to realize he was talking to me.

I gathered myself and moved on without answering his question, although I could have told him plenty. I knew more about what I was staring at than he did. Sitting inside the little shop, waiting to have his picture made, gussied up like he'd never been in all his live-long days, was my old cattle-drive coach driver. A man named Leon Thaw, he had been born and raised in Mobeetie, Texas. The best shootist far and wide, his reputation had been

sealed by getting tossed out of a Wild West Show
in Amarillo and warned against ever coming back
for getting up and outshooting J. B. Hickok. Twenty-
six years old and getting no older, he was the husband of a seventeen-year-old Emeline Thaw and
father of baby Millie. The last I had seen him, he was
skinny as a broomstick, but swearing that he
would make Fort Worth before I would.

"You take off on your own, Wilkie John, you'll
be lucky to ever see me again," he said. "But if you
do, I'm sure to be sitting up in some fine hotel
sipping whiskey and waiting for you."

I walked by the building again on my way back
to the Black Elephant, and I could see Gentleman
Jack, the Jack Rabbit, standing next to my unlucky
friend Leon, jotting down notes in a little brown
book. Talking to the photographer, he leaned over
and rubbed on Leon's face. That's when it hit me
that he was truly good and dead, for Leon would
have never allowed such a thing. Not that I had
any tears to give him. He hadn't been like a
brother to me. Truth is, he had tried to kill me on
one occasion, and I couldn't help seeing his current
predicament at least partially as being well deserved.

As I walked along Main Street and made my
turn on Fourth, I couldn't help shaking the feeling
that the tables had turned and it was now me that
was being followed. I watched in the glass windows
of the passing businesses. I saw nothing but my own
reflection, looking thinner and older and maybe a
bit more worried than expected.

CHAPTER THREE

"Wilkie John," Gentleman Jack said. "Must it be both? Why can it not be Wilkie? Or John? You can even pick."

We were sitting at the third blackjack table on a slow Tuesday night, which meant the dealer was at the bar chatting up one of the girls and we were sitting alone. My appearance at the table had been requested by the Jack Rabbit himself, earlier in the afternoon. I had been beside myself since then, standing in front of the mirror in Madam Pearlie's room, practicing answers to every question I could think up. Now, I was sitting three feet away from the man, he was looking me dead in the eye, and all my cool had suddenly evaporated.

"I've always just been called Wilkie John," I said.

That actually wasn't true at all. I had been called all kinds of things. Wilkie. Will. Wilkes. John. Johnny. Liquorish. Whiskey. I was in the *Texas Panhandle News* under the name John Liquorman and Whiskey

John, so Wilkie John would do just fine, thank you.
I didn't see what the big problem was.

"Okay, Willie Boy," Jack said, "you expect me to
believe you did not come into town with the coach
from Mobeetie, the same coach your good friend
Leon Thaw showed up dead in."

I had never been called Willie Boy, and I didn't
like it at all. On the other hand, part of me was fas-
cinated by this man, and his calm manner worked
to keep my hot head in check.

"That man is no friend of mine," I said.

If I hoped to trick the system, he was having
none of it.

"Willie, I'm willing to give you that one. You
know why?" He leaned across the table and low-
ered his voice from steady, quiet lilt to full whisper.
"I don't guess good friends put bullets in each
other's noggins, do they?"

So it turned out that the derby hat was tilting
because some part of the top of Leon Thaw's head
had been taken off with a bullet. I only knew two
things: One, Leon was more the cattleman's hat
type. Two, it hadn't been me that pulled that particular trigger. Last time I saw Leon, he was fully
intact and talking back.

"The two drovers on the drive were located.
One was dead and buried just outside Meridian.
Fella named Ira Lee Liquorish, I believe it was.
Now ain't that a peculiar thing?"

I was a balloon and he was a pin.

"The cook, from what I can tell, seems to have

died before you even hit Wichita Falls. Why, it's a wonder even two of you survived."

I wasn't sure if he was amused by the story he was unfolding or by my reaction to it. Either way, I didn't like the way he was smiling at me. I figured by the way he was telling it that Simeon Payne had survived and was back in Wichita Falls. That made some sense, because last I had heard from him, he was turning back and heading for home. Still, I could scarcely imagine Simeon hanging around in Wichita Falls.

Things had already been going south for the cattle drive when we reached that damned spot in the trail. Our cook, a Mexican named Jacobo, had come down with food poisoning just days out of Mobeetie. Tainted chili, he said. The whole bunch was thrown out. Rivers of chili. Jacobo talked about going back over the border to his family, but he needed the dinero.

"I will go on to Wichita Falls and see," he said. "If I'm better then, I continue with you. If I'm not so well, we find a new cook, I collect my pay and get out of your way."

We even discussed turning the whole drive back to Mobeetie. How things might have changed if we had. It all came down to Ira Lee and Simeon. The *Jefe* and the *Segundo*. Ultimately, it was Ira Lee's drive. They conferred and decided to push on for Wichita Falls.

"Jacobo will be fine by then," Simeon said.

"If not, he's right," said Leon. "There's bound to be cooks in Wichita Falls."

On we went. You know, there are times in life when you have to make decisions. Sometimes it's a fork in the road. Sometimes it's a dancing partner. You choose one, and if it proves out, you become something you weren't before. You're a successful business man, or you're the husband of the prettiest girl in town, or you're a cattle driver. You choose wrong, you're every sad son of a bitch drinking his life away in every bar and brothel between Boston and Austin. I was well aware of this. I was also aware that I was sitting in a brothel with a very bad hand of cards and a poker face that had just betrayed me.

"Ira Lee Liqourish was my big brother," I said. "He was twenty years old."

I didn't feel like admitting to this was admitting to anything important to Gentleman Jack. Whether it was important to me wasn't any of his business, and I couldn't see how it was any link to the dead stage driver with the tilted derby.

"Let me ask you two more questions, Willie Boy."

It seemed like as good a time as any to remind him.

"Wilkie John Liquorish," I said.

He kicked his chair back at an angle and rested one big black boot on the chair next to me.

"If I were to prove that a certain man pulled the trigger that shot the bullet that took our friend Leon Thaw's head off," he said, "do you think that man ought to hang for his actions?"

I knew that old trick. I had seen the same approach play out in a courthouse in Mobeetie. If the man on trial said "no, that man shouldn't hang," it made him look either morally suspect or just plain guilty. If he said, "yes, that man should hang," he was tossing the dice on his own mortality. Not many men could do it with any air of confidence.

"Yes, that man should absolutely hang before sundown," I said.

I don't know if Gentleman Jack was expecting that response. His boot wiggled, but he kept his calm. I didn't smile, but I didn't cry either.

"That he should."

He nodded and said it again. I looked him square in the eye and willed myself not to blink. After some looking back, his eyes moved down to the table, perhaps imagining the hand he was playing had become just a little less copacetic. If that was the case, I knew the feeling.

"And what if he killed fifty, sixty, more even. Men, women and children, free men and slaves, preachers and sinners alike? What might be due a culprit like that?"

That boggled the mind. I had once run into John Hardin in Gonzales, and even he couldn't boast numbers like that. It seemed biblical.

"I suppose only Jehovah himself could do numbers like that, sir."

Jack seemed satisfied enough with that.

"I suppose that's right."

He was stone cold and still, but his foot was twisting in its boot next to me, like it could barely keep from giving me a swift one in the side. It hurt my feelings that this most interesting and engaging man from New Orleans had taken such a strong disliking of me. I made note that I should do what I could to rectify it. I also thought it might be prudent to look into moving on out of town, even if I had developed a bit of an attachment to it.